André Caroff's
MADAME ATOMOS

The Revenge of
Madame Atomos

André Caroff's
MADAME ATOMOS

The Revenge of
Madame Atomos

Translated by
Michael Shreve

A Black Coat Press Book

Acknowledgements: Thanks to Françoise Carpouzis & Catherine Losserand.

Visit our website at www.blackcoatpress.com

Table of Contents

Introduction

This volume collects the ninth and tenth install-
ments of the saga of Madame Atomos, a series of 17
novels published between 1964 and 1970 in the *Angoisse*
horror imprint of French publisher Fleuve Noir. Our in-
troduction to Volume 1 contains a biography of its au-
thor, André Carpouzis, a.k.a. André Caroff (1924-2009).
More information about Fleuve Noir and its popular
brands of science fiction and horror can be found in the
introductions to the other volumes translated from their
imprints and published by Black Coat Press: Richard
Bessière's *The Gardens of the Apocalypse*, Gérard
Klein's *The More in Time's Eye* and Kurt Steiner's
Ortog.

The saga of Madame Atomos (her real name is
Kanoto Yoshimuta) is about a brilliant but twisted middle-aged female Japanese scientist who is out for revenge against the United States for the bombings of Hiroshima and Nagasaki—where she was born, and where
her family died in the nuclear holocaust.

Madame Atomos seeks to repay the United States
by unleashing deadly new threats, such as radioactive
zombies, giant spiders, a madness-inducing ray, flaming
tornadoes, etc. The heroes opposing her are Smith
Beffort of the FBI, Dr. Alan Soblen, and Yosho
Akamatsu of the Japanese Secret Police.

Volume 2 introduced the character of Mie Azusa,
a.k.a. Miss Atomos, a younger version of Madame

Atomos, groomed to continue the fight in the event of her death.

In Volume 3, after Mie fell in love with Smith Beffort, she joined the fight against the deadly Madame Atomos who, in the meantime, had returned from the dead.

In Volume 4, Madame Atomos overreaches and the US Army finally destroys her powerful flying fortress. With her organization in shambles, she is forced to re-group, while increasingly devoting all her energies to achieve revenge on Smith Beffort and Mie.

In Volume 5 Madame Atomos continues waging war on the United States, first by turning the hapless residents of Baltimore into blood-thirsty monsters, then by unleashing uncontrollable wild fires over Nevada...

Now read on...

Jean-Marc Lofficier

ANDRE CAROFF

Mme ATOMOS CROQUE le MARMOT

ANGOISSE

Éditions
"FLEUVE NOIR"

THE REVENGE OF MADAME ATOMOS

Chapter I

Smith Beffort tore the page off the calendar and was astonished to see that the month of November had started 17 days earlier. His face froze. In August, Madame Atomos had literally disintegrated in the police headquarters in Canby, Oregon, where she was being held prisoner. It was stupefying, unlikely and utterly unexpected. Still, the diabolical woman had really disappeared from the room in which four men were guarding her. Beforehand, Madame Atomos had given herself the satisfaction of telling how she planned to escape. Naturally, no one believed that she could disintegrate herself there and reconstruct her human form almost instantaneously in her lair on Atomia Island.

Since this magic trick—teleportation by disintegration, whose principles violate no laws of physics—the FBI had been forced to search for the location of Atomia Island. They had inspected every island in the Pacific and particularly in the Hawaiian Islands with no success. Needless to say that this was a huge job. How could they find an underground shelter in an archipelago spread out over almost 1000 square miles?

"How indeed?" Beffort mumbled.

Just then Dr. Soblen walked into the kitchen. Being the Befforts' guest for the last couple of weeks, Soblen was recuperating from his trip to the Pacific where he was helping in the search. When he heard Beffort, he said, "You're talking to yourself, Smith?"

Beffort frowned and shook Soblen's hand. "Yes," he admitted. "If this continues, I think Madame Atomos will end up making me senile. Did you sleep well, doc?"

"Yes, thanks. Tell me, Smith, in spite of what everyone thinks, are you still afraid of Madame Atomos coming back?"

Beffort's smile had no joy in it. He pointed to the coffee pot and the table set for breakfast. "Help yourself."

"Answer my question first," Soblen insisted.

Beffort spread his hands, palms up, and said, "I'll believe she's dead when I see her corpse."

"So," Soblen said calmly, "you're going to spend the rest of your life tearing your hair out. In our present state of knowledge, we can admit that Madame Atomos could have disintegrated herself, but we must refuse to believe that she actually did..."

"Okay," Beffort interrupted, "we've already talked about this till the cows come home! Eat some toast—it's something solid."

Soblen sat down, poured himself some coffee and started buttering his toast. "Is Mie still in bed?"

Beffort pointed to the clock, "Do you know that it's not yet 6 a.m.?" Soblen had a little jolt. Beffort sat across from him and went on, "You're here on vacation but you talk aloud in your sleep all night long and you get up at the same time as me. Is that proof of your peaceful state of mind?"

"At my age..."

"No way! In truth, you can't stop thinking about Madame Atomos. Last night you yelled out her name a dozen times. Doc, you're in no position to lecture me."

Soblen buried his nose in his toast.

"Of course," Beffort continued, "you would die before admitting it, but Canby really shook you up. Madame Atomos was at our mercy and then all of a sudden, poof! Nothing in her chair but a pile of clothes. For a scientist, that's pretty unusual, isn't it?"

Soblen shrugged his shoulders and defended himself, "That's not the issue. I simply claim that Madame Atomos could not have reconstructed her human form and so we're chasing a ghost."

"Excuse me," Beffort corrected. "*You* are chasing a ghost! Me, I haven't budged from here since August—you can jot that down in your little notebook."

"You're stuck in a rut."

"That doesn't mean we're not in the same position. I knew that you wouldn't find Atomia Island and that you would come back here to see how I was doing. So, you can see that I'm biding my time. I'm just waiting for Madame Atomos to show herself and in my opinion, it won't take long."

Soblen smiled frugally. "For a patient man," he said sarcastically, "you're pretty nervous! At night you hear me dreaming, but I hear you pacing for miles between the bathroom and the second floor landing. Plus, I think it's your stomping that keeps me awake. You should take some tranquilizers!"

Smith Beffort sat back and lit his first cigarette of the day. "In conclusion, doc, we're all on hot coals and the tension is mounting the closer the theatrical moment comes for Madame Atomos to reappear. The normal cycle of the famous three months is almost up. It's always been at the end of this time that our enemy launches a new attack against the United States."

"Yes," Soblen tried holding firm, "but she had never disintegrated herself before!" He was stubborn as a mule.

"Damn," Beffort said, "if you were so sure she was dead, you wouldn't be so stressed all the time."

Soblen drained his cup of coffee, wiped his mouth ceremoniously and murmured in an irritated voice, "You see, Smith, you can't swear to anything when it comes to Madame Atomos. Probabilities give her a one in a million chance of success at teleportation by disintegration and it's precisely this slim chance that bothers me. We know that Madame Atomos has domesticated the atom, that she invented a terrifying disintegrator ray, that she can protect herself with a magnetic shield and submit hundreds of innocent people to her will by sticking a motor-brain in their heads. We know she uses flying saucers that are capable of astounding speed, that she gave immortality to some people and that she has at hand extraordinary inventions that we know nothing about. In all this we also know with almost mathematical certainty that Atomia Island is somewhere in the Hawaiian Islands and nevertheless, we can't find a trace of it. So, how do you expect me to sleep soundly?"

After a short silence, Beffort said, "Basically, we're only now starting to be honest! So far we've been careful not to reveal our worries. Let's stop this farce and admit that Madame Atomos is now capable of disintegrating and reintegrating herself at will."

"Let's admit that."

"So what's stopping her from suddenly materializing right in front of us, here and now, and wiping us out with one swipe of her ray gun?"

Soblen shook his head. "Impossible. As a prerequisite she would need an accomplice here."

"Why?"

"Because teleportation has to have a computer at the departure and a second computer at the arrival. Theoretically, it should happen like this: you feed the potential traveler's genetic code into the first computer and he's disintegrated. Meanwhile, the code has been sent to the second computer, which reconstructs the traveler in flesh and blood on arrival. Therefore, for Madame Atomos to materialize suddenly before us, a computer would have to be hidden somewhere in the kitchen to reconstruct her."

Beffort tapped the ash off his cigarette and said thoughtfully, "If I understand correctly, the trip happens at the speed it takes to transmit electromagnetic signals, that is the speed of light. Suppose that Madame Atomos expands her system…"

"Expands?"

"Yes. If she can travel in this way, why not also let her servants do the same? I can just see the whole Atomos Organization moving around like lightning and striking where we least expect it. All it would take is an accomplice to sneak a computer into the point of arrival."

Soblen scrunched up his nose and said, "It wouldn't even have to be hidden. At zero hour it would just have to be wherever they want. The disintegrator computer that Madame Atomos used to vanish from the police station in Canby was the size of a watch. The reconstruction computer can obviously be the same size so that anybody could put it anywhere without attracting any special attention. Hell, Smith, this is a serious concern!"

Beffort stubbed out his butt in the ashtray, stood up and started pacing with his hands in his pockets. "Now, doc, you understand why I stayed home instead of going with you to dredge the Pacific. Madame Atomos' hatred of Americans is completely focused on me and my family. She swore to kill us and she won't stop until she's accomplished her sinister plans. So, if our guesses are right, from now on I have to be suspicious of everyone. Every person who caters this house might be carrying a reconstruction computer."

He sat back down across from Soblen and added, "Our best protection is that very few people know we're living here…" He counted on his fingers out loud. "You, Akamatsu, J.E.E., Witter, Hyde and Owen Bernitz. Six men whom I fully trust but whom Madame Atomos knows."

Soblen puckered his mouth. "And the neighbors?"

Beffort flipped his hands, resigned. "It's impossible for us not to look like oddballs to them. We practically never leave and the deliverymen have never crossed the yard. The neighbors have to be wondering what's going on behind the high walls and your arrival must look like something of the utmost importance. But it's inevitable. For Madame Atomos to find out that we're living in the suburbs of Williamsburg, it would take a miracle. She'll be searching at the other end of the United States, in the deserts, mountains and forests, but she'll certainly never imagine that we're only 400 miles from New York!"

Dr. Soblen sighed. Now Beffort was put on the defensive. While some people were trying to find the location of Atomia Island, Beffort was thinking only of Madame Atomos' next attack and, like a soldier, was preparing for the shock by digging trenches. It was just an image but in Soblen's eyes this way of proceeding looked more like surrender.

However, Beffort had full power in the fight against the sinister Japanese woman and her Organization. The navy, air force and the Green Dragon Force added up to a formidable deterrence power. Why let them lay down their arms while the enemy was working in the wings on a new attack whose consequences might be catastrophic to the United States?

"I don't understand, Smith," Soblen spoke frankly since he never minced words when the situation started to look dire. "You're acting like a man who is scared."

Beffort raised his eyebrows. "But *I am scared*! For months I've feared for the life of my wife and son who are the main targets of Madame Atomos. Everyone is congratulating each other because the USA is calm thanks to the diversion that the Befforts create in the sinister woman's mind, but no one thinks of the danger that's looming over us. Their reaction is all too human. Two or three lives mean nothing if you put in the balance the millions of people whom the Atomos Organization might strike down after we're eliminated. Because that's the whole problem, doc—for Madame Atomos to continue to ignore the USA, we have to stay alive." He raised a finger and spoke gravely, "The day after she kills us, she'll annihilate the United States! Don't you see, I'm not just scared for my family?"

Soblen nodded. "I didn't see things like that," he admitted, "but in that case, why not find a safer hideout?"

Beffort smiled and rubbed his weary face, explaining, "Doctor, we have to be reasonable and understand that Madame Atomos could get tired of looking for us if it takes too long."

Soblen's eyes widened. "Are you insinuating that you're deliberately staying within her reach?" Beffort nodded and Soblen raised his voice, "You're tempting the devil!"

"Madame Atomos is the devil personified and we're playing a great big game of chess with her. Except that she cheats and all the pawns that we capture she replaces from our own reserves. Now you're not so sure, but at the start of our conversation you claimed that Madame Atomos was dead. Well, you can't imagine the number of men and women who have disappeared since August."

"How do you know that?"

"I've read the papers and Eddy Witter keeps me up-to-date on the reports filed with missing persons. Now, in two and a half months almost 2,000 people have vanished without leaving the slightest trace. What do you make of that, doc?"

Soblen grimaced. "If I believe you, I'll have to conclude that Madame Atomos is rebuilding her Organization. Recruiters are kidnapping American citizens and probably taking them back to Atomia Island where they are operated on to put a motor-brain in their skull. Afterward, they become slaves of the Great Brain, which is just an extraordinary electronic machine controlled by Madame Atomos..."

"Okay, doc! You've learned your lesson by heart," Beffort observed. Then he pointed at the calendar and said, "It's November 17. I'll bet my bottom dollar that we'll hear news from Madame Atomos before the end of the month."

Soblen stayed quiet. He knew Beffort was right.

Chapter II

On the same day at 8 a.m., Miss Dolly McIntyre closed the door of her apartment, caught the elevator and went from the 12th floor down to the lobby of the building located at 455C Washington Street in Boston. Miss McIntyre was a superb blonde full of inviting curves. With her very free spirit she always looked on the bright side, lived in the present and did not care at all about what the future held in store. Of course, she was only 23 years old so she still had plenty of time to think about her golden years.

Dolly worked in a travel agency. She was constantly in contact with businessmen who had fat wallets, which she emptied using her charms. In short, she felt happy and had no complexes. Nevertheless, Dolly chose her partners carefully. Strange as it may seem, she was not what you would call "easy". So, no one could boast of breaking the ice with her without first being physically attractive to her. Some young ladies like young men. Dolly was drawn to men in their 40s or 50s, with graying temples, experienced in love and who knew how to treat her with uncommon tenderness. Dolly always felt like she was the man's daughter, protected and free to let loose in all kinds of frivolity. Her partner forgave all her whims with a cute little grunt.

On the other hand, Dolly hated the young pretty boys with more and more effeminate manners, who looked bored watching her while they played sluggishly with their long straight hair. To them she was just another girl. Besides, the demands of these young apathetic and unmanly boys were stupendous. They wanted this, said no to that, etc.

T.B. Clark knew of Dolly's disgust for the young men her age. Clark was the "Mister" of the moment. Right now he was parked at the other end of Washington Street in his shiny orange Cadillac waiting for his young lover to show up so he could drive her to work as he did every day. There was already a lot of traffic and a veritable wall of cars separated the two sidewalks. To cross the street the light had to change.

The front door of the building finally swung open and Dolly appeared. She was ravishing. Even more— sensational!

She smiled, waved to Clark and came down the sidewalk toward the light at the crosswalk. About halfway down she stopped for no reason and stood still on the edge of the sidewalk, looking at something off in the distance that only she could see, but that completely captivated her attention.

T.B. Clark followed her eyes, saw nothing special and suddenly had the weird feeling that something was wrong with Dolly. At that precise moment an old Chevrolet pulled up to the young lady and a guy in his early 20s got out. Long hair, pale skin... exactly the type Dolly could not stand the sight of. The young man walked up to Dolly, took her arm and led her to his old beater. Dolly sat calmly in the passenger seat. The guy walked around the Chevy, sat behind the wheel and instantly took off.

T.B. Clark sat there dazed. He had just witnessed something unbelievable and was swimming in utter confusion. Anger finally got the better of him, but it was much too late. Clark had a fast car, but the traffic kept him from making a U-turn. He was forced to go to the intersection and wait at the red light, letting the pedestrians cross before starting in pursuit. He sped like crazy down Washington Street and got to Dedham with no sign of the old Chevy.

The Chevrolet had turned west a long time before. It cruised slowly through Quincy and continued in no hurry toward Hingham Bay. Dolly and the young man had not spoken a word when the car stopped at pier 2, reserved for pleasure boats. The young man cut the engine, helped Dolly out and then led her gently to the yacht that had obviously been docked in the same place for a long time. It was called the *Lanaï*.

Dolly followed the man to a cabin, which he made sure to lock, covered the window and turned on the light. After that he took a black uniform and short, black boots out of a closet and put them on the bunk before walking over to Dolly, who was still strangely passive. Unemotionally and unforcefully he took off the girl's fur coat and then her dress; he popped off her bra and then slipped off her panties and girdle and stockings; then he removed her pumps. All this without meeting the least resistance or receiving any help, just a flaccid indifference that would have been alarming under any other circumstances.

Naked now, Dolly stared blankly at the young man piling up her clothes in the closet. Afterward she let him help her put on the black uniform and boots and then with thoroughly empty eyes she watched him while he lifted a trapdoor in the corner of the cabin. The young man, still silent and stone-faced, came back to her and pushed her to the ladder that sank into the belly of the small yacht. Dolly shimmied down into the hold in front of the man. He climbed down after her and lifted the cover of a tube that stuck through the yacht's hull. This tube was two and a half feet in diameter and furnished with another ladder.

Dolly and the man climbed down another 20 rungs and into the operating room of the submarine that was huddled up against the hull of the *Lanaï*. The young man handed Dolly over to the six waiting surgeons; he turned around and immediately climbed back on board the yacht.

Ten minutes later the old Chevrolet, equipped with an emitter that paralyzed the will, was cruising the streets of Boston again in search of new, healthy and beautiful servants for the Atomos Organization.

T.B. Clark gave up his search, went to his office and worked unproductively until noon. Everyone annoyed him a lot as he did not get a minute to himself to phone the travel agency where Dolly worked. When he finally got the chance to call, it was past noon. The agency was closed and no one answered the phone. Seriously worried, Clark got back into this car and drove straight to 455C Washington St. He left his Cadillac in the parking lot, found a phone booth and, to assuage his conscience, dialed Dolly's home number. To his great surprise the girl answered right away.

Clark was well bred, he said, "I waited for you this morning for nothing, huh?"

Dolly laughed her head off. "Oh, I'm really sorry, Tony, but the most extraordinary thing happened to me! Can you believe that out of the blue I ran into my brother? I haven't seen him in at least five years…"

Clark was shocked silent. He had imagined everything but this.

"Where are you, Tony dear?" Dolly murmured.

22

"Downstairs," Clark answered stupidly.

There was a short silence before Dolly complained, "Don't you want to see me?"

He got a little emotional lump in his throat. He was 42 years old and Dolly was certainly one of his last (maybe the last) conquests and she had a lot more power over him than she imagined. When she talked to him in that pouty voice, Clark melted and always felt like he was 20 again. "Of course I want to see you, Dolly."

"Well, are you coming up," Dolly whispered.

"I'm on my way!"

He hung up. Dolly did the same, undressed quickly and slipped on a see-through negligee. After unlocking the door of her apartment, she lay down on the living room couch.

She had never acted like this, but she was ready to do all kinds of things that she had never done before, even though she did not know it because she no longer really existed. Miss McIntyre was just another one of Madame Atomos' creatures, controlled by the motor-brain, like a robot, on a specific wavelength through electromagnetic impulse. Thus, she had just received orders to bring Clark up to her room. The Organization was recruiting and the Great Brain wanted to see if the man could be of use. The programming wanted *healthy* and *beautiful* for its future victims, but it said nothing about *young*...

Clark rang, got no answer, tried the door and opened it. He closed it behind him and entered the living room. Seeing the pose his young mistress had struck took his breath away.

"Hello, Tony."

Clark stepped forward, already burning with desire, unaware that Dolly's eyes were sending back his image to the Great Brain. Over on Atomia Island, thousands of miles from Boston, a file was speeding into a programmer, passing from one sector to another, until it ended up in a sorting tray with one word printed on it: *Good*.

The order was sent in a flash to the motor-brain that the surgeons on the submarine had buried in the girl's brain. Dolly smiled and patted the couch. "Get comfortable, Tony dear."

Clark was undressed in the blink of an eye. When he was naked, Dolly turned on the paralyzing emitter they had given her and Clark froze in the middle of the living room. Now he was ripe for the operation.

The next day T.B. Clark was completely out of circulation, but Dolly McIntyre, promoted by the Great Brain for headhunter of the Atomos Organization, went to the travel agency as usual. Naturally, Clark's wife informed the police about her husband's disappearance. Under normal circumstances, when it was just a normal citizen, the police would do nothing before the legal delay of 48 hours. However, it happened that T.B. Clark was a big fish, his wife's brother was a senator and she loved him a lot. All this combined to land the matter directly on the desk of a G-man named Clay. He was the director of the Boston FBI and so considering the fact that too many Americans had disappeared over the last two months, he immediately decided to deal with the Clark file personally.

Clark was a cautious man. He had jealously hidden his tryst with Dolly but when it comes to affairs, it is very difficult, nary impossible, to fool a personal secretary for long.

Through Clark's secretary, Clay quickly and easily got the address of Dolly McIntyre and two telephone numbers: one was her home number, the other of the agency where she worked. He asked no questions and went directly to the agency. When got there, he asked a ravishing young blonde where he could find Miss Dolly McIntyre.

The blonde smiled and said, "I'm Dolly McIntyre. What can I do for you?"

Clay avoided thinking about all the things this wonder could do for him and flashed his badge. "Mr. Clark has disappeared," he said.

"Oh dear!" Dolly exclaimed.

Clay leaned over the counter where he got a bird's eye view of the girl's cleavage and almost forgot what he had come there for. Good God, it was about Clark! "When did you last see him?"

Dolly batted here eyelashes. "The day before yesterday, I think," she stuttered. The problem was (and the Great Brain did not know it) that Dolly did not know how to lie. Right now she was under the Great Brain's control, but she still retained a certain amount of intellectual independence. Here is where you might say the Atomos Organization was not exactly perfect. When the young lady stuttered, the Great Brain had no way of catching up. If it interfered, it might cause more problems with unexpected consequences.

A machine, even an electronic one devised by Madame Atomos, was still just a machine!

Naturally Clay raised an eyebrow. "You think? If I were you, I think I'd be sure, don't you?'

This time the Great Brain must have taken the reins. It sent a little impulse to Dolly's motor-brain so she could answer with complete self-control, "But I am sure! It's just a way of speaking… Say, I hope nothing serious has happened to him?"

"We don't know anything. How was he?"

"Like always."

Clay felt something was not right. From the personal secretary he had learned that Clark probably saw his mistress every morning. Logically, therefore, and since Clark had disappeared the day before around noon, Dolly must have seen him that morning.

Clay was a good G-man. Miss McIntyre's attitude seemed strange (though he could not say why), so he decided to put off his interrogation until later in order to get as much information as possible from his subject. After all, he had come here on instinct. The mistress of a man as important as T.B. Clark deserved more light on the situation before being grilled under the blinding lamps of the FBI!

Clay put on a satisfied smile and very politely said goodbye, to take his business elsewhere, that is, he was soon in front of the building where Dolly lived. Well, you would have had to be totally blind not to spot Clark's shiny Cadillac parked in the lot next door. Clay mumbled to himself, then called headquarters and waited patiently on the sidewalk. Five minutes later two specialists showed up. Clay led them to Miss McIntyre's door and they quickly found a key to open the lock. In the apartment the three men made a thorough search. Clay was not at all surprised not to find Clark, but he was surprised to find his clothes.

"Weird," he moaned.

"And what do you think this is?" one of the break-in specialists asked. He was holding a small, square box with a screen on it, two knobs and a very short antenna. Clay grabbed the thing and examined it, with a troubled look because the antenna did not look quite right.

"Turn the knob…"

"No! You can go. I'll take care of closing up here."

The specialists left after giving the key to their boss. Clay used Dolly's phone to call James Edward Evans in Washington. They tried to put him on hold, but he said it was urgent and got put straight through to the FBI's head honcho.

"What's eating you, Clay?" J.E.E. asked.

"If you know where Smith Beffort is," Clay said in earnest, "I think you'll want to contact him immediately!"

"Okay, but what about?"

"I'm on a trail that stinks of his Atomos to high heaven!"

"Go on…"

"A guy's disappeared," Clay summed up, "and his mistress claims she hasn't seen him since the day before yesterday…"

"Stop!" J.E.E. interrupted. "That has nothing to do with us."

"Wait. At the girl's place I just found the guy's clothes and I'm holding some weird little box with a grid screen, two knobs and an antenna. Given Beffort's latest instructions to us, it seems to me that finding a contraption like this deserves…"

"Okay! You're sure it's not a radio or tape recorder or maybe…"

"No!"

"And the girl?"

"Exactly. It was her behavior that made up my mind. If she were normal, she would never have said she had no news from her sugar daddy when she had to know I would immediately spot his car in the lot next to her building. To all appearances, she killed him with an accomplice."

"Blood?"

"Not a drop, but his underwear and t-shirt. Statistics show that a man very rarely leaves these things with his mistress, right? Unless…"

"That goes without saying," J.E.E. cut in bitterly. "Where are you right now?"

"At the girl's apartment."

"Go back to your office and try to find out what that black box is. Beffort will call you in a few minutes."

"Okay."

J.E.E. hung up. Clay did the same, tucked the box under his arm and left, being careful to lock the door behind him. He had left Clark's clothes where they were. There was no way for Miss McIntyre to know that her love nest had been violated.

Clay pressed the elevator button and waited for it to arrive. When the doors finally opened a young man with long hair and pale skin came out. Clay stepped aside to let him pass, but the guy pointed the antenna of a black box at him and turned the knob. Clay understood instantly, but the ray was too fast for him. Although he wanted to jump away, the G-man stood frozen. A kind of veil fell over his eyes and he suddenly lost his willpower and all desire.

The young man led him by the arm into the elevator. Then he pressed the button for the first floor.

Chapter III

After J.E.E.'s call, Smith Beffort called the FBI headquarters in Boston. He was not expecting much from a conversation with Clay because for months now all the federal agents were suffering from acute Atomositis and Beffort had already followed up on hundreds of dead-end leads.

At headquarters they told him that Clay had not come back yet and they asked him to leave a phone number. Beffort said he would call back in 30 minutes and hung up. Six people had his phone number, which was more than enough.

"What's happening?" Mie asked.

Beffort frowned. "A guy in Boston think he's on the trail of the Atomos Organization… How's Bob?"

"Better. We certainly won't need to call a doctor."

Little Bob had a slight cold. Soblen smiled. Like all parents of an only child, the Befforts panicked when their kid had a runny nose.

At 11 o'clock Beffort phoned Boston again, but Clay had still not shown up. They were sure that he was not at Miss McIntyre's anymore and they were presently searching his usual hangouts. Beffort thought that the Boston bureau chief had made a mistake and was trying to get it forgotten. Typical.

He told them that they should advise Clay to get in touch with Evans and he hung up with every intention of thinking no more about it. But 15 minutes later Evans called him. He did his best to sound calm, but his voice trembled with repressed excitement. "Still no news from Clay, Smith?"

"No and he still hasn't come back to the office."

"That's exactly what surprises me," J.E.E. said. "When he called me, he was all worked up because of this famous black box. At the time I thought his imagination was getting carried away and I believed it up until a little while ago."

"What changed your mind?"

"Clay was at this Miss McIntyre's when he called. Now, since then it appears that nobody's seen him. I wonder if he really did have a hot lead."

Beffort said nothing. He was thinking. Until now Madame Atomos' attacks had been unpredictable. If Clay had stumbled upon the Organization while it was preparing its next offense against the USA, they would have to do him in.

"Don't you think," J.E.E. proposed, "you should take a little trip to Boston?"

"Certainly, certainly."

"Not too enthusiastic, Smith? You're worried about Mie and Bob's safety, aren't you?"

"Why ask if you already know? On the other hand, I know that I can't very well stay here forever playing bodyguard. Listen, Evans, if you want me to go back to the front lines with peace of mind, you have to watch this house closer than the pupil in your own eye!"

"Damn it," J.E.E. exploded, "I've offered you a security team a hundred times, but you never wanted to talk about it. How do you expect me to protect your family if you refuse to let my men inside your house?"

"Remember the bungalow in Burns[1], Evans?" In spite of a group of experienced G-men, the Atomos Or-

---

[1] See *Madame Atomos Prolongs Life* in *The Mistake of Madame Atomos*.

ganization were able to kidnap Mie and Bob without too much difficulty."

"It was an accident!"

"Let's not brag about it, okay? That can't happen again no matter what!"

"Okay," J.E.E. said with interest. "So, will you be kind enough to tell me what magic the FBI can use to protect your family from a distance? Personally, I admit that I…"

"Not from a distance, Evans, but discreetly. When you attack an entrenched camp, you first start by killing the sentinels. At Burns the Organization just put them to sleep, but the result was the same. Our house here is not alone and we have nosy neighbors. If a team of G-men turns up here, everyone will know about it!"

"I don't know Williamsburg, but I imagine it's not a village, is it?"

"It's got a population of 7000 and the business district and shops all fit on one city block. I chose this small town precisely because anything out of the ordinary is immediately detected. Thus, a commando team from the Atomos Organization would have a slim chance of getting to my front door without me knowing."

J.E.E. took a breath and said, "If you're so well informed, then why do you need me?"

"I was talking about a commando team, Evans. But we're still vulnerable to individuals. I just had a talk with Soblen and we concluded that Madame Atomos is perfectly capable of surprising us."

"How?"

Beffort explained to him how Madame Atomos could use a reconstruction computer and J.E.E. was speechless. "You see," Beffort wound up, "the situation will not be pretty if the Atomos Organization finds out where we're staying."

"For the moment you have no reason to turn pessimist! Who says that the Organization will find out that you're in Williamsburg?"

"When you talk about Atomos, you're talking about infernal power! Don't try to kid me. I'm thoroughly convinced that our hideout is hanging by a thread. Can you swear to me that right now one of Madame Atomos' servants isn't listening to our conversation?"

J.E.E. did not argue. Five months earlier, the security services of the FBI were stunned to learn that a young woman named Susan Doolittle, a switchboard operator at headquarters, was, without even knowing it herself, a member of the Atomos Organization. And that was the whole tragedy: 50% of those with brain surgery by the Organization continued to live normal lives. Now, there was only one way to recognize them: the surgery left a very particular half-moon scar on the scalp. But this mark was always hidden under the hair and it was almost impossible to spot it without examining the suspect up close. Of course, you had to have suspicions beforehand and how can you be suspicious of someone who has not changed any of their usual habits? It was a vicious circle.

"Let's get back to our first subject," J.E.E. said. "I mean protecting Mie and Bob. Personally, I'm for a massive defense, but you're against it. What do you want me to do?"

"Not much, Evans. I simply want you to bring me four or five guard dogs trained at Quantico[2]."

"Yeah?" Evans was bewildered. "That's it?"

[2] Quantico, in Virginia, the US Marine Corps base where the FBI agents are also trained.

"That's all I need," Beffort assured him calmly. "Make sure the animals are specialized in guarding and attacking silently and they are slavishly obedient. I want to be able to leave them in my yard and be sure that no one can enter without being ripped to shreds on the spot."

"Men can do that just as well!"

"No. Men think before killing."

"And if a kid from the neighborhood sneaks in there out of curiosity?"

"The surrounding wall is over 13 feet high and it has shards of glass on top—it's a real deterrence. If a kid tries to climb over, it would only be after receiving orders from the Great Brain."

J.E.E. did not comment. He knew that the Atomos Organization used children, too. "Okay. The dogs will be there this afternoon. Now, Smith, tell me what will happen if Madame Atomos shoots a paralyzing ray at your house?"

"The ray only has a range of 500 yards," Beffort reminded him, "and we know it can't penetrate anything more than 12 inches thick. Well, the walls of this house are thicker than that and the windows are triple-paned—they can stop a bullet. Considering the fact that the ray loses power the farther away it is, I think we're safe. To be effective, the shooter would have to open fire from the yard. And he would meet the dogs first."

"If he paralyzes the dogs?"

"Soblen and Mie will know right away that something's wrong. We have paralyzing rifles here, too, Evans."

"If they attack at night?"

Beffort sighed, "All precautions have been taken. If you need to know details, okay. An alarm will go off if someone touches the top of the wall. So right now I have everything but the dogs."

"All right, you'll have them soon. When they get here, can I expect you to leave for Boston?"

"You count on it."

J.E.E. hung up. Beffort put his telephone down and said, "I have the feeling that Evans is getting old."

Soblen looked up from his newspaper. "You should talk, Smith! 20 minutes ago you wouldn't stop talking about guaranteeing your family's security knowing full well that I'm in charge of it. I'm not sensitive, but you have to admit that it could be taken the wrong way."

Beffort did not even smile. Soblen was just posturing. Deep down inside he was no more confident than Beffort.

Around 5:30 p.m. a UPS delivery truck stopped in front of the Befforts' house. A deliveryman got out, checked his order and decided to ring at the gate. A few seconds went by before the gate cracked open. The man said something to an invisible person, went back to the truck and started unloading the two big crates with the help of the driver.

The first crate had the following stickers: Fragile, Electric Appliances, Top, Bottom. The other crate, which looked heavier, apparently contained some kind of record player/TV combo.

The two men carried the crates onto the property. The gate instantly closed behind them so that the closest nosy neighbors were left unsatisfied. In the yard, the deliveryman, who was in fact the dog trainer from Quantico let the dogs loose. Six Great Danes with terrifying fangs, quiet as shadows, immediately gathered together behind their master. At the trainer's request Beffort went to get Soblen, Mie and little Bob.

"No one else?" the man from Quantico asked.

"No," Beffort assured him.

"Who's going to be really in charge of the dogs?"

"Me and Dr. Soblen," Mie Azusa-Beffort answered.

The trainer took two metal tubes out of his pocket. "Ultrasonic whistles," he explained. "The dogs are trained to respond to its call. Now you have to get to know one another."

The trainer spoke to the dogs in a strange language while letting them sniff the clothes of Mie, Bob and Soblen. Like that the big dogs identified who they were supposed to defend and then they started taking possession of the place by lifting their legs against the outer wall.

"There you go," the trainer said. "Now they know you. Still, I advise you never to touch them and try not to go out at night. If a visitor has to come in, meet him at the gate and always hold his arm to show the dogs that he's a friend. If you act otherwise, the visitor will have no chance of getting out of here alive."

"Charming!" Soblen piped up.

"They're not house pets, doctor, but guard dogs. They're used to living outside, but we should still think about shelter..." The trainer's experienced eye quickly spotted the ideal place. "Under the porch stairs will be perfect."

Out of one of the crates he pulled six blankets and six big food dishes. As he was taking a card out of his pocket he said, "The dogs only eat once a day at exactly 3 p.m. This card has their diet. Don't go giving them treats. Stick to the menu."

He went to spread the blankets under the stairs and put the dishes nearby. The dogs went up and sniffed. Strangely, they stayed in pairs, almost shoulder to shoulder. The trainer said, "They always hunt in pairs. If you whistle, they'll all come. If one of them is missing, watch out because that'll mean he's dead. If a pair doesn't answer the call, be on your guard, too. That'll mean the animals are waiting somewhere in the yard and there's a threat around. Be careful because they never growl."

"How will they alert us?" Soblen asked, eyeing the Great Danes warily.

"You have to keep an eye on their rounds."

"Right now they're not moving." The trainer clicked his tongue. Two animals immediately went to lie down under the stairs. At the same time, the two other pairs trotted off in opposite directions along the wall. A minute later they reappeared, crossed in front of the gate and continued their silent, monotonous patrol.

"Now," the dog trainer said, "they'll keep going for months if necessary. Periodically the pair resting will relieve one of them and so on and so on. You don't have to do anything concerning the guard. These dogs have been doing this since they were born, or almost, and they know no other life. They'll come to eat in pairs and take turns sleeping, but four of them will always be watching over you. They won't stop their routine unless you use your whistle. Do you want to give it a try?"

Mie put the whistle to her lips and blew into the opening. Naturally, no one heard a sound, but the six animals came right away to Mie's feet. They waited, ear pricked up and nostrils flaring. It was pretty impressive.

"If you were being attacked," the trainer said, "your attacker would already be dead with his throat ripped out. So, don't whistle for nothing. To let them go, just click your tongue a few times."

Mie clicked and the dogs left.

"Okay!" Smith Beffort said with satisfaction. "I think I can leave with peace of mind. By the way, can you pack me into this crate? I'd rather get out of here on the sly."

Chapter IV

It was 9 p.m. when Smith Beffort walked out of the Logan International airport on the outskirts of Boston. He took a taxi, was driven to FBI headquarters, paid the two dollars on the meter and waited for the taxi to drive off before entering the federal building.

Since J.E.E. had told them that Beffort was coming, the local FBI chief, Bert Chandler, the second in charge under Clay, was waiting in the lobby to greet him. The two men shook hands and went straight up to Chandler's office. Beffort was told in detail how Clay had disappeared and was quickly convinced that Dolly McIntyre was in it up to her neck.

"Since Clay vanished, what have you done?"

Chandler became sullen. "Evans advised me to sit tight until you arrived. I did what he said, but we've continued looking for Clay and we've kept Miss McIntyre under surveillance."

"Perfect," Beffort approved. "I know you haven't learned anything about Clay, but with the girl it may be different?"

Chandler shook his head, discouraged. "So far she's acted like anyone else. She left the agency at 6:30 p.m. and went directly home on the bus. Since then she hasn't moved." He looked up at Beffort and added, "In my opinion, we won't get anywhere like this. If I could arrest the girl, I bet I could wring the truth out of her before midnight!"

"Be careful!" Beffort warned. "Don't forget that this is not your run of the mill case. Clay thought Miss McIntyre might be hooked up with the Atomos Organization. If he was right and I'm here to check that, then we can't do anything rash. The fact that Miss McIntyre went home after Clay's disappearance proves that she feels perfectly safe. Now, logically, she should be on the run."

"She's not thinking," Chandler groaned.

Beffort stood up, walked across the room and turned to his colleague. "You don't know how right you are, Chandler. If she's really a member of the Atomos Organization, then it's obvious that the Great Brain has complete control over her. To put it simply, let's just say that she's being radio-controlled by an electronic machine that can't predict everything. Well, two men have evaporated after seeing Miss McIntyre, who at the same time becomes the prime suspect. But the Great Brain only judges things by their appearance and won't make any decisions as long as we leave the girl alone."

"So," Chandler could not believe it, "we have to let her run wild?"

"For the moment, yes. But I'm not here on vacation and sooner or later she'll lead us to the Atomos Organization's secret headquarters in Boston."

"You're taking a big risk," Chandler said, "The Organization will spot you right away."

Beffort opened his suitcases and said, "In here I have everything I need to look like I want. Warn your men that they're about to get a chubby-cheeked man with a moustache and glasses in their sights."

Disguised like that, Beffort looked like any other traveling businessman, but oddly enough, he seemed nice. Not that traveling businessmen are not nice, mind you, but for Beffort it was something new. He could have felt uncomfortable, out of his skin, awkward and with a complex. However, the goal he had set evaporated most of the annoying obligations his new character required. To be convincing, a character study always has to look natural and when Beffort pulled his rented Buick up to the curb, everyone could tell that Dolly McIntyre's curves were the only reason for the sudden stop.

Beffort lowered his window and said, "Wherever you're going, doll, it's on my way!" He was really only interested in the girl's reaction. He had spent the last night learning pretty much everything he could in such a short time about a young woman living alone.

Dolly glanced at him, saw right away that he was her type, and smiled. Her reflex was immediately recorded by the Great Brain, which freed up a computer to assess Beffort. A file soon started circulating from one sector to another until the card fell into the sorting box with the one word printed on it: *Good*.

An impulse rushed into Dolly's motor-brain and she stepped forward, saying, "I'm going to Tremont Street."

"Great!" Beffort boomed cheerfully, opening the door. "What luck! I'm headed that way!"

Dolly sat next to him casually. When she crossed her legs, her skirt hiked up. Even being radio-controlled, she was ravishing, still as much of a vamp and Beffort knew he was playing with fire in two ways. On the one hand, he risked, like anyone, going soft for the young woman's youth and beauty because he knew she was a victim of Madame Atomos. On the other hand, Miss McIntyre, even though a victim, would not hesitate to kill him if the Great Brain gave the order.

"You're probably in a hurry, right?" he asked.

"Not too much. I start work at 9 o'clock."

Beffort headed for Tremont Street. Through Chandler's quick investigation he had found out that Dolly had not gone to the agency on the day of T.B. Clark's disappearance.

"You know," he said with gusto, "I've been hanging out in front of your building for a few days now."

"Go on!" Dolly said. She was not really reacting normally. The Great Brain was guiding her to a specific goal: neutralize the man in the Buick and bring him on board the *Lanaï* docked at Pier 2 in Hingham Bay. This was not easy because Dolly did not have the will-paralyzing emitter anymore. Clay was carrying it when the longhaired young man met him and since then no servant had been able to bring it back to her. And now, being the headhunter of the Organization, the young woman was supposed to live like nothing was wrong. At the moment she was going to the travel agency where she would work all day long. Therefore, the man in the Buick was supposed to be lured with enough enthusiasm to come back to see her in the evening. It must be said that in this the Great Brain knew how to pick its servants because Dolly was not lacking allure.

"I was waiting," Beffort continued, "for you to be alone…"

Dolly snapped out of her meditation. The Great Brain had just given her the program to follow and she was set for the day. "I'll say," she smiled, "you've got plenty of spunk, don't you?"

"Generally," Beffort claimed without a hint of arrogance, "I always get what I want. What time do you get off work?"

"6:30."

"What are doing this evening?"

Dolly pulled her skirt up a little, tossed her hair back and said languidly, "Uh, nothing special. What do you have in mind?"

Beffort forced himself to stay cool, but it took a serious effort. Dolly was seducing him outright, pulling out all stops, and even though she was dressed, she was revealing as much as if she were nude. It was beautiful work, almost an art, this way of stretching the fabric over her perfect curves.

Beffort assured her, "I'm full of ideas. For starters, we could have dinner in some trendy joint?"

Dolly frowned and slid over on the bench seat. Her body was suddenly touching Beffort's. Just then the Buick was cruising down a calm little street lined with gardens.

"Stop for a minute," Dolly whispered. "I don't need to get to work early."

Beffort pulled over to the curb, put on the handbrake and slipped his arm over the girl's shoulders.

"The restaurant," she said, "doesn't turn me on."

Her lips puckered and Beffort leaned over to kiss her. He managed to keep under control: while his left hand paid the usual homage to Dolly, his right hand discreetly explored her skull containing the dreadful motorbrain. Since he knew where to look, he found the dreadful half-moon scar with no problem. There was no doubt about it now.

Dolly wriggled free and whispered in his ear, "Tonight, why not come over to my place? I live alone and it'll be cozier for us to talk, don't you think?"

She was amazingly sensual. Beffort was not quite sure anymore if he was really playing a role. He had not been in a situation like this for a long time and even though he was a federal agent, he was still a man. But his mission was precisely to get intimate with the girl…

"Okay!" he said. "I'll buy a chicken and a bottle of champagne."

Dolly took his hand and spun his wedding ring, which he had not thought to take off. "And your wife?"

"Don't worry. I don't live in Boston."

"Business trip?"

"I'm here for a couple of weeks… So, we're good for tonight? You're not going to stand me up?"

Dolly offered her lips again as an answer and this time he let loose the passion she inspired in him. Dolly pushed him back, looked at the clock on the dashboard and said, "It's almost 9! Quick, take me to 7 Tremont Street!'

Beffort started the car and sped away, regaining his calm little by little. This girl got his blood flowing so he would have to be very careful tonight at her place. Still, he was not forgetting that she was controlled, that every word and gesture was dictated to her by the Great Brain. But the erotic charm her body emanated was real and that was what he had to fight against.

While he was musing, Dolly put on her lipstick, fixed her hair, smoothed out her skirt and straightened her blouse.

All of a sudden Beffort remembered the famous neutralization hour when the servants of Madame Atomos became themselves again. It was a necessity that the Organization had never been able to get rid of. After 23 hours of duty under the constant control of an electronic machine, the servants of the Great Brain needed to turn back to normal so that nature could regenerate them according to its own laws. During these 60 minutes of neutralization, the motor-brains were turned off and Madame Atomos lost complete control of her creatures. Moreover it was due to this neutralization hour that Mie Azusa-Beffort and other members of the Organization had been able to be operated on in the Atlanta clinic. But at that time, they knew that the neutralization always took place between 9 and 10 in the morning and they could prepare the transportation and operation with certainty. Since then, Madame Atomos had changed everything. Nevertheless, the neutralization hour still existed, by necessity, but when?

Beffort started thinking about Dolly's work schedule. If she worked in the agency all day long, she needed to be lucid. Well, the neutralization made the subject comatose, unstable, unable to follow through on any concrete action. So, Dolly probably had to transform during the night...

"Why don't we have lunch together?" Beffort proposed, sounding her out.

It was barely noticeable when Dolly tensed up. She answered, "No way! Between 12 and 1 p.m. I have to watch the agency!"

"You have to watch the office when everyone else is having a nice lunch? Why's that?"

Dolly smiled nervously. "Someone has to answer the phone. A travel agency has to be available to its clients all the time... Thanks, we're here. See you tonight at 6:30."

Beffort stopped. Dolly caressed his cheek, opened the door and jumped nimbly onto the sidewalk. Beffort watched her sway into the agency. He sat there without moving for a long time after she had disappeared. He wondered if the neutralization hour might just not be between 12 and 1 in the afternoon.

Chapter V

At 12:05 Beffort phoned the agency. It rang a dozen times, but nobody picked up.

"Seems like you were right," Chandler commented.

Beffort hung up and donned a big hat. He had changed his look and was now a Texan farmer. He had a salt and pepper moustache and thick sideburns covering his cheeks. To top off the disguise he had put on a tartan overcoat borrowed from the FBI wardrobe and brown leather boots from the same place.

Chandler handed him a keychain. "My car's in front of the building."

Beffort took the keys, went out of the office and down to the first floor. He climbed into Chandler's Ford, started it up and sped off to Tremont Street. He stopped directly in front of the agency, got out of the car and limped, for show, to the front door. As he was expecting, the agency was closed. Now he just had to find out where Dolly McIntyre was hiding. It was of the utmost importance because if she really was free of the Great Brain's control, it would mean that the Atomos Organization was vulnerable between 12 and 1 p.m.

The agency was not big and through the window he could easily see that it was empty. There was a dark recess, probably to hang coats, but Beffort could not see inside it. Still, he did not think Dolly was hiding in this closet. He did not think so, but he would not have sworn to it.

He knew pretty well what the robots felt during the sudden pause when The Great Brain left them to themselves, waking up suddenly in a place they did not re-

45

member coming to. Dolly was waking up somewhere familiar. Nevertheless, she must have known that time had not stopped since the day before and been anxiously asking herself what had happened in the meantime. And how strongly did she feel that she was really living for only one hour a day? If she guessed the truth, could she stand having undergone an operation? It could be, but anyway, the poor girl must have been drowning in an awful panic.

Beffort walked away from the agency, still limping to fool any would-be observer, and went down the street examining the restaurants closely and checking out the back alleys. He had to be very careful as long as he was not absolutely sure that the Atomos Organization was neutralized. And there was only one way to be certain: find Dolly before 1 p.m.

He wandered around until 12:40 and was starting to give up hope when he saw Dolly sitting at a table in the back of a snack bar, staring blankly at her plate. Beffort kept an eye on the young lady while pretending to consult the six menus hanging strangely by a string in the window. For anyone unaware, Dolly was just pouting over her lunch. For Beffort it was clear that she was trying not to attract attention to himself. She was acting like someone suffering from an embarrassing sickness, maybe contagious, of unknown origin, and, at the very least, shameful.

Beffort entered the snack bar. It was pretty crowded but there were still a lot of empty tables. Beffort chose a place next to Dolly, grabbed a plate, took a ticket, paid the bill and went to sit at his table. After a minute he turned toward the young lady. Since he was so close, his movement drew her attention and their eyes met.

"Hey," Beffort drawled in a heavy Texan accent, "don't you work in that travel agency on Tremont Street?"

Dolly nodded once and turned back to her plate. She did not want to talk to anyone and no doubt regretted being recognized. Her personal problem was more important than anything else. Maybe she thought she was crazy?

"Say," Beffort pressed her, "don't you remember me? I came to see you this morning to organize a trip to Europe and you told me to come back this afternoon... I didn't know your office was closing. Since I was left high and dry, what time do you reopen?"

Dolly examined him carefully. Of course she did not remember him and this only made her troubles worse. "The agency opens at 1:30," she forced herself to say.

No matter how hard she tried, she did not recall what happened this morning, or last night, or yesterday afternoon... In fact, her last precise memory dated back to exactly 23 hours ago. Like today, she found herself sitting at a table in a snack bar before a full plate, totally ignorant of how she had wound up there. Sometimes the fog dissipated a little and she told herself that her name was Dolly McIntyre, that she lived at 455C Washington Street, that she worked in a travel agency on Tremont Street... Then she repeated the name T.B. Clark without being able to put a face to it and she wondered who he was.

"You're not too talkative," Beffort grumbled, playing the Texan farmer with conviction. "This morning at the agency you were nicer. By the way, you still haven't told me if this Clark guy is your husband or friend or what." He tried to nudge her gently back on the right track.

Dolly abruptly looked back up at him. "Clark?" She was totally lost.

Beffort figured that she had not belonged to the Atomos Organization for a long time. She was still traumatized by the brain operation. During the neutralization hour she did not manage to recover herself entirely. That would come gradually and her agony would be horrible when she figured it out.

In the meantime, there was nothing Beffort could do for her without risking her death. At 1 p.m. the Great Brain would take control of her again. If, for any reason, she did not respond to its call, it would kill her on the spot.

He did not answer Dolly's question and she did not repeat it for one simple reason: she had already forgotten it. Beffort wolfed down his lunch, got up and left without Dolly looking over at him.

At 1:02 the young lady was on the street. Her expression had changed completely. Now she looked very lucid, self-confident and extremely cheerful. However, she did not walk quite normally; she looked a little off-balance, a little hesitant… It was a subtle vision of a spring mechanism that took the experienced eye of Beffort to catch because only the servants of the Organization had it.

Instead of going directly to the agency, Dolly made a long detour strolling through the streets. Beffort followed her at a distance, not really knowing what to expect, but sure of having achieved a great victory over Madame Atomos: from now on he knew when the neutralization hour took place… All of a sudden and for no apparent reason, Dolly turned around, sped up and went back toward Tremont St. Beffort glued himself to a storefront window, let her pass and got on her tail again, being twice as careful.

Dolly crossed the street and went to the end of Tremont where she turned off suddenly into a narrow street. Beffort lost sight of her and sprinted to the corner just in time to see Dolly climb into an old Chevrolet. The young woman sat next to the driver, a young man with long hair and pale skin, but the car did not move.

From his vantage point, Beffort could see Dolly and her weird companion perfectly. He was sure that they had not said a word to each other before the girl got out of the car holding, as well as her purse, a heavy-looking, square package.

Beffort did not waste his time trying to know the purpose of this brief encounter. The old Chevy was on a one-way street that came out on Tremont. He ran to Chandler's Ford, jumped in and turned the engine over just as the other car materialized at the corner. Beffort spun the wheel and got on the tail of the old heap. He did not bother about Dolly: she would stay at the agency all afternoon and, as agreed, he would see her at 6:30 p.m.

At the same time, but 5000 miles to the west of Boston, a rather mundane scene was playing out in one of the underground rooms on Atomia Island. This square room (about 65 square feet) was split in two by a grill extending from the floor to the ceiling, from one wall to the other. One half contained an armchair in which Madame Atomos was sitting. The other side of the grill was furnished, all the way down to a rug and reconstructed fireplace. But it was a complete mishmash. They had not even bothered to match colors: white, wooden chairs

49

next to a wicker crib, a shag rug lying by Spanish throw rugs… In truth it was a bunch of ugly odds and ends.

In the middle of this crowd of junk was a monstrous mannequin made of chunks of meat. A metal armature held up this gruesome doll, whose shape roughly resembled a child.

At 1:30 p.m. Madame Atomos raised her hand and pressed a button on the back of her armchair. On the opposite side of the grill the fireplace screen slid into its housing and revealed a 3 by 2 foot rectangular opening. Two seconds ticked off and then a tiger traipsed through the hole. It was a huge beast, powerful and silent…

On its arrival, a shriek rang out and the repulsive doll started moving forward between the rugs by means of an electronic mechanism operating a small cart. It was very clear that the tiger had been trained to run after its meal. With a tremendous leap, it crossed the distance separating it from the chunks of meat and sank its fangs into the doll, which collapsed under the weight…

The old Chevrolet cruised slowly, apparently at random, through Boston for 30 minutes. Smith Beffort followed it cautiously all the way to Hyde Park Avenue, wondering what all the seemingly pointless twists and turns meant. Around 2 p.m. the Chevy stopped at the edge of Hyde Park, near the river that ran down the southern part of the huge park, but the longhaired young man stayed in the car, ready to wait.

To be safe, Beffort stopped much farther back between other parked cars. He started thinking that the young man was acting like this to see if anyone was following him. It was the typical kind of precaution the Atomos Organization took when an operation was in progress.

Nothing happened for a long time. Beffort lit his last cigarette. He was very anxious and smoking far too much in order to calm his nerves because he knew he was on the right track. Sooner or later the old Chevy would lead him to the refuge of the Atomos Organization.

Up ahead, for the first time since he had parked his car, the young man showed some interest in a young lady pushing a stroller and holding the hand of a little girl walking next to her. The girl could not have been more than two or three years old. In the Chevy, the guy fidgeted around and then an antenna stuck out of the car. In that instant Beffort did not make the connection, but the young lady and the girl froze simultaneously in the middle of the path. Then they turned around and walked very naturally to the Chevrolet. When they reached the sidewalk the young man got out casually, took the woman by the arm and the girl by the hand, and led them into the back of his car. After closing the door he went back to get the stroller, which he folded up and put in the trunk. In no time at all he was back behind the wheel, pulling away from the curb and driving right past Beffort, heading east.

Everything happened slowly and Beffort could see that the young lady was very calm. Not knowing that Madame Atomos was using a will-paralyzing emitter, there was no way for him to know that the young man had just captured two new victims. The woman would enter the Organization doing the same thing as Dolly McIntyre. The little girl would be sent to Atomia Island—From now on the tiger could continue its training with living subjects!

The old Chevrolet crossed Milton, Quincy and entered Hingham Bay through Weymouth. It drove to Pier

2 and stopped in front of the *Lanaï* where the young man brought out his passengers. A few seconds later the trio had crossed the gangway of the yacht and disappeared from Beffort's view. The G-man left his car and strolled along the pier, catching the name of the yacht, which made his heart skip a beat. Lanaï was one of the Hawaiian Islands. A yacht here by that name was certainly no coincidence. This might mean that Atomia Island was around the island of Lanaï… or that Madame Atomos had changed the name to keep her ultimate refuge secret.

Beffort strayed off to walk by the old Chevy. He leaned over and saw that the guy had left a square box with an antenna on the front seat. He knew immediately that this object fit the exact description that Clay had given to J.E.E. on the phone before he disappeared. He glanced around to make sure no one was watching and snatched up the device. Then he hurried back to his car, started it up and sped off toward downtown. Now his most urgent task was to find out what this mysterious box was all about.

20 minutes after Beffort left, the longhaired young man reappeared on the deck of the *Lanaï*. He walked back down the gangway, onto the pier, and climbed back into the Chevrolet. Conditioned as he was, there was no reason for him to think about the emitter for the moment. He had to get back to the city to find more victims. When the time came, when he needed the device, he would reach out and, of course, grab nothing but empty air. Then the alert would be given to the Great Brain and straightaway relayed to Madame Atomos, but how could either of them imagine that Smith Beffort was behind the disappearance?

Without knowing it, Beffort was sitting pretty.

Chapter VI

While Beffort and Chandler were busy in the FBI laboratory with a handful of electronic specialists, some G-men boarded a Coast Guard gunboat and started staking out the *Lanaï*.

In the lab, the eight men were huddled around the bizarre box whose telescopic antenna had retracted. Beffort explained, "The problem is we can't take the thing apart to see what's inside."

"Why not?" Chandler asked.

"If we do, and I'm speaking from experience, we may alert the Atomos Organization instantly. In this box you can bet there's a signal waiting to go off if we take off the cover… if not a bomb that will blow us to smithereens."

"Nice," Chandler grumbled.

Beffort smirked and said, "When something's got the Atomos stamp, don't ever expect any good, Chandler. This device was made to destroy, that's for sure."

"What?"

Beffort turned to the engineers. "In your opinion…" he invited.

One of the men shook his head, "Impossible. We're not magicians. This contraption might do anything, anywhere, at any time and we won't be able to determine its use just by looking at it. We're like surgeons: we have to open up to say for sure."

Beffort sighed. "Stalemate. But anything else would surprise me. How can we know what this box does if we can't even make it work?"

The engineer said, "There's one way. We have a chamber here to test explosives. The explosion is contained and half a ton of TNT can be set off without danger."

"Okay, but how do we work the box?"

"Mechanical arms. You can watch through a special wide-angle sight. Even if this thing is stuffed with TNT, the chamber won't be scratched. In my opinion, it's doable."

"Okay!" Beffort accepted. "Let's go!"

The group went to the basement and into a rectangular, concrete room in the center of which was a huge metal tube built from floor to ceiling like a chimney. The tube was 15 feet in diameter on the outside, but only 6 on the inside; the difference due to the armor and the padding to buffer the shockwave from the explosion. Beffort had the opportunity to see a similar set up in Houston at the space center. The model here was smaller but no doubt big enough for the present experiment.

The specialists placed the box on the floor of the chamber, closed the heavy door and invited Beffort and Chandler to watch the procedure through the sight. Beffort saw a mechanical arm detach from the padded wall and stretch out slowly until its three pincers were over the box. The antenna was pulled out and the knobs turned. Nothing happened.

"A bag of tricks, eh?" Chandler said, being convinced that they were wasting their time.

Beffort did not reply. In a flash he remembered how willingly the young woman and girl in Hyde Park had followed the young man with long hair. Now that he had time to think calmly, the episode seemed extraordinary. As far as he could recall, the first time the woman passed by the Chevrolet, she paid no attention to it. Then the young man pulled out the antenna and the woman and girl stopped in their tracks, turned around…

"Say, Chandler," Beffort proposed, "would you mind going into the chamber?"

Chandler shrugged. "I'm not scared, but what's the point?"

"Just an experiment. Let's say you could try some routine action like untying and retying your shoes or throwing your keys down and picking them up and then just sit down."

"Are you kidding?"

"No. We'll reset the box back to zero."

"Okay," one of the specialists said, "let's do it." He worked the commands of the mechanical arm and the antenna went back into its housing while the knobs were reset.

Beffort opened the door and said, "I'll just ask you to start your performance when the device is working again. If my hunch is right, you won't even be able to lift your pinky."

Chandler laughed, "I'll take that bet at 10 to 1. For starters, I'm the one who'll start it up. Now shut the door."

Beffort swung the heavy door closed, turned the lock and went back to his observation post. Chandler motioned that he was starting the experiment. He pulled out the antenna, turned the knob and stepped back. He leaned over to untie his shoelaces, but did not finish the movement. He was stuck, bent over, as if petrified, apparently unable to stand up or move at all.

"Damn!" the engineer exclaimed. "Looks like you were right."

"Stop everything! Quick!" Beffort shouted.

The mechanical arm shot out, pushed down the antenna and reset the knob. Chandler instantly untied and retied his laces. After that he threw a key down, picked it up and sat on the floor with a little, triumphant smile. Clearly he had absolutely no idea that he had been paralyzed for nearly 30 seconds.

Beffort opened the door. Chandler came back saying, "So, what do you think about that?" He suddenly saw the expression on their faces and his smile turned into a smirk. "Don't tell me I didn't do what I was supposed to!"

Beffort told him what had happened, adding, "You didn't move because no one was there to give you orders. But if a member of the Atomos Organization had been holding the box, you would have done anything they asked. This device destroys the willpower of whoever is in its range, including the operator, unless they have a motor-brain controlled by the Great Brain!'

"Which means," the engineer concluded, "that we all would have been neutralized if we had turned it on anywhere but here. Luckily there's 10 feet of armor between us and the waves."

In the ensuing silence, Chandler mumbled, "So, that means we can't use this diabolical invention against the Organization."

"No," Beffort agreed, "and we'd better destroy it before it starts turning on by itself."

"Don't worry about that," the engineer assured him. "In five minutes there will be nothing left but a heap of burnt scrap iron."

Beffort and Chandler left the specialists to deal with the emitter. They went back up to the first floor and climbed into the car parked across from the lab.

Beffort headed downtown and said, "Now, at least, we know what danger is threatening us when some stranger points an antenna in our vicinity."

"As long as we see him in time…"

"Of course. Besides that young man I told you about, I wonder how many robots are running around Boston? Because we have to admit that Madame Atomos is launching her next attack against the United States in your city."

Lost in thought, Chandler did not comment and the two men kept silent all the way to FBI headquarters.

Once in Chandler's office, Beffort got rid of his farmer costume and turned back into the character Dolly was expecting to see at 6:30. After that he got on the phone to call the secret base of the Green Dragon Force and then J.E.E.'s office in Washington D.C. On the first call to Owen Bernitz, he ordered him to gather his troops and get to Boston on the double with weapon and baggage. He asked J.E.E. to call Yosho Akamatsu in Tokyo and mobilize Witter and Hyde. The three men should contact Beffort as soon as possible at the FBI in Boston.

"Hell," J.E.E. said, "it's a call to arms, isn't it?"

"Precisely. We have to nip the attack in the bud, whatever Madame Atomos is fixing up. This time we're lucky to be on the right track before anything's been fully unleashed."

"What kind of track?"

"A yacht moored in Hingham Bay, plus a young man who's a member of the Organization and this famous Dolly who I'm meeting in half an hour. Don't forget to tell Akamatsu about the emitter, okay?"

"You can count on me, Smith. Be careful and good luck!"

Beffort hung up. He had just done everything in his power to foil the sinister plots of Madame Atomos. To-night Owen Bernitz and his men would land in Boston is small groups. They would be armed with paralyzing guns and would put out of service any members of the Organization carrying the terrible square box.

Likewise, Witter and Hyde and then Akamatsu would enter the game, all of whom had been fighting Madame Atomos from the start and their experience would weigh heavily in the balance when it came time to settle the score...

Beffort left Chandler to handle the telephone and went to meet Dolly McIntyre.

At the Beffort's house in Williamsburg, Soblen, Mie and little Bob were starting to get used to the dogs, who, it must be said, were interested in nothing but their assigned task. Since their arrival they had not stopped making their rounds in the yard, watchful and silent, tak-ing turns with amazing regularity, sleeping in pairs and eating the food that Mie prepared for them.

"Fantastic," Soblen said, observing them, "you'd have to see it to believe it. With guards like this we can sleep soundly, don't you think, Mie?"

The young lady stopped peeling the orange for Bob, looked up and said, "I'm not as calm as you, doctor. Mr. Evans just called to tell us that the Atomos Organization is preparing something in Boston. We're not so far from there..."

"Oh, it's a good 600 miles!"

Mie rubbed her son's cheek and unconsciously put her hand on the butt of the paralyzing pistol that she car-ried in her belt. "Distance means nothing to Madame Atomos," she said gravely. "Since Smith left, I've stopped living... Every time something happens, it's when he's gone. So, when he leaves us, I always think that Madame Atomos is taking him away in order to make us more vulnerable."

Soblen made an effort to smile. "Nonsense!" he tried to sound casual. "There's nothing to fear here. Give that orange to Bob instead of mashing it up! He's falling asleep... While waiting to put him to bed, I'll make sure we're locked up tight."

Soblen left the living room and went to make a quick but thorough inspection of the doors and windows on the first floor; he came back with his mind at rest. Night had come on a little while before and through the thick windows the dogs looked like ghostly forms in their brief passage across the front yard. Soblen looked away. Eventually he would end up with the weird feeling that the yard was full of dogs. He was not seeing six anymore, but twelve... Ridiculous!

In the living room, Bob was sleeping on top of his orange slices. "I'm going to put him to bed," Mie said tenderly. "Are you coming, doctor?"

Being single and, of course, without children, Soblen had a tendency to spoil his godson. He was the one who picked up Bob. He took him in his arms and went up to the second floor talking a strange baby language that at least had the advantage of making Mie smile.

There were three rooms on the second floor: Bob's room next to his parents and the guest room across from them, which was empty for now. While Mie put her son to bed, Soblen checked all the shutters—on that score, there was nothing to fear. He went back to kiss Bob, whose eyes were already closing, and then adjusted the heat, as well as the small nightlight artfully installed in the fireplace.

Mie tucked in her son, dragged Soblen into the hallway and said, "I'll take the first watch tonight."

Soblen protested weakly, just for show, but he needed sleep and finally accepted. A watch had been agreed upon to keep an eye on the dogs: Soblen and Mie would replace each other every two hours. It was no holiday!

Around the same time, a man stopped his car in the Williamsburg Inn parking lot, one of the three exclusive hotels in town, and then brought his suitcase up to his room, which he had reserved under the name of Harrison. When he came down, he filled in the registration form, wrote that he came from Philadelphia where he worked as a supervisor at an osteopathy school. His job must have made him spend long hours indoors because his skin was pale and his walk a little jerky.

Harrison got back in his car and oddly enough started driving at random through the town. He made a quick tour, came back to where he had started and right away took off on a new route.

An hour later, Harrison stopped his car on a quiet, little street, turned off the lights and lowered the window. Then, totally unexpectedly, he laid his head back on his seat and closed his eyes. To a police car passing by he could have been a tired traveler, taking a snooze before continuing on his way. In reality, Harrison was not sleeping at all. Between his half-closed eyelids, he was watching the Beffort's house and all the images he caught were sent directly back to Atomia Island.

Madame Atomos had found her target!

Chapter VII

Still in Chandler's Ford, Beffort headed for the agency. He quickly understood that he was late for his rendezvous with Dolly McIntyre. It was the end of the workday and the streets of Boston were blackened by cars and pedestrians. And the night had come, along with a cold, incessant drizzle sweeping through the streets, which did not help traffic.

At 6:40 Beffort finally turned onto Tremont Street. At first he did not see Dolly and thought he had spoiled his best chance to trace back to Madame Atomos. Still, he drove up to the agency, whose lights were out, and saw the young woman waiting patiently in the entrance next door. With a sigh of relief, Beffort stopped in front of her and waved. Dolly smiled, waved back and came to the car. She was carrying both her purse and the infamous square package that the longhaired young man had given her, but now Beffort believed he knew what the package contained.

Dolly climbed in and said right away, "I almost didn't recognize you! This morning you were in a Buick, weren't you?"

Beffort realized that in his haste he had just made his first mistake. Pressed by time he had completely forgotten about his rented Buick parked in the lot of the federal building.

"It wasn't mine," he said casually, "but a company car. And this is one of theirs, too."

"I don't mind," Dolly smiled, "because you told me you didn't live in Boston but the Buick's plates were from here. I hate liars!"

She leaned over and kissed him. Beffort told himself he was lucky. Without the mistake, it would probably have looked like the Buick was his. But Dolly's remark proved that the Great Brain had an eye on everything and that Beffort had to be constantly on his toes.

Dolly turned around and put her purse and package on the backseat. Beffort shifted into first, drove slowly, and asked, "You really don't want to go to a restaurant?"

Dolly looked at him with surprise. Beffort saw that he should not push it too hard. A beautiful girl was offering him her hospitality for the night and he was talking about a restaurant! His attitude might seem suspicious under such conditions. Of course, he could not say that his main objective was to stay alive until noon tomorrow at the next neutralization. For this it was absolutely necessary that he keep the girl from using the device in her package. And there was no way of him stealing it away between the agency and Washington Street.

"I have what we need in my refrigerator," Dolly said, "and unless you eat like an ogre…"

"No!" Beffort cut in. "I wasn't thinking of myself. I simply wanted to celebrate our meeting with a special night out. After all, everyday life is pretty boring. You were working for nine and a half hours non-stop and I thought of doing something nice for you."

Dolly smiled and caressed his cheek. "You're sweet. You know, you haven't even told me your name? Me, I'm Dolly."

"My name's Samuel, but you can call me Sam. So, we go to your place?"

"Okay! You know where it is."

Beffort sped up, thinking feverishly. If he let himself get cornered by the girl, she would use her terrible box and he would be turned into a robot. There was still the possibility of pulling out his paralyzing pistol, but neutralizing Dolly meant alerting the entire Atomos Organization.

"In spite of everything, I'm going to buy a chicken and a nice bottle of something," Beffort acted naturally. "Nobody can say I went over to your place empty-handed."

"You're stubborn! I have everything we need at home."

"I know, I know, doll, but I'm wearing the pants here, right?" As he was talking he pulled up to a drug-store and opened his door. "Don't move. I won't be five minutes."

It went unanswered. He entered the drugstore, which was jam-packed, fought his way through the crowd and dove into a telephone booth. Dolly could not see him from where she was and he hoped that he had not been followed by a member of the Organization. Anyway, he had to take the risk.

He dialed Chandler's number, got him on the line right away and said, "Beffort here. Listen carefully, Chandler, and don't interrupt me. In six or seven minutes I'm going to stop your car in front of a store on Washington Street. The car will be empty for a minute. One of your boys has to be there and steal the square package on the back seat. Possible?"

"Certainly," Chandler kept it short. "A car is following you."

"That wasn't in the plan…"

"Your hide is very important to J.E.E. and I'm only following orders. Sorry."

"Okay," Beffort groaned. "For once it's a good thing."

"And how! I know exactly where you are and I can even tell you that after you left Dolly picked up her purse and package. My boys are updating me every minute. In my opinion, the girl won't leave the package in the car to run into a store with you."

Beffort clenched his jaws. Chandler was probably right.

"Listen," Chandler proposed, "leave it up to us and just try to ignore us."

"You must be joking!"

"My men aren't idiots! They'll swipe the package before you get to 455C Washington Street, don't worry. Still, you have to get Dolly to go shopping with you no matter what."

"Okay," Beffort accepted begrudgingly. "I'm leaving it in your hands. See you!"

He hung up and looked at his watch. He had not gone over his time limit and he could still buy a chicken. He did it quickly, without looking at his choice, and sprinted back to the car. Dolly had not budged, but, as Chandler had said, her purse and package were now in her lap. Beffort walked around the Ford and opened the door while inspecting the street. He thought he spied the FBI car pretty easily, but he would not have bet on it.

"Here's the chicken!" he said cheerfully, climbing behind the wheel. "Unfortunately this store doesn't sell champagne."

"Let's skip it," Dolly smiled.

"No way!" Beffort protested. "This is a red-letter day! Cigarette?"

Dolly helped herself. Beffort lit hers and then his own. He was trying his best to slow things down, to show that he intended to have a good time at a lazy pace. Logically, it was the opposite of what the Great Brain wanted. Dolly must have received orders to render her companion powerless as soon as possible.

"Shall we go home?" Dolly murmured. She was leaning on Beffort and using her charms exquisitely.

"Not before buying a bottle! Don't tell me you don't like champagne, sweetie?"

"I love it."

Beffort now drove to Washington Street. He spotted a grocery store, stopped the Ford again and decided, "Come with me!"

Without giving Dolly the chance to respond, he walked around the car, opened the door and took the girl by the arm, obliging her to get out. He was gently insistent and it was becoming hard for her to refuse him anything. Dolly let him take her, but she did not let go of her purse or package. Beffort pretended not to notice, hiding his disappointment, and led her into the store. Like the other, it was crowded; it was the busiest time of the day. This one was a self-service and its aisles were bustling with carts pushed by people who paid no attention to anyone else.

Beffort grabbed a cart and followed the crowd crawling toward the aisles. He was clumsy, often bumping into other people. He ended up turning to Dolly and saying in frustration, "Can you push his thing for me? I feel like I'm pushing a stroller!"

He did not give her the choice. Dolly put her purse and package in the rack and took her station in a good mood. Under the bright lights, she was almost white, but it was not because of the lights. Every minute she was losing a little more of what made her a human being. Her organism was working in slow motion, only under electromagnetic impulse, and in a few hours, she would have the sickly appearance of the oldest members of the

Atomos Organization. Beffort fought against the pity she inspired in him because as long as she had a motor-brain, she was extremely dangerous and invulnerable. Of course the paralyzing ray could render her harmless, but only fire could destroy her...

"Come this way, Dolly, I see the champagne."

She followed him docilely to the shelf. Beffort was thinking that Chandler's men would take advantage of the crowd to steal the package. He was hoping that they were nearby and could jump at the opportunity he was giving them.

He raised his arm, grabbed a bottle of champagne and held it out to Dolly. "Here!" He purposely held it too far. Dolly stepped forward and turned her back to the cart for a split second. Her body was in the way and Beffort had to wait for her to move before he could see the cart again. Then he had to keep himself from swearing: the package was still there!

Dolly was already heading for the checkout. Beffort followed her and paid for the champagne. Dolly left the cart and picked up her purse and package but left the bottle to Beffort, who looked around and met the eyes of a man in a gray overcoat. The guy winked at him and disappeared instantly.

"Well, Sam, are you coming?"

Beffort took her arm, walked out of the store and went back to the Ford. Worried now, Beffort wondered what that guy's wink meant.

Dolly giggled but was a little irritated, "You really aren't in hurry! I don't see lovers like you very often!'

"Sorry. Where I come from, people are a little slow... But we're going to catch up on lost time, believe me!"

Nervously he turned the ignition, but as he pulled away the car started bouncing. Beffort stopped. Now he knew what the wink meant.

"What's wrong?" Dolly asked.

"Flat tire," Beffort explained. "Sorry, doll, but I have to change it. What bad luck!"

"Darn! Will it take long?"

"Hey, if I find the jack right away, I think I can do it in fifteen minutes. As long as the spare isn't flat and…"

"Oh no!" Dolly moaned. "Our evening is ruined!"

Behind Dolly, Beffort saw the guy's face framed in the window. He winked again, waved his hand around pointing to Dolly and then got lost in the crowd.

"Listen," Beffort proposed, thinking he had correctly interpreted the silent language of the G-man, "I won't put you through this. Why don't you go ahead and I'll join you after I've fixed the tire."

Dolly seemed to hesitate.

"We're hardly 200 yards from your place," Beffort insisted. "By the time you put the champagne in the fridge, cut up the chicken and set the table, I'll be there. Okay?"

"Okay," the young lady suddenly decided. "I live on the 12th floor. See you soon, Sam dear."

She gave him a kiss, snatched up the chicken and champagne and got out of the Ford. Beffort watched her walk off. Then he got out and went to look for the jack. He found everything he needed in the trunk and without much enthusiasm started setting up the jack.

After a minute, he felt someone next to him. He looked up and saw the winking man who asked, "Do you need some help?"

"Gladly," Beffort accepted. It was an excuse to talk without raising the suspicions of any would-be observer.

The G-man squatted down and held the tire, whispering, "Everything's okay. We switched the package with an identical one and the girl didn't see a thing."

"Bravo! I fell for it, too. How'd you do it?"

"Chandler had already figured that the package was important. During your first stop in the drugstore, my partner strolled by the car where the girl was waiting. The object in question was in her lap. It was about the size of a box of cookies, ordinary wrapping paper and held together with tape. While you were calling Chandler, my partner bought what we needed at the drugstore and we made a copy that we switched in the grocery store. Chandler was kept up-to-date on our project and that's why he suggested you take the girl with you to go shopping."

"Good work," Beffort admired sincerely. He went to put the flat in the trunk and brought back the spare. "The flat is your work, isn't it?"

"It was the only way to tell you without the girl around," the G-man explained while helping him put the spare on. Then he added, "Now we're at your disposal. You're going to the girl's place, right?"

"Yes, because the success of my plan depends on her. On the orders from the Great Brain, she might take off at any time and that's exactly what I want to avoid. My only goal is not to leave her before tomorrow at noon."

"What can we do for you?"

"Do you have paralyzing guns?"

"Of course!"

"Then fix it so that nobody enters Dolly's apartment. But do it discreetly, which means without being seen. The Great Brain is will probably react when is sees that the package is nothing but a box of cookies, but it won't understand yet what happened and so might not suspect me. However, since Dolly can't take me on alone, I think it'll send someone to help her."

"Why do you think the Great Brain is so set on you?"

"Not especially me," Beffort smiled. "The Atomos Organization brings people in by the dozens and I would be as good a recruit as T.B. Clark or Clay. Tomorrow, if you're unlucky enough to meet up with a servant of the Organization, it'll be your turn. Right now, no one is safe from the Atomos danger, so keep your eyes and ears open."

The G-man smiled weakly, "Be careful. By the way, who should we be looking for in particular?"

"Watch out for a longhaired, pale young man," Beffort said as he put the jack away. "If he shows up on Washington Street, give him a good dose of the paralyzing ray!"

"Don't worry, we'll stop him."

Beffort nodded, but was not convinced. For the audience, he shook the volunteers hand and offered him a cigarette. He asked, "In case I need you, I'll call Chandler. What's your name?"

"Benchley. But remember that we'll be in the building. At the slightest sign…"

"No," Beffort stopped him. "No clumsy heroics. If I need help, I'll call Chandler, who will contact you immediately by radio. Otherwise, don't move no matter what. Got it?"

"Got it."

Beffort got back in the Ford and took off. Now all he needed was a whole lot of luck.

Chapter VIII

Dolly closed the door of her apartment, put the chicken and champagne on the kitchen table, took off her jacket and then opened the package. At this moment, like the other 23 hours in the day, she was just a robot, so she was not startled when she saw the box of cookies instead of the will-paralyzing emitter, but on Atomia Island, an alarm ran through the computers and electronic sorters. The Great Brain's programming was not prepared for this kind of incident because it should not have happened.

Everything was programmed for Dolly to use the emitter against her visitor. The punch cards showed that the longhaired young man had given Dolly the good package with the device. He had then disappeared between 1:15 and now. Since Dolly could not be suspected and no one had touched the package, the Great Brain was faced with an insolvable enigma. In a case like this, it had to resort to primitive methods and consult a human brain. The relays started working immediately and a signal went off in Madame Atomos' office.

The diabolical woman got up, walked over to the machine with the flashing light and took the printed card sent by the Great Brain. Right away she guessed that the FBI or the Green Dragon Force, even Smith Beffort in person was behind the substitution. A logical deduction. Dolly McIntyre had done everything possible to look suspicious and it was normal that the Americans had decided to use her to attack the Organization.

Madame Atomos sneered. She had organized all this with the sole hope of bringing Smith Beffort to Boston and it seemed that her plan was working. Nevertheless, there was nothing to prove that Beffort had left his house in Williamsburg. In fact, and in spite of the remarkable means of information at her disposal, Madame Atomos had no idea where he might be. She only found about the Beffort's hideout 12 hours ago and Harrison, her servant, had not been watching the house for long.

Another alarm shook Madame Atomos out of her thoughts. The Great Brain was informing her that Dolly McIntyre was now inactive, that is, unable to act, and that could produce dangerous results.

Madame Atomos went into her command post next to the office and stood in front of a big board with red and green lights. Red for the men and green for the women. Each light represented a servant and was marked with an identification number. Dolly's was 2615. Madame Atomos started the network that allowed her to take control of any robot, pressed the button 2615 and sat in front of the TV, which would show everything Dolly saw; and before the speaker that would repeat everything she heard; and next to the microphone—here the operation was reversed because even though Dolly would be speaking, she would only be translating the words that Madame Atomos spoke into the microphone.

The screen clouded over, cleared up, and Madame Atomos suddenly found herself in Dolly McIntyre's apartment in Boston. She was not there in flesh and blood, but she could use all her senses as she wished. Thus, strange as it may seem, Smith Beffort, totally unaware, was going to have a private rendezvous with his formidable enemy who, on her side, was ignorant of his true identity...

Beffort rang the door of the apartment, listened to it purring quietly, then heard footsteps. A few long seconds passed before Dolly's distant voice said, "One second, I'm coming!"

Beffort lit a cigarette and leaned against the wall. He took a little mirror out of his pocket to check his disguise again. His moustache was holding up, as well as the sideburns rounding out his cheeks. As for the big, tinted, thick-framed glasses, they completely hid the expression in his eyes and eyebrows. In any unexpected situation, Beffort was sure that the Great Brain could not recognize him.

Suddenly the doorknob turned from the inside, it swung open and Dolly appeared in the doorframe, wearing a flustering negligee that liberally showed off her curves. She smiled sweetly. "Come in, Sam."

Beffort entered. He was more and more apprehensive and wondered how he would manage to avoid succumbing to the girl's charms without giving himself away. "You've got a nice place," he said flatly.

He turned around and saw Dolly staring curiously hard at him. Beffort could not guess that Madame Atomos was getting acquainted, but he felt that the belated examination was not normal. "If my face is smudged, I'm sorry," he said, changing the pitch of his voice a little. "Changing that damn tire was some work... By the way, I would love to wash my hands."

Dolly took his arm and led him to the bathroom. "Make yourself at home, Sam. There's some pajamas that should fit you."

She did not hide what she was expecting of him. To refuse or get stuffy would risk alerting the Great Brain. Even if he had to cheat on Mie, Beffort had to go all the way now. Besides, it was not exactly an unpleasant prospect, far from it.

"Is the champagne chilled?" he asked casually while undressing.

"It is," Dolly smiled. "Say, you're a lot stronger looking than I imagined!" She examined him shamelessly. Beffort was fainting from embarrassment, but the situation made him uncomfortable. He was forgetting that Dolly, even though ravishing, was just a robot and acting under orders.

Beffort cleverly snuck the paralyzing pistol into the pocket of his coat, using it as a screen, and hung his clothes on the coat rack. He said nonchalantly, "I don't mind you admiring my physique, but it's still not something I'm used to doing in front of a woman."

Dolly giggled, left and closed the door. Beffort took off the rest of his clothes and slipped on the pajamas marked with the initials T.B.C. He thought that Dolly and the Organization were not being very careful. Certainly, everyone knew that T.B. Clark was Dolly's lover, but to keep his clothes after he disappeared was going a little too far.

For the first time, Beffort had the vague feeling that something was not quite right. But he had no time to delve into it, and there was no turning back without setting off the alarm in the Great Brain.

He buttoned up the pajama shirt, washed his hands and hid the paralyzing pistol under the bathtub. He suspected that Dolly would search his things the first chance she got.

"Are you taking a bath in there?" Dolly shouted.

Beffort put on the slippers (no doubt the ones Clark wore when he stayed with Dolly) and left the bathroom. In the living room, Dolly had just set the table, cut up the chicken and lowered the lights.

"Come over here, Sam, and take off those awful glasses."

"I'm very shortsighted," Beffort claimed, "if you please, I'll keep them on for dinner."

On Atomia Island, Madame Atomos gave up out of boredom. She did not know who this man was, did not care, and wondered how the Great Brain could have selected him as a future member of the Organization. Shortsighted!

She gave Dolly back to the Great Brain, reprogrammed Sam as a negative, and went back into her office. For her, this myopic man, and relatively old to boot, could not enter the Atomos Organization.

The Great Brain, at the request of Madame Atomos through the other relays, delegated one of its innumerable computers to the task of resolving the problem posed by the disappearance of the two emitters. For, the most recent news that came inexplicable late was that the longhaired young man had just reported that his device was also missing from his car.

Madame Atomos recorded the bewildering news, evaluated the situation and found to her surprise that this information had been communicated two hours earlier. The card file was sitting on her desk, intact. Therefore, Madame Atomos, the supreme master of the Organization, had unconsciously neglected to follow up on this matter like common sense demanded.

Madame Atomos sat down, jaws clenched. Now there was no doubt about it: since she had voluntarily disintegrated to escape Smith Beffort and his men, she had lost some mastery over her mental facilities. For a woman like her, it was a tragic revelation. Thus, she realized that she had not done everything she should have with respect to Dolly McIntyre and her companion. The Great Brain had alerted her specifically about the disappearance of the emitter and she had completely forgotten about it in the course of events!

Madame Atomos fought against panic. She stood up and turned on the speaker system to the clinic on Atomia Island. There was a crackling sound and then a voice said, "Doctor Minao here."

"Minao," Madame Atomos said dryly, "I think I'm sick."

"What do you mean?" the doctor was alarmed. He belonged to the team of Japanese volunteers who were fighting by principle against the United States. With his colleagues, he had constructed the fantastic motor-brain, the disintegrator ray, the electromagnetic shield and the Great Brain. But, all this had been possible thanks to Madame Atomos' extraordinary genius and the fabulous sums of money she put at their disposal.

"Since my disintegration," Madame Atomos said, "I have memory lapses, troubles with my eyesight, dizziness... You have to fix this, Minao! Right now I'm unable to continue the new battle that I just started against the Befforts! I'm going to program the Great Brain, but you know that this can't last... How much time, in your opinion?"

"I don't know, Madame. We'll have to examine you. It might simply be overwork..."

"No! It's more serious than that!"

You don't argue with Madame Atomos. Minao just spoke softly, "I can't heal you over the telephone, Madame. When you're ready, come down. We'll all be here to clear up your troubles."

Madame cut off communication, swallowed a tranquilizer (which she was doing more and more often) and went to the programming room. For one hour she checked that everything could keep working without her for several months. This had happened before, but in the case of unexpected events, the Great Brain would obviously come up short. It was only a machine and had just proven it by refusing to deal with the matter of the missing emitters.

Madame Atomos made one final adjustment and took the elevator directly to the clinic. Dr. Minao and his assistants were waiting for her there. Madame Atomos held back a sigh and went into the examining room.

At 455C Washington Street, in Dolly McIntyre's apartment, Smith Beffort was struck by one surprise after another. Even though the girl seemed to be programmed for seduction, her attitude had just taken an abrupt turn for the worse. The excuse was a sudden migraine.

"Be a doll, Sam, and leave me alone... I have an awful headache..."

Beffort hemmed and hawed, just for show, but ended up going back to the bathroom. He came out soon afterward, dressed from head to toe, pretended to be in a bad mood, which he absolutely was not, and said, "What a rotten evening!"

Dolly did not even bother to answer. The Great Brain had ordered her to get the man to leave, that's all.

"What about tomorrow?" Beffort said with his hand on the doorknob.

"Impossible," Dolly replied, uninterested. "I'm going to California tomorrow."

"Vacation?"

"Yes."

"Okay, in that case, I'll say goodbye."

Dolly remained silent. Beffort went into the hall-way. Something he did not understand had just hap-pened. Was, perhaps, the Atomos Organization on the skids?

Chapter IX

In the hallway of the building, Beffort found Benchley standing guard. A little ways down the street, the FBI car with the radio was parked, ready to receive any messages coming from headquarters.

"What's wrong?" Benchley sounded worried. "A fly in the soup?"

"Miss McIntyre just received different instructions concerning me," Beffort explained, "but we're going to continue watching her. Don't move from here."

"Same orders?"

"No. Let the visitors come, whoever they are. We're only worried about Dolly from now on. Whatever she does, it's absolutely necessary to keep her in sight until tomorrow at noon. If you need me, I'll be in the car."

Beffort left and walked down the sidewalk. Just before getting in the car he looked up to the 12th floor. He was half expecting Dolly to watch him leave and was very interested to see that she was not so curious. The Organization had definitely turned their back on him.

Beffort was not complaining since it was going to make his job easier, but knowing the methods of the Organization, he could not help being surprised at the new policy it was following. Concerned about this, he climbed into the car with Benchley's partner and asked, "Anything new?"

"Chandler let us know that Owen Bernitz arrived in Boston with his team and everything's calm with the *Lanaï*... hey, did you strike out with the chick?" His little smirk told much about what he thought about Dolly.

Beffort shrugged. "If you've slept with a girl with a motor-brain, you'd change your tune, pal. Unless you're turned on by corpses... Call Chandler for me, would you?"

The G-man took the mic and called in. Chandler's voice came right back over the speaker. Beffort took the mic and told him about the unexpected turn of events. He ended by saying, "I don't understand because it's the first time, to my knowledge, that the Great Brain has changed the program of one of its servants in the middle of a mission."

"Maybe it thought you were dangerous?"

"Clay was dangerous and they eliminated him. That's generally what happens to those who get in the way of the Organization's projects. Listen, Chandler, there could be a bunch of other explanations, but I think that Madame Atomos has just finished up recruiting new servants. She must have enough manpower and is going to go into action."

"In Boston?"

"Highly likely! Tell your boys to keep their eyes open and inform you immediately if they witness anything out of the ordinary. Things are going to heat up and it'll probably start in Hingham Bay."

"If you're talking about the yacht," Chandler said, "I can assure you right now: a gunboat is there and ready to send it to the depths if need be. Plus a team of federal agents is lying in wait on the seawall..."

"Great," Beffort cut in, "you can tell them to go hang out somewhere else. Owen Bernitz and his men are going to take their place."

"But..."

"Don't argue, Chandler. The Green Dragon Force knows how to fight against the Organization and your boys will be more useful in the city. To each his own work."

"The gunboat?" Chandler asked stiffly.

"Leave it where it is, but make sure they don't open fire without orders. If I'm not mistaken, your boss is on that yacht, as well as T.B. Clark, not to speak of the young lady and girl kidnapped in Hyde Park... By the way, do you know who they are?"

"No. No one's reported them missing yet," Chandler said with indifference. "Owen Bernitz is here."

"Let me speak to him."

There was a short silence and then the hoarse voice of the old gangster said, "Hello, Boss! So, another round?"

"You know it, Owen. Did you hear my conversation with Chandler?"

"Yes. I've already sent Stutton, Baxter and Simms to take a walk down Pier 2. The other guys are spread out around town. If I got it right, we gotta neutralize the A.O. robots if they want to play rough?" Bernitz spoke his mind and did not mince words.

"That's it," Beffort agreed, "but wait a little before starting a brawl. I'm on the tail of a girl who should go into action shortly. If we're lucky, she won't move and I'll use the neutralization hour to put a bug on her..."

Bernitz did not ask for an explanation because he knew what Beffort was talking about: it was a tiny device that gave off a signal every 15 seconds and that could easily be hidden behind a coat lapel, in a shoulder pad, etc. Whoever carried it could be followed anywhere, except, and this was the case for the members of the Organization, if they changed their clothes. But when they did change, it was always inside an Atomos Organization shelter. Therefore, the operation would bear fruit.

But it obviously had to take place during the neutralization hour so that the Great Brain did not know about it.

Concerning Dolly, Beffort's plan was more complicated. This time he wanted to keep the tracer on her when she changed into the uniform of the Organization servants. For that, there was only one way: hide the emitter on Dolly's body. It would not be easy, but Beffort had an idea.

"Okay," Bernitz said. "We'll try to take it easy…"

He stopped suddenly. Beffort heard a muffled conversation and then Chandler shouted, "Beffort, I just received a message from pier 2. Clay just got off the *Lanaï*! It's unbelievable! What should we do?"

"Above all, order your men not to approach him. He's part of the Atomos Organization now and is walking with a motor-brain."

"Are you sure?"

"Aye aye aye, Chandler, I know Madame Atomos has never let one of her prisoners go without operating on them before. Clay is certainly going to go back to headquarters. He'll tell you some plausible story to explain his absence and start working again as if nothing had happened. Pretend to believe him, don't let him know that you know, and make sure that he finds out nothing about our current operations. This last point is crucial. If Clay learns what's up, the Great Brain will be informed instantly."

"Damn! If you think that's going to be easy! Once at headquarters Clay will be in control of the epicenter of the information network for Boston and the region."

"Change all that!" Beffort barked. "Get in touch with the city police and use their headquarters. Hell, Chandler, don't tell me you're twiddling your thumbs! Figure it out and fast! When you've switched your system, call this car, which from now on you can consider as my mobile headquarters."

"Got it," Chandler said in a monotone.

Beffort signed out, gave the microphone back to the G-man and turned his head just in time to see Benchley running up. He was very excited when he dove into the car and said, "I've been trying to signal you for two minutes! The longhaired guy just went up to Dolly's. Look, his car is sitting in front of the Ford."

"Was he alone?" Beffort asked.

"Yes, but he was lugging a package exactly like the one we stole!"

The news made Beffort think. If the Organization was giving Dolly another paralyzing emitter, it meant that the recruitment period was not over yet. Very soon other Boston inhabitants would disappear without a trace. And it was likely that they would be taken on board the yacht to be operated on. The worst thing was that there was nothing they could do about it. If Dolly and her partner were taken out of action, dozens of servants would be there to take their place. Moreover, by neutralizing Dolly and the young man, the Great Brain would know that the FBI was on the trail and it would automatically change its tactics.

Recognizing once again his powerlessness made Beffort raging mad... for nothing. "Let's wait," he said. "Right now Dolly's are best bet."

Clay arrived at the headquarters 30 minutes after he left pier 2. He seemed to be in good shape, giving hell to the guard who was stunned watching him, sprinting up to his office and when he got there Chandler shouted, "Well, I'll be! Where have you been?"

"Hello," Clay said cheerfully. "Good old Chandler, you can prime yourself to blow up Mama Atomos! I discovered enough clues to disintegrate her Organization!"

For a few seconds Chandler wondered if Beffort had not made a grave error in claiming that his boss was in the other camp now.

Clay sat behind his desk and said, "You know that I suspected T.B. Clark's mistress, that Miss McIntyre?"

"I know," Chandler confirmed, hesitant.

"Well, I went to her apartment. I found out for certain that the girl had made her lover disappear. Why do you think?"

"I don't know."

"Because she's part of the Atomos Organization, Chandler. But let me tell you how I found the pot of gold. Coming out of Miss McIntyre's building I spotted a guy playing with that famous square box in his car, which intrigued me. I waited, thinking something would happen, but after playing with it for a little while, apparently with no results, the young man put his old Chevy on the road to Newton... Do you have a cigarette?"

Confused, Chandler handed him his pack. Everything made fairly good sense in Clay's story, except the last detail about the old Chevrolet leaving for Newton.

"I understood right away that this young man was part of the Organization," Clay resumed with energy, "and I rushed to my car. I got on his tail, we crossed through Newton and then Waltham and finally stopped after Riverview in front of a really remote house."

He was speaking pretty wildly and, whether consciously or not, sounded melodramatic. Chandler was embarrassed for him and knew now that Beffort was right. Usually Clay was sober, in his words as well as gestures. For anyone who knew him, it was easy to see that he was not acting normally.

"There," Clay continued, "I had two choices: either follow the young man or give it all up and alert headquarters. As you can guess, I chose the first because it was the most logical, considering the fact that the guy could disappear if I left."

Chandler was only half listening. He knew that Clay was telling him a completely fabricated story and he simply wondered where it would end up. Because if Clay were not being controlled by the Great Brain, he would not feel the need to justify his absence. He was the FBI director in Boston and as such could leave on any mission he thought useful without telling his subordinates about it.

"So," Clay kept on, "I let the young man enter the house before slipping in myself. I'll spare you the details of how hard it was for me to enter without being seen… Once inside I noted that the house was deserted and all the precautions I had taken were in vain. Because, strangely as it might seem, the guy had disappeared!"

He waited for a reaction with such intensity that Chandler felt obliged to say something. "That is strange indeed."

Clay looked satisfied and continued, "Naturally, I searched the whole house for a place where the guy could be hiding. I didn't find one. However, in the cellar I found a trapdoor that I opened, uncovering a flight of steps that disappeared, inexplicably, into the underground. What would you have done in my place?"

"I would have gone down," Chandler fired back. He knew that Clay was testing him, on the orders of the Great Brain, of course, to check his credibility.

"That's what I did," Clay said. "And I came into an extraordinary maze that I just barely found my way out of. Meanwhile, I realized that all the underground rooms and tunnels stuffed with electronic equipment were the primary refuge of the Atomos Organization in our area!"

"No way!" Chandler kept playing the game.

"Yes, indeed, my old Chandler. We have to inform Smith Beffort immediately. Do you know where he is?"

Chandler suddenly realized that this whole fantastic story had been invented to justify this last question. Through Clay, reduced to a machine, the Great Brain was trying to get information about its most mortal enemy.

"Beffort?" Chandler said. "But he had nothing at all to do with T.B. Clark's disappearance. You were in charge of the matter and Washington was only informed because you wanted to. This is the first I've heard of Miss McIntyre belonging to the Atomos Organization… And I can tell you it's real curveball. After your disappearance, I dropped everything to look for you."

Clay smiled. "Tell my wife that I'm back, Chandler. I'm going to phone J.E.E. immediately to explain the situation to him. Go on! Scram!"

Chandler did not have to be told twice. He dashed into his office, stalled Clay's line and called Washington himself. He quickly told Evans what had happened and that he wanted to know where Beffort was, and to launch all the FBI forces at the Riverview property.

Evans reacted on the spot. "I understand, Chandler. Put the poor guy on the line. I'll be hard on him, but I have to since he represents the Great Brain!"

Chandler hung up and ran straight to the radio-transmission room. In spite of the danger that Clay's presence presented, he had to alert Beffort at all costs.

Chapter X

"So," Beffort said coldly. "He's acting exactly as I expected, isn't he?"

"Exactly, but he's looking for you and doing all he can to drag all our forces to Riverview!"

"Don't panic, Chandler, and count on J.E.E. to stop his hostility. Clay can be muzzled. In spite of his post, he has to follow Washington's instructions and he will. Keep an eye on him, make sure that he doesn't find out anything about our plans and he'll end up slowing down. When I'm talking about Clay, I'm obviously thinking about the Great Brain."

Chandler let out a little sigh and asked, "Are you still on Washington Street?"

"Yes," Beffort was curt, thinking time was dragging.

"Okay!" Chandler concluded. "Good luck."

He left the room and was headed back to his office when he remembered that he was supposed to call Mrs. Clay. The poor woman must have been on pins and needles. Chandler wondered what he was going to say to her. Certainly Clay was in good health, seemingly in his right mind, but how would he act in front of his wife? And if Chandler remembered correctly, the Clays had a little girl.

Chandler knew his job would not be easy, so he came up with something like, "Your husband is back at the office, Mrs. Clay. He's in good shape, but don't be surprised at his behavior." He winced. How could he tell this woman that her husband was nothing but a robot, a living-dead, and that in all probability it was incurable?

Chandler looked up Clay's home number, grabbed the phone and asked the operator to put him through to Mrs. Clay. A few seconds later the operator told him the number was not answering. As Chandler checked the number again, he also glanced at the address and a shiver ran down his spine: the Clays lived next to Hyde Park!

"Good God!" Chandler swore. "That would be awful!" He had just thought that the young woman and child whom Beffort had talked about... No report of their disappearance had been made, which was surprising... unless it was the Clay family!

Chandler left headquarters, climbed into a fleet car and sped off toward Hyde Park. Ten minutes later he pulled up in front of 42 Milton Street. On the 6th floor, nobody answered the doorbell. He rang at the neighbors and learned that they had not seen Mrs. Clay since she had left with her daughter for her walk in Hyde Park. Chandler thanked them and went back to the car. Now he had to tell the sinister news to Clay.

In the depths of Atomia Island a horrible tragedy was being prepared. The huge room split by a grill resounded with a child's wailing. The decoration had not changed, except that Madame Atomos was not in the armchair on the unfurnished side of the room; and the moving doll had been taken out. Now the Clay's little girl had taken its place. She had been separated from her mother for a while, kept alone in this wicked place, and was crying out her fear and grief. At four years old, a shadow is menacing and the total silence made a terrible noise.

All of a sudden a small, round object fell down the chimney, bounced and rolled across the floor. It looked like a ball and the little girl stopped sobbing. She scrambled out of the armchair where she had curled up, took a step forward…

In a flash the tiger sprang out of the ball, which in reality was a computer, and its hideous muzzle lunged for the little girl.

There was a scream and then silence again in the room, which was filling up with the repulsive stench of blood.

In Boston Beffort and the two G-men had to wait close to two hours before seeing the longhaired young man come out of the front door of the building.

"He's not carrying the package anymore," Benchley said. "What do we do?"

It only took Beffort a few seconds to answer, "We have to follow him. Benchley, take Chandler's Ford and stick to this guy. In case of an emergency, remember to alert the police headquarters and not the FBI."

"Got it," Benchley said. He got out, changed cars and got on the tail of the old Chevrolet.

Ten minutes later Dolly appeared on the sidewalk. She had changed her look, was wearing pumps with dizzying heels, a dress and a mini coat.

"Funny look," the G-man commented.

"I guess she really wants to look like a chick," Beffort agreed. "Strange that she's not carrying the package."

Dolly stood before the door and did not move. A minute later a taxi, which she had obviously called, stopped in front of her. She got in and the taxi headed for downtown.

"Get going," Beffort ordered.

The taxi crossed Boston from south to north before it stopped at the end of Summer Street, not far from the piers of Mills Peninsula, in a place that was utterly deserted. A few scattered streetlamps lit the seawall and revealed the jagged outline of warehouses built in an off-limits area, casting moving shadows on the dark water, sawed off by the hull of a cargo ship near the wharf.

"For a girl who wants to pick someone up," the G-man said, "this place doesn't have a lot of prospects."

Beffort did not answer as he watched Dolly get out of the taxi. She did, in fact, walk awkwardly, but this might have been due to the too high heels that were not a good fit for the uneven pavement. The taxi restarted and disappeared toward downtown again. Dolly did not turn around, just kept staggering toward the seawall.

Beffort had the feeling that something was fishy...

The G-man suddenly remarked, "Say, it's weird that the girl is going out without her purse. Hey, what's she doing?"

Dolly had just stopped at the seawall. She abruptly kicked off her pumps, threw off her mini coat and her wig and the pale face of the young man was lit up under the streetlamp. He glanced at the FBI car, broke out laughing and dove into the ice-cold water that swallowed him up under a little spray of foam.

The G-man made for the door, but Beffort held him back. "Nothing rash!"

"The guy's going to drown!"

"Don't worry about that, pal. Get your car back on the road instead. We were spotted by the Organization and our lives will be worth nothing if we stay here. Damn, if Benchley didn't have a car, Dolly would be lost for good! I wonder what all this adds up to?"

The more time passed, the more Beffort felt that the Atomos Organization was not using its usual methods. Madame Atomos had to know that the *Lanaï* was under surveillance. The way the young man just sacrificed himself proved it. So, why was she dragging things out? What did this weird roundtrip to Boston mean? And especially, what had become of Dolly?

"Let's call headquarters," the G-man advised while driving toward Savin Hill. "Maybe Benchley has already given some news to Chandler."

"First," Beffort decided, "get me to a post office open at night, if there is one in this neighborhood."

"Sure, pretty close. It's none of my business, but if you want to call someone, why not do it from a police station?"

"Wherever… it doesn't matter. The main thing is that I do it very soon."

The G-man understood by his tone that it was an emergency. He stepped on the gas and braked three minutes later across from a police station. Beffort entered and identified himself and what he wanted. They led him to an empty office where the telephone bypassed the operator and he dialed the number of his house in Williamsburg.

On the second ring someone picked up. Beffort hung up right away and dialed again… It was their code. This time Mie spoke up loud and without fear, "Smith, what's wrong?"

"Nothing. I was just worried for no particular reason. Is everything all right there?"

"Yes. Bob and the doctor are sleeping and the dogs are circling the house… I'm sitting near the window… all the lights are out. It's eerie, but I'm not worried. What's new in Boston?" She did her best to sound relaxed, but her voice shook terribly. The Atomos menace was gnawing at her…

"Nothing special," Beffort lied. "I think it's all a false alarm. If it keeps up, I'll be back tomorrow or the next day. How's Bob's cold?"

He fell back on small talk so as not to alarm his wife, who herself did not dare confess her fear. In this way, the conversation quickly became boring and Beffort felt no better when his wife hung up. He did not know where the premonition came from, but he was expecting disaster.

When he got back to the car, he got on the radio to Chandler, who told him he had no news from Benchley. "But," Chandler added, "I know who the woman and girl from Hyde Park are."

"Yeah?" Beffort's mind was elsewhere.

"It's the wife and daughter of Clay! It doesn't seem to surprise you... Do you know that they're probably still on board the yacht and we might be able to save them? Why are we doing nothing instead of attacking the Organization?"

He finally stopped talking and Beffort asked coldly, "How many servants of the Organization do you know of, Chandler?

"Dolly McIntyre, the longhaired young man..."

"And Clay," Beffort finished for him. "Well, are those the ones you want to attack?"

"The yacht..."

"It'll be empty!" Beffort barked. "If, by chance, you find Clay's wife and daughter, you'll be meeting two new servants of the A.O., one point is all. Besides, you should know that the young man just jumped into the freezing water of Mill Peninsula and Dolly's on the run. What Organization do you want to attack, Chandler?"

Chandler did not answer. He had flown off the handle, but Beffort was much more furious than he was.

"Keep your aggression in your pocket and stuff a handkerchief in it," Beffort said more calmly. "We've been fighting shadows for years and you're not the one who's going to take down the Organization from your office. Get on your radio and try to find out if Benchley has been seen by your men. For now that's my number one concern. When you know something, call me. Good night."

Beffort cut off and the G-man said, "You just told Chandler that the yacht would be empty."

"To each his own work," Beffort said. "Chandler's going to have enough problems with Clay. Besides, that's an issue for Green Dragon Force now." He smiled, offered a cigarette and said, "You're going to have front row seats, friend. Maybe it'll be better if I call you by your name?"

The G-man started the car and said, "My name's Daniel Westlake, but everybody calls me Danny."

"Okay, Danny, step on it! Benchley might just be swallowing his birth certificate right now!"

Benchley had followed the old Chevrolet to pier 2, where he was not sure what to do. Dolly, who was still dressed as the young man, had just disappeared inside the yacht. In the night, Benchley could make out some shadows that he knew were the Green Dragon Force and so he rightly figured that his presence was unnecessary. He thought he should contact Chandler in order for him to bring Beffort up-to-date on the situation but the Ford he was driving had no radio, which made him groan. He had to find a public telephone.

He turned around, drove down the pier and found a booth on Sea Street. From there he called Chandler, who asked him to hold the line while he informed Beffort by radio. The call reached Beffort as he was leaving Mill Peninsula. He told Chandler to order Benchley to stay near the pier and to warn Owen Bernitz that the next attack was going to be against the yacht. Chandler relayed the messages so that when Beffort's car arrived at the marina, everything was ready for the offense against the *Lanaï*. The gunboat was blocking the port and ten men from the Green Dragon Force, armed with paralyzing rifles, were lying in ambush behind the seawall.

Owen Bernitz walked up to Beffort and said, "Everything's okay, boss." He furrowed his brow and added, "Kinda weird that this boat is sitting here like this with no lights, eh? It's like there's no one on board…"

"It's to see if we're here, Owen. Gather your men, we're going in!"

The group advanced in a line down the pier and when it came up to the *Lanaï*, the yacht suddenly went up in flames. The blaze was too quick and too widespread not to have been set off on purpose. The fire rapidly shot across the deck, spurted out of the portholes, which were cracked by the heat, and devoured the superstructures with amazing speed.

"Gas!" Bernitz shouted.

Beffort withdrew gloomily from the incredible heat coming off the boat. He realized that Madame Atomos, by destroying the yacht and killing Dolly McIntyre, had just wiped out all leads that could have brought her enemies down on her.

In fact, only Clay could accomplish that now.

Chapter XI

Eddy Witter, one of Madame Atomos' oldest enemies, had been told in plenty of time that Beffort needed him in Boston. Nevertheless, J.E.E. was very worried about Mie and Bob, so he asked him to make a detour to Williamsburg to check if all six dogs were still protecting the Befforts.

Witter knew the methods of the Organization perfectly well. He got to Williamsburg around midnight—at the same time that the yacht was sinking with its crew in Boston—filled up his tank and headed slowly for the house. He had no intention of paying Mie a visit. He was there incognito, to J.E.E.'s knowledge, but unknown to Smith Beffort, who would certainly not have appreciated the initiative.

Smith feared above all that a visiting friend would involuntarily lead a servant of the Organization to his house. Witter knew how to deal with this. All along the 200 miles or so of travel, he had taken unimaginable precautions to shake off any would-be followers. In Williamsburg he went through another series of checks. The city was asleep, the streets deserted. It took no time for Witter to be sure that he was not followed, so he went to the Befforts' neighborhood.

Wisely, the G-man left his car on a nearby street and walked very cautiously, staying in the shadows. The night was dark and cold. Witter raised the collar of his overcoat and slipped his hands into his pockets. He found the area bleak and was therefore on his guard. He snuck along the hedges, examining the parked cars and his heart jumped a little when he spied the man who seemed to be sleeping in one of them. If it were not so cold, Witter would certainly have found the presence of the man less alarming. In the present case, considering the fact that the car was parked across from the Befforts' house, the G-man knew right away that Mie, Bob and Dr. Soblen were in a precarious situation.

Witter hid behind a tree and concentrated his attention on the sleeper. He did not see his face and could barely make out his outline. The man was not facing Witter and was leaning back against the headrest. He did not move an inch and really looked like he was sleeping... And then Witter noticed a detail: the windows of the car were completely clear. As if the guy was not breathing or giving off any heat at all to warm up the air inside! And yet, the windows of the car were all shut tight. Weird!

Witter backtracked and returned to his Dodge, which he inched up to the corner. He turned off his headlights, turned slowly, and finally stopped when the suspicious car was in sight. Then he turned it off. If this guy was not dead and cold for a long time, he could only be a servant of Madame Atomos! But there was a doubt that Witter could not take the risk of checking out because if dead, the guy was obviously no danger; if a robot of the Organization, he would react violently and set off the alarm in the Great Brain, which would change its plans...

Witter decided to wait it out. He was sure that it was the wisest decision.

In the house, Soblen was now on watch. Mie and her son were sleeping on the second floor and the dogs continued their rounds of the yard. Sitting behind the living room window, Soblen unconsciously counted the number of time the dogs passed in front of the porch. He felt useless and was starting to miss his laboratory. The dogs would obviously let no one pass by. They were trained for it, would kill at the least alert and would stop their rounds if anything bothered them—a security that kept suspense at bay and left Soblen's mind empty, lulled imperceptibly into a sweet, dangerous tranquility.

But the situation was such as Madame Atomos had prepared for him. Neither Soblen or the dogs nor Witter were capable of perceiving the sneaky approach of the miniaturized flying saucer coming out of the sky. It came directly from Atomia Island, was the shape and size of a car tire and carried only a computer that was no bigger than a tennis ball.

The hour was at hand and the Beffort's son was going to die. Madame Atomos had sworn to it. For this, the terrible woman was forced to postpone her vengeance against the United States and had mobilized her entire formidable Organization. To accomplish her plan, she had to eliminate Smith Beffort. Since the man had always escaped her blows, she was going to get to him through his son and hit him harder than if she took his life.

Madame Atomos, or more precisely the Great Brain, knew for certain that Smith Beffort was in Boston. It had been confirmed by the longhaired young man who, disguised as Dolly McIntyre, had thrown himself into Mill Peninsula. Then through Dolly's eyes the Great Brain had made sure that Beffort and his Green Dragon Force were busy with the yacht. The *Lanaï*'s disappearance cut off the trail that could lead them to Atomia Island.

As for Clay, he would have to die soon.

And in Boston, everything was settled.

In Williamsburg, it was dead calm. The Great Brain knew this through Harrison, who had been watching the Befforts' house for hours. After Bob's death, Harrison would go back to Atomia Island on board a submarine. The sub was the same one that had latched onto the hull of the *Lanaï*. Right now it was swimming peacefully off the coast of Norfolk and would be in Batten Bay at the meeting point to pick up Harrison.

Therefore, the flying saucer, the bearer of death, came down to the roof, hovered over the chimney, opened its trapdoor and dropped the computer, which rattled down the flue. It bounced noiselessly out of the fireplace and rolled over the floor until it came to a stop in the corner of the room where little Bob was sleeping.

At the same time, on Atomia, another computer registered the genetic code of the tiger, which vanished from its cage in a flash. The operation went off magnificently, without a hitch, with mathematical precision. However, the tiger was trained to attack a child standing up and screaming in fear. Now, because of the time, the Great Brain was well aware that Bob was sleeping. Consequently, everything had been prepared to wake him up. The saucer descended another few feet, flipped over and literally rolled down the tiles of the roof before rising up and disappearing.

The noise was tremendous. It was as if a rain of lead shot had suddenly struck the house. The dogs stopped their rounds, Soblen leapt onto the stairs and Mie jumped out of bed. At the same time, Bob started crying and sat up in his bed. The room had only a night-light. Scary shadows danced on the walls. Mie burst into the room just as Soblen reached the landing.

"Did you hear that?" the doctor shouted on the run.

Mie's heart was pounding when she answered, "Yes, but it didn't come from Bob's room!"

Soblen appeared in the doorway. He was gripping the paralyzing pistol and his face was twisted in anguish. With a quick glance he saw that everything was all right, but Mie's arms were dangling at her sides. "Your gun," he groaned. "Go get it while I watch Bob."

With a touch of panic Mie left the room and ran into hers. She rushed to the dresser, grabbed the pistol and turned around... At that very second a horrible cry rang out and then the crash of overturned furniture. Petrified, Mie heard the strangled voice of Soblen and of Bob, unrecognizable...

She finally shook herself out of the paralyzing daze and ran into the hallway, deafened by a hideous wail. Soblen appeared, bloody, staggering, with nothing in place of his right arm but a ragged stump. The doctor took one step forward before collapsing in the hallway. He was trying to speak, but no words escaped his lips, just that frightful wail bearing witness to his unbearable pain.

Mie stepped over him, into the room, and howled. A huge tiger was devouring some shapeless thing that must have been her son! Traumatized, she did not even have time to pull the trigger of her pistol. Her strength gave out, her mind keeled over and she plunged into a bottomless abyss.

A minute later the tiger, blasted by the computer, collapsed on what was left of little Bob, and then the computer disintegrated and there was nothing left but a small pile of dust.

In the hallway, bathed in blood and horror, Soblen was crawling toward the telephone...

Witter was too far from the house to understand even the most insignificant detail of the tragedy. He saw lights filter through the shutters on the second floor, but that was nothing out of the ordinary. Afterward he did not have time to think of anything but the car he was watching. For no apparent reason, it had just pulled away from the sidewalk and was heading back into Williamsburg. When it passed by Witter, in low gear, the G-man saw the man behind the wheel very clearly. It was brief, but Witter saw enough to know for sure that he was a member of the Atomos Organization.

From that moment, Witter had the same reaction as Beffort had with Dolly McIntyre: stick like glue to this servant of Madame Atomos.

The two cars left town, turned east and drove fast for an hour until they entered Newport News and took the James River Bridge, which crossed James Bay into Bartlett. After that the car Witter was following turned south, took Highway 17 for almost two miles before turning off onto a back road that led to the sea. Witter obviously did not know that this was where his prey was supposed to board a submarine, but knowing how Madame Atomos worked, he figured he was going to lose him anytime now.

He looked around feverishly for a way to continue his pursuit, even if he had to go to sea. He told himself that there was no way and decided to inform Washington if his fears came true.

At Batten Bay Witter knew that he was right: less than 100 yards away, the servant of the Organization jumped out of his car and got into a dingy with an outboard motor in which another man was waiting for him. The dinghy skidded over the water out of the small harbor and was soon out of sight.

All this happened so quickly that Witter could do nothing, even if he had wanted to. Without missing a beat, he turned around, raced to the police station that he had spotted earlier, and demanded authorization for a telephone while flashing his FBI badge.

In four minutes he was in contact with J.E.E.'s office and the secretary asked him to wait a minute because the boss was on the other line. Witter was champing at the bit, as the secondhand of his watch ticked off.

He was about to swear at the secretary when Evans' voice exploded through the earpiece, "Damn it, Witter, where are you?"

"At Batten Bay, I..."

"What the hell are you doing there? I ordered you to watch the Befforts' house! Do you even know that Bob is dead, Mie's half crazy and Soblen is in a coma with an arm torn off?"

It was such a brutal blow that Witter was dumbstruck.

Furious, Evans went on, "They just found the remains of a tiger in the place! That's what mutilated Soblen and ate little Bob! Meanwhile, what were you doing, huh? Tell me!'

Witter fought back the nausea that was washing over him. "I was following a servant of the Organization..."

"Where did you spot him?"

"In front of the Befforts' house... but he didn't leave his car at all."

"He's probably the guy who was supervising the operation. Where is he right now?"

"On the water in a dingy that's heading out to sea. I think he's getting ready to board a bigger ship that'll take him to Atomia Island, so do whatever it takes for the US Navy to follow this lead instead of chewing me out! Because maybe I didn't see the tiger! And what were the dogs doing?"

This remark brought J.E.E.'s anger down a notch or two. He said wearily, "That's exactly what we're wondering. The beast seems to have come out of nowhere to fulfill the awful duty given to it by Madame Atomos and we won't know any more unless Soblen can start talking."

"Smith?"

"He doesn't know yet," Evans mumbled.

"You have to tell him! While you're at it, tell him about this guy I followed to Batten Bay and who we absolutely can't lost track of. If we act fast, I figure he'll lead us to Atomia Island."

"Why do you think that?"

"After what Madame Atomos just did, she knows that she can take some time to get ready. She's going to stay calm for a while and we won't hear from her for months. But in reality she's recuperating her servants. Believe me, we've never had a better chance. Tell Smith. He's the only one who can use the navy, air force and all the forces the US has…"

Unsure, Evans remained silent. He wondered how to tell Beffort the tragic news.

"Well?" Witter insisted. "What are you waiting for?"

"Nothing… okay, Witter, I'll alert Smith and the navy."

"Norfolk?"

"Of course…"

"Tell them not to leave without me! I'll be there in ten minutes!"

"Okay," J.E.E. said. He hung up and right after dialed the number of Admiral Greens. Without admitting it, he was putting off having to call Beffort in Boston.

Chapter XII

When Smith Beffort arrived in Williamsburg, Dr. Soblen had just died and his wife was lost in sleep treatment. Floating in a strange trance, Smith wanted to see the remains of his son. They gave in to his wishes after long discussions and Beffort stayed more than an hour before the corpse of the innocent victim.

When he left the hospital, J.E.E. had to step in front of him to get his attention. "Smith?"

Beffort gave him a frightening stare. "You're here, Evans... Thanks for coming."

His eyes wandered over to the line of cars parked along the edge of the lot. They were all full of G-men and the Green Dragon Force. Beffort recognized Charles Hyde, Owen Bernitz and, just behind Evans, Yosho Akamatsu, who had just arrived from Tokyo. Everyone was silent, frozen.

"Smith," J.E.E. resumed, "you can see that Eddy Witter isn't here."

Beffort blinked. "More bad news, Evans?"

"No, Witter is fine. Right now he's on board an escort vessel following a submarine by sonar..."

Beffort woke up a little. "A submarine belonging to the Organization?"

"Yes. It's heading south... Cigarette?" Beffort took one automatically. Evans gave him a light and continued, "It's going to take an awfully long time, but we think it's going back to its base in the Pacific."

"Atomia Island? If it really is off the coast of Hawaii, the submarine will have to pass by Cape Horn! Do you realize that, Evans?"

J.E.E. led Beffort gently to his car. For the moment, he only wanted him to think of something else. "Now Smith, we have time. The navy will keep on its trail for months if it has to, and the submarine won't escape. If it's going to Hawaii, it could get there sooner than we think. It's fast. Admiral Greens is almost sure that it's an atomic boat…" He opened the door of his car. "Climb in. We're going to hold a little conference even though it's late. All the men here need you to draw up an action plan against Madame Atomos. This time, Smith, we've got her, trust me."

Beffort nodded. Killing Madame Atomos personally would certainly bring him great relief.

J.E.E. piled on one conference after another to keep Beffort under pressure, but reality was there with its demands. First it was the double burial of Soblen and little Bob, then Mie's health troubled Smith a great deal. The young lady could not get back on her feet after the sleep treatment. She barely recognized her husband, expressed no desire, refused to get out of bed and was slowly changing into a stubborn invalid.

Only Smith could have convinced her to come back to normal life, but he did not feel the need. He could not help her, even dreaded the moment when he would be alone with her in another home. The shadow of Bob was between them like a silent reproach. They had played with his life, had, in a way, sacrificed it… Of course it was to save the United States, to lure Madame Atomos into a trap, to save hundreds of human lives while they were at it, but it was still true that a child, their child had died needlessly.

Madame Atomos was no longer heard from, nor her Organization. Clay was dead and they had found the body of T.B. Clark in a Boston cellar, but the submarine was still on its way. The navy was following it doggedly and over the next few weeks it was reported off the coast of the Antilles, Brazil, the Falkland Islands and then it crossed Cape Horn and headed back north without once resurfacing. Later it veered off its course, toward the northeast, passed the equator and finally headed straight for Hawaii.

Admiral Greens launched two submarines after it and announced that they would be on its tail in less than 24 hours. So, Smith Beffort went to the clinic where Mie was leading a more or less vegetative existence. She had not changed; her eyes looked veiled.

Beffort sat on the edge of the bed, took her hand and said, "Tomorrow we'll know where Atomia Island is."

He was hoping for a reaction, a start, but got only an apathetic stare. Nothing, not even vengeance, interested Mie Azusa-Beffort anymore.

"The Island is probably in the Hawaiian Islands," Beffort had the feeling that he was talking to a wall, "and the navy is on the tail of the submarine."

Mie lowered her eyes and asked, "Akamatsu?"

Surprised, Beffort said, "He's here in Williamsburg. He asked authorization to see you several times, but you refused."

"Now I would be glad to talk with him. I miss Japan, Smith."

Beffort sighed in relief. This was the first time since Bob's death that Mie expressed a desire. It no doubt meant that she was starting to revive. "Yosho can come this morning if you want. By the way, I'll let you know that you can also see James Edward Evans, Owen

Bernitz, Charles Hyde, Ralph Stutton, Art Baxter, Lucky Simms…"

"No," Mie cut him off curtly. "I don't want to talk to anybody but Akamatsu. At least for now." She stared at her husband. "You're obviously going to be leaving for Hawaii soon?"

"When Atomia Island is located, yes."

"This submarine can't escape?"

"I don't think so. All precautions have been taken for it not to know it's being tracked, so it has no reason to change its course."

Mie lowered her eyes again. Beffort felt like she was trying to hide from him the interest aroused in her mind by the news, but he immediately rejected this groundless idea.

"What will happen when you know its location?" Mie asked with a little more indifference.

"That depends on a lot of things. If it's somewhere inhabited, which is likely, our job won't be easy. We'll have to evacuate first, set up an airlift to go faster, and all this would cause a ruckus that could alert Madame Atomos."

"Why evacuate?"

Smith's eye flashed. "Atomic bomb," he said. "We're going to blow up Atomia like a little gopher hole. That's where the Great Brain is and the laboratory where they make the weapons that might annihilate humanity tomorrow. Even if Madame Atomos manages to flee, she'll be without resources."

"So, you think she'll escape again?"

"Yes! I'm afraid so," Beffort answered sincerely. "She only needs a few seconds to disintegrate and teletransport to the other side of the world. We can't do anything against that, but I'll say it again, if we destroy

Atomia completely, Madame Atomos will never again be able to use her flying saucers or her disintegrating rays or her electromagnetic shield! Before beating an enemy, you have to disarm them. That's what we're going to do to Madame Atomos."

This spirited confession did not have the anticipated effect. Mie fell back into the sluggishness that had become her normal state and seemed to take refuge in a defensive drowsiness that nothing and no one could disturb. She was calm there, safe, with no obligations or responsibilities; they cared for her, watched over her and protected her tranquility. For who or what would she make the necessary effort to return to the land of the living?

Beffort accepted defeat. He hoped now that Yosho Akamatsu could do better. He was Japanese, like Mie, and had a typical Asian philosophy that the young lady connected with more easily... Moreover, if she had asked to see him, it was probably to fulfill a need to talk with someone of her race, to be with him to examine the problems that she could not clear up alone.

Beffort kissed his wife, who kissed him back with unexpected passion. She held him tightly for a moment and finally whispered, "Patience, Smith, I'll get better."

Beffort smiled. "I know. See you soon, Mie... I'll come back to see you when I get back from Hawaii."

He caressed her hair and left quickly to hide his emotion.

Yosho Akamatsu stayed with Mie for three hours before he went back to the Motor Inn around 1 p.m. He was clearly worried, but he tried to look relaxed when he saw Beffort.

"Well, Yosho?"

"Your wife is fine, my friend, don't worry. She needs time to accept Bob's death, to understand that no sacrifice will bring him back to life. Let's say that this is a mandatory period of meditation."

"I understand, but what did you talk about?"

Akamatsu waved his hand in the air. "About Japan in general and Tokyo in particular. Mie was eager to know what was happening in the country. A kind of homecoming to find herself again... Do you realize that your wife has never been back to Japan since her kidnapping and operation? She brought up memories dating back to when she was studying singing at the Takarazuka School, she talked about Mikonosuke Watanabe, that young servant of the Organization who kidnapped her in the middle of Tokyo so that she would become Miss Atomos... In short, our conversation was just small talk... Say, Smith, are we going to have lunch?"

The Motor Inn had become temporary HQ for the FBI and the Green Dragon Force and was literally swarming with armed men waiting impatiently for Admiral Greens reports. They knew that the submarine of the Atomos Organization was still nearing the Hawaiian Islands, but since morning it had slowed down considerably and was gradually veering off to the west. If it continued like this, it would end up pretty far from what they believed to be its goal.

Still, they were ready for anything. At the Patrick Henry airport, located a few miles from Williamsburg (20 minutes away by car), several big troop carriers were prepared to take off instantly to bring Smith Beffort and his men to the front line. Likewise, Admiral Greens was rounding up his fleet. Because of the forces in play, the attack on Atomia Island would either end in a brilliant victory or, if Madame Atomos fended them off, in a devastating disaster.

Beffort and Akamatsu sat at a relatively remote table. Beffort tried to talk about Mie again, but Akamatsu skillfully dodged him and remained vague. A little later J.E.E. joined them, said that four atomic bombs were at their disposal and that Atomia Island would be reduced to dust.

Beffort was only half-listening. He suspected Akamatsu of hiding something from him and thought that Mie had made him swear to keep the taboo subject a secret. Of course, Beffort realized that he had no real reason to believe that Mie was preparing some action without him knowing. It was just a feeling, a kind of premonition.

At 5:25 p.m. the A.O. submarine was nearing a granite island, flat and bare as bones, measuring barely one mile by one half. Latitude 14°12', Alt. 20 feet, in the middle of the Pacific Ocean, and rather far from all the inhabited Hawaiian islands.

At 6:12 p.m. the submarine went through a gap cut out of the reefs, 40 feet under water, and slowly approached the island. A little later it slipped into an underwater cave, kept its course for an instant and finally resurfaced in the underground pool on the edge of Atomia Island.

A team of 25 men, plus Harrison, left the ship and went into a control room under the direct supervision of the Great Brain. There they were identified and sent straight to the workshops. The Great Brain reset the control panel in Madame Atomos' office to zero. That meant that all the servants of the Organization, with no exceptions, had come back to base. Madame Atomos sneered gloomily, lowered the lever that controlled the hermetically sealed exits of the city, and fell back wearily on the bed she was lying on.

Doctor Minao and his colleagues had advised her to stay in bed and rest. She was on the brink of a nervous breakdown, had to stop her research, get more sleep, etc. Madame Atomos knew perfectly well that she could never get rid of the hatred she felt toward the Befforts and that was the main thing eating away at her. Little Bob's horrific death was a meager consolation for her. Now, she needed the life of Mie Azusa and she was already figuring out how she could reach her goal.

Her hatred, however, did not make her neglect her own security. The sinister woman was constantly wearing a transmission computer around her neck that already contained her genetic code. In case of danger, all she had to do was move her hand up and she would be instantly disintegrated and sent to a reconstruction computer in Savannah, Georgia.

Of course, Madame Atomos was convinced that she would never need to use this system as long as she was on Atomia. All her power was here, all her fortune, her laboratory... Everything that had taken 20 years for her to acquire, to perfect and that she would be unable to replace if destroyed.

She closed her eyes, tried to fall into a refreshing sleep, but could not. Madame Atomos (like Smith Beffort) had antennas. She felt a threat hovering over Atomia, but (also like Beffort) it was just a feeling, a kind of premonition.

Chapter XIII

At 6:30 p.m. Admiral Greens' last report fell like a bomb among the occupants of the Motor Inn. Very succinctly Greens gave the exact position of Atomia Island and asked for Beffort's instructions. Ten minutes later, J.E.E., Akamatsu, Owen Bernitz and Smith Beffort located the island on a detailed map of the Pacific. The island was called The Rock. It was an arid block surrounded by dangerous reefs and only visited by birds.

During past searches made jointly by the navy and FBI—the very searches that Dr. Soblen had been on—no one dreamed of landing on this spot. The Rock was like a desert where no possibility of refuge was visible, so they just flew over it.

"Unbelievable," J.E.E. grumbled. "Madame Atomos can't be crazy enough to build her headquarters on such a vulnerable island. Greens must be mistaken."

Beffort shrugged. "It's precisely because everyone thinks like you that Madame Atomos has never been bothered. Personally, I imagined Atomia Island differently. I saw instead an inhabited land, with roads, an airstrip and a relatively big population where the servants of the Organization could pass unnoticed... Psychologically, it's a success. Without that submarine, Madame Atomos could have lived in peace under The Rock for years."

Yosho Akamatsu said, "I totally agree with your optimism, Smith. But the navy followed the sub to this island and who says that it's really Atomia?"

"That's what I think," Owen Bernitz said. "Before pelting The Rock, we gotta know if Mama What's-her-face is really stuck down there."

A short silence ensued. Everyone could feel the absence of Dr. Soblen. Usually, Soblen was the moderator in this kind of discussion. He had common sense, a cool head, knew better than anyone how to analyze a situation, and drew foregone conclusions. From now on, they were going to have to make decisions without him.

"I think," Beffort said, "that there's at least one way to know if The Rock is just a layover or a real base. Over the last three months, we've been searching for Atomia. I know the navy took aerial photographs of the Hawaiian Islands. Evans, can you see if any of them were made of The Rock?"

J.E.E. called Washington on the phone, learned that there were, indeed, a dozen shots of the The Rock and asked that they be sent urgently.

30 minutes later the 12 photos were in Beffort's hands. He laid them out on the table, scrutinized them and said, "Does anyone see a bird in these photos?"

Evans, Owen and Akamatsu shook their heads. Beffort took the map and its detailed descriptions and read, "The Rock is only visited by migrating birds that are found in large numbers throughout the year." He looked up and said, "This information was written in January 1955 and is therefore prior to Madame Atomos' first apparition. Can you explain to me why this bird island has suddenly transformed into inhospitable land? Look: in the 12 photos, taken at low altitudes, you can clearly make out the detailed topography, but there's nothing to show that birds have been here recently. Now, it's not a submarine that would chase them away. No, it's the meteoric departures of flying saucers..."

"Okay!" Evans interrupted. "Enough already, Smith! No proof could be more conclusive. When the animals flee, it's because man has come... All we have to do is order the bombing of the Atomia."

Beffort shook his head. "Easier said than done, Evans. An atomic bomb won't do any good unless it hits right in the heart of Atomia. Dropped from a plane, it might only nick the rock. In my opinion, we're not out of the woods yet."

"Damn," Owen Bernitz said. "What are we gonna do?"

"First," Beffort decided, "we have to get a closer look. We leave immediately for Hawaii!"

They were all together on the aircraft carrier *Georgia*, which also carried Admiral Greens. The ship had been anchored off the coast of Hawaii since the day before. It was the closest ship to Atomia seeing that some areas of the waters had been declared a zone of operations, but the distance separating it was still over 300 miles.

All this in order not to alert Madame Atomos whose wariness had become legendary...

Three in the morning had just tolled. Fatigue was starting to weigh on the men's shoulders and in the voices of Greens and the air force general Salem. The two of them were arguing over the honor of dropping the bomb, trying to snatch the decision by proving that their plan of action was better.

Beffort asked them to be quiet, got Akamatsu's and Evans' advice, and then said, "I think Admiral Greens' plan is the best suited to the situation." He saw Salem's face drop and Greens' blossom. He added coldly, "However, neither of you will be the hero of the day. If

Atomos is disintegrated, we have to send a remote-controlled torpedo to carry the bomb. That will be up to a specialist, not a sailor or a pilot."

"A remote-controlled torpedo?" Greens was alarmed. He had recommended the use of his submarines and realized to his displeasure that his plan had just been modified.

"A submarine would be detected by Madame Atomos' radar and sonar," Beffort said.

"It'll be the same with a torpedo!"

"Possibly, but if it blows up before reaching its target, we'll have no human victims to mourn over. A ship heading for it can't get closer than 3 miles. We just have to find a way to guide the torpedo beyond such a distance. It has to go through the passage cut in the reef, into the underwater grotto and explode under The Rock. Naturally, we'll attack during the neutralization hour, that is at 12:30."

"I can supply the ship but not the men or the torpedo!"

"The torpedo and the remote-control specialist will arrive from Houston around 9 a.m. In 15 minutes the atomic charge will be in place. All you have to do is transport it 3 miles from Atomia before noon."

"Impossible," Greens declared categorically. "No ship can cover 300 miles in three hours."

Beffort smiled. "That's where we're going to see a close collaboration between the navy and air force. Leave right away, Greens, without a minute to spare. Salem will go all out to get the torpedo and the specialist on your ship in good time."

"Nothing could be easier," Salem started smiling.

Beffort stood up and looked at his watch. "Now, enough talking. Enjoy the rest of the night, gentleman. We'll meet again after Atomia is destroyed!"

The men left the *Georgia*, which cast off right away and headed south.

The dawn came blazing over the windless ocean as the sun slowly wrestled up over the horizon, climbing into the clear blue sky like a big red balloon. In the range of 300 miles from Atomia Island, the sea and sky were empty. Only the *Georgia* sailed toward its goal at full speed and even then Admiral Greens was not sure that they would reach it in time.

At 9 a.m. the plane from Houston landed as planned on the Honokohua runway, located on the west coast of Hawaii, and the specialist found himself surrounded by Beffort and his men. His name was Cooper and he was tall, determined, and up to now worked at the space center, helping to launch satellites into orbit. When Beffort explained to him what he had to do, Cooper narrowed his eyes in worry.

"All depends on the condition of the sea," he said simply. "A torpedo is easy to handle, but its behavior varies almost automatically with the elements. If there's a storm, The Rock will certainly be hit, but you shouldn't expect to get a bull's eye."

Beffort flicked his butt away furiously.

"Can we postpone the operation?" Evans asked.

"That'd be dangerous," Beffort said. "Madame Atomos might suddenly change the neutralization hour, for security reasons, and we'll be sure to come up against an impregnable defense. But right now the sea is calm and the weather forecast is clear skies all morning. If we run into bad luck and things go haywire, I still think that, in spite of everything, we have to go the whole nine yards."

He stared at Cooper, who had never had contact with the Atomos Organization and, strangely, was the one destined to destroy Atomia. At that moment, Lieutenant Commander Sommer entered the room. He was the one in charge of following the submarine from Norfolk to The Rock and had witnessed its passage between the reefs and its disappearance into the grotto.

Beffort introduced the two men and said to Cooper, "Captain Sommer will go with you and give you the necessary information to make the operation run smoothly. We leave in an hour. I'll leave you to work everything out."

Followed by Akamatsu and J.E.E., Beffort went to the radio room where Witter and a group of officers were waiting for news from the *Georgia*. So as not to awake Madame Atomos' suspicions, he had decided that no changes would be made to normal airport operations. To impose radio silence would have been the biggest blunder. Thus, the *Georgia* could communicate, without too much fear of being recognized, and give its location every 30 minutes.

"Where is it?" Beffort asked.

"Still far," Witter scowled. "Greens thinks that he won't get there before 1 p.m."

Beffort jumped. "Tell him to step on it! He absolutely has to arrive before the end of the neutralization hour!"

"He can't go any faster…"

"How's the sea?"

"Flat as a pancake. Nothing to worry about on that score. But Greens insists that the plane land on his bridge as soon as possible."

"Okay. Let him know that we're taking off with the materials immediately."

Witter raised his eyebrows. "You're going to the party too?"

Beffort pulled out his wallet and showed him a picture of Soblen holding Bob's hand. Through gritted teeth he said, "What party are you talking about, Eddy?" Then he left without another word.

At noon Atomia was still not in sight. The *Georgia* was shaking dangerously under the pressure of its engines and on the rear bridge Greens felt every vibration like a little pain. Since its departure the aircraft carrier was sailing at 34 knots and that was pure madness! As fast as a destroyer escort!

With binoculars glued to his eyes, Beffort asked, "You really can't push it any faster?"

"No!" Greens howled. "I'm at the limit! We left Hawaii too late! Instead of letting me hash it out with Salem, you should have…"

Beffort walked out on him and off the bridge. The torpedo was prepared, as well as the remote-control device. The sea was still dead calm, everyone was at his post… Paradoxically, all they needed was their target!

Beffort went up to Cooper. "When the torpedo has been dropped, how long until it hits home?"

"Between 4 and 5 minutes," Cooper answered without the slightest hesitation. He blinked and said, "The *Georgia* will have to be quick to get out of range of the radiation."

Beffort nodded, worriedly. At three miles from the epicenter of the explosion, the aircraft carrier would be directly threatened by the bomb. Of course, everyone had glasses and except for the men on watch, the whole crew had been ordered to their quarters to limit the risks. And Greens was going to head his ship north after the mandatory stop that Cooper needed to get a good shot, but who could tell what would happen after the explosion?

The silence over all the huge ship was telling. None of the men were sure of getting out alive.

At 12:30 a shout came from the lookout. "Land in sight! Dead ahead!"

Beffort ran to the bridge, aimed his binoculars at where Greens was pointing, and made out a dark mass, cut off, barely sticking out of the water. It was like a monster lying in wait, a ferocious sleeping beast but whose awakening would be sudden and terrifying.

"We'll be there in 15 minutes," Greens said coldly.

Beffort made no comment. They still had to stop the ship, ready the torpedo, adjust the remote-control, take aim...

When everything was ready, they would only have a few minutes before the end of the neutralization hour.

Chapter XIV

At 12:56 the torpedo shot out of its tube, dove into the water and started cutting through the sea. The *Georgia* turned easily, set its curse for the north and sailed off at full speed as Cooper and Sommer, standing on the bridge, surveyed the destructive device speeding toward The Rock.

At that moment, Madame Atomos was just coming out of a deep sleep. She had had a weird dream. Mie Azusa-Beffort was in the form of a lioness and chasing her, Madame Atomos, who was a mouse… Madame Atomos sat up and instinctively looked at the control boards. Everything was fine. The electromagnetic shield was up between Atomia and the sky and all the exits were hermetically sealed. Just then, only Madame Atomos and Dr. Minao, with his collaborators, could defend the island, which would be relatively easy given the means of protection they had. If some missile were shooting out of the air, it would be instantly detected and destroyed by the computers on duty. Nevertheless, like in everything, nothing was absolutely perfect in the island's defense system. Thus, and no doubt because it was unlikely, they had not allowed for an underwater attack.

Madame Atomos lay back down and unconsciously caressed the computer hanging around her neck… and the impossible happened!

A warning light blinked on the control board and a siren started wailing dismally in the sleeping city. Madame Atomos jumped out of bed, turned on the 25 TVs and searched frantically for the danger on the screens. She first saw a ship and its plume of smoke, but it was far away, clearly heading north, and anyway no immediate danger. Then, on a screen from an underwater camera, she saw the long, cylindrical shape that had just shot through the breach in the reef. It was coming on fast and Madame Atomos felt her blood freeze in her veins. Whatever she did, she could not stop this missile!

For a second she was hoping the torpedo would crash into The Rock, but a brief image showed it entering the grotto. Two seconds later the torpedo reached the pool and hit the submarine...

Madame Atomos brought her hand up to the disintegrating computer, flipped a tiny switch and disappeared like magic from her office.

A split second later the atomic bomb exploded under Atomia and the entire island flew into the sky in thousands of fragments of rock, metal and human debris.

The shockwave rattled the *Georgia* and a burning wind hurled over the ship. Then a huge mushroom cloud rose up into the blue sky, rolled up violently, spread out and scattered deadly radiation in all directions. But the *Georgia* was out of range and by the time the cloud vanished, Beffort could see that Atomia was completely wiped off the surface of the Pacific.

In Savannah, in an old antiques shop that had been closed for a long time because of illness, Madame Atomos had just been reconstructed by a second computer. The terrible woman stood in the protective shadows in the back of the dusty shop, alone, henceforth deprived of all her special powers and with only enough money to survive...

Then, as nobody would expect, she burst out laughing!

Over the next few hours, one undeniably important detail proved to the Americans that the Atomos Organization had really been destroyed by the nuclear explosion. In Palm Beach, in a glass coffin, the corpse of the Boss, which had mysteriously remained intact after his death[3], abruptly decomposed and turned to dust. Well, Madame Atomos had sworn to steal it one day in order to make him part of her Organization. She had preserved him for this end. Today, if the Boss was finally joining the other victims of Madame Atomos in death, it was obviously because she herself had stopped living.

An explosion of joy rocked the United States after the announcement of the news and they let the world know that the Befforts had finally won the battle against the sinister Japanese woman. This lasted several days and then they talked about other things…

Beffort arrived in Williamsburg with Akamatsu and Witter and went straight to the clinic where Mie was convalescing. He asked to see her and the receptionist's eyes widened as she said, "But I don't understand, Mr. Beffort, your wife checked out the same day you left for Hawaii."

Beffort was floored but Akamatsu put his hand on his shoulder and said, "Sorry, Smith, but I gave Mie my word that I wouldn't tell you anything before this moment. Come on, there's a letter from your wife waiting for you at the post office."

They got back in the car and as they drove to the post office Akamatsu explained, "I don't know what Mie

---

[3] See *Miss Atomos*.

said in the letter, but I can tell you now about our conversation."

"I suspected you were hiding something from me," Beffort groaned.

"I wasn't at liberty to tell you the truth," Akamatsu defended himself. "Mie called on me because she counted on my friendship and discretion. To betray her would have been a crime."

"Okay. I don't hold it against you, Yosho. If you did it, it was obviously because you figured my wife had good reason... What did she ask you?"

Akamatsu turned a corner, stopped at a red light and confessed, "She asked me to get a car for her and a paralyzing pistol. Her plan was to leave Williamsburg and disappear for a little while so Madame Atomos would come looking for her. Like that the terrible woman might end up forgetting about you. She told me, word for word: *You know, Yosho, I've already lost my son and I don't want to risk losing my husband.*"

"Ridiculous!" Beffort exploded.

"Yes and I thought it was just an excuse, but how could I refuse what she was asking of me?"

"Damn it! But she knew that we were getting ready to attack Atomia. I told her myself! And she didn't react at all. It was like I was talking to a wall."

Akamatsu was driving again. "She was putting on an act, Smith, because when I saw her, she was very lucid. I think she'd been preparing this for weeks, carefully weighing the pros and cons. Of course it's all a result of Bob's death, whom neither the FBI nor the Green Dragon Force could protect."

"Let's say," Beffort spoke grudgingly, "that I understand that my wife no longer trusted me to protect her, but what does she figure on doing?"

Akamatsu shook his head. "I know absolutely nothing about it, Smith. I got her a car, a paralyzing gun and a checkbook from your house. If you want to know more, you have to read her letter. And you can do that now—we're here."

Akamatsu stopped the car in front of the post office and Beffort got out. He crossed the wide sidewalk and entered the building. A letter in his name was waiting for him in general delivery. It was Mie's handwriting. He did not open it right away, but went back to the car and asked Akamatsu to drive him to the Motor Inn. After they arrived, he shut himself in his room and tore open the letter.

The letter was dated the day before and had been sent from Washington. Mie said:

My love,

You're going to be surprised at my sudden departure. Forgive me for not speaking to you about this. I did it because I was sure that you would try to stop me.

Since the death of our son, I knew that I would find no rest if Madame Atomos didn't pay for her crimes. Well, in spite of all your efforts, I clearly saw that you wouldn't kill her using the methods at your disposal. The Green Dragon Force was effective at the start, when Madame Atomos didn't know who they were, but now our enemy knows most of its members and can block its blows.

Moreover, everyone is running around without real passion, chasing Madame Atomos as if she were some petty criminal, and too often obeying contradictory orders that spread them all over the United States. As proof, just look at the perfect example of her taking Bob away from us: while you were in Boston, Madame

Atomos quietly did what she needed to do to kill our child!

In short, regrets are useless and vain. I've decided to launch a personal assault on Madame Atomos.

I know that Atomia has been destroyed, but I also know that Madame Atomos escaped the catastrophe. Don't ask me why I'm so certain of this because I won't be able to say. It simply seems impossible to me that Madame Atomos didn't anticipate that Atomia could one day be bombed, her work destroyed and she herself threatened with a violent death. Right now you're obviously thinking that you pulled off a great victory. It's true if you're thinking that the Atomos Organization has been disbanded and the world has nothing to fear from the awful, terrifying weapons that almost destroyed it. However, nothing will be really over as long as Madame Atomos is alive.

Her criminal genius is such that she can easily rebuild a force that, although not as strong as the Organization, will hound us doggedly day after day and inevitably end up killing us.

From now on I refuse to play the role of victim. I'm going to go on the offensive. I surely don't have your strength, Smith, or your skills, but I'm a woman! Madame Atomos has never had to fight a woman, but she knew how to use them to accomplish her sinister plots, which proved effective. I have a healthy bank account, a formidable weapon and I'm fueled by an unquenchable thirst for vengeance!

Smith, dear, Miss Atomos has just been reborn! She'll often work outside the law and that's one of the reasons that compelled her to leave without you. Don't condemn her too quickly if she commits acts that you

*disapprove of. Anyway, she is still yours and will come
back to you when Madame Atomos is no more.*

I kiss you tenderly.

It was signed: *Miss Atomos!*

Beffort stood up, opened the window because he
needed air and then swore his head off. Only a woman
would have such ideas!

Chapter XV

Over the following week, Beffort had no news at all from his wife. He had gone back to his old apartment in Washington D.C. and was on pins and needles waiting. An APB had been sent out by J.E.E., but Mie Azusa—pardon, Miss Atomos—appeared to have vanished into thin air.

It was December and Washington was sleeping under the snow when Beffort learned that his wife had withdrawn a large sum of money from her bank account. He ran to see Evans.

"Mie's in Savannah," he announced as he burst in. He held out the bank slip to Evans.

"She was there three days ago," the FBI chief corrected. "That's another story!" He handed back the paper and said, "If I were you, Smith, I wouldn't worry. Your wife is still in shock from Bob's death. In a little while she'll see that she's acting crazy and come straight back here." Then he tensed up and murmured, "But didn't Madame Atomos have an antique shop in Savannah?"

Smith grimaced and sat on the edge of the desk. "Now you're getting it, Evans, bravo! Mie isn't taking this adventure lightly. She remembered this refuge and went to see if Madame Atomos was hiding there. Damn it! To take all that trouble, she has to be convinced that our enemy is safe and sound. In the end I wonder if she might not be right?"

Evans shrugged. "Atomia has been disintegrated and all hypotheses are allowed concerning its occupants. It could be that Madame Atomos no longer exists. But it could also be that she escaped the catastrophe. Bets are open, Smith. Personally, I think she's dead. As far as I can tell, we haven't heard news from her for a long time. If she were alive, wouldn't she be taunting us?" He paused, saw that Beffort was preoccupied, and said, "Now, if you're worried, you can still fly out to Savannah on our charge…"

"Thanks," Beffort said. "I was hoping you'd say that!" He rushed out of the office, got back home to pack a bag and hurried to the airport.

In Savannah the shop was closed. Beffort had the local FBI chief open it and went in alone. The place smelled musty and spider webs hung from the ceiling, stretching between all the old objects of questionable value. But in the back of the shop, before a table that was clean as new, Beffort stopped short seeing two sheets of paper ripped out of the same notepad, but covered in two different handwritings.

The first sheet read: *Too late, Mr. Beffort!* and it was signed by the hand and with the name of Madame Atomos.

The other message was in Mie's writing: *You see, Smith, I was right!*

Beffort's legs gave way and he dropped into a chair. His wife had become crazy or dreadfully reckless. She was thinking to meet up with Madame Atomos and put her down for the count, but the opposite was likely to happen. Madame Atomos was evil personified. She would quickly notice that Mie was on her trail and do whatever it took to get rid of her…

Miss Atomos versus Madame Atomos!
Unbelievable!

Turned to jelly, Beffort left the shop and took a plane back to Washington. He already felt overwhelmed by the events.

Eight days later a letter posted from Crescent City fell onto J.E.E.'s desk. Since it was not addressed to him but to the name of Beffort, he gave it to a secretary who put it in the G-man's box.

Beffort arrived at the office at 9:30 a.m. He had slept badly, tossed and turned all night, only managing to fall asleep when the sun rose. He was worried about Mie, whom the police still could not find, and feared above all that they would discover her corpse on some vacant lot.

He opened the letter without thinking, paying no particular attention to the envelope or typed address. But he literally jumped out of his chair when he recognized the inimitable handwriting of Madame Atomos. From Savannah, she had crossed the United States to the west, which meant that she still had certain resources at hand and that she was probably ready to return to crime.

Beffort read:

Mr. Beffort, I think that my letter won't surprise you too much because you have surely found my little note in Savannah.

Today I'm in Crescent City. Tomorrow I'll be somewhere else, untouchable, and taking advantage of these nice little jaunts to fill up my war chest. This is the first time that I've mingled so closely with your countrymen and I admit that the experience is fascinating.

I never imagined that such a rich people could also be so incredibly gullible! Since Atomia ceased to exist, I've already stolen more than $40,000 from the Americans. It's true that I don't hesitate to kill them if it's nec-

essary. And it's almost always necessary! I'm carrying out my vengeance on a smaller scale, certainly, but it's only a temporary occupation.

In one or two months I think I'll be ready to resume my attacks against the United States. I know, it's astonishing news! Of course, I won't be able to use the disintegrator ray anymore, or the paralyzing ray, or even the electromagnetic shield. Believe me, I miss that because these little gadgets were my pride and joy! Nevertheless, I will get some firepower using more conventional methods. You know, one can kill very well with grandmother's old recipes. You see, in a certain way, I'll be quite happy to have to resort to old-fashioned methods. I was getting a little soft among all those ultra-modern weapons that gave me the debilitating feeling of being at the peak of my power and of not being able to invent anything new!

In fact, it was too easy. I just had to press a button to wipe the United States off the map and that's why I never resolved to do it.

Now, however, everything will be much more interesting because of the complications I will encounter in taking my revenge. But if the methods will change, the slogan remains the same, Mr. Beffort: Hiroshima, Nagasaki! Compliments of Madame Atomos!

I wish you and your wife a quick and particularly gruesome death!

Beffort reread the letter three or four times. The Atomos affair had taken a strange twist, totally unexpected, and no one could say what result would be…

In any case, Beffort was absolutely sure that the newspapers would be sporting the following headlines: *Miss Atomos vs. Madame Atomos!*

André Caroff

LA TÉNÉBREUSE Mᵐᵉ ATOMOS

ANGOISSE

FLEUVE NOIR

THE EVIL OF MADAME ATOMOS

Chapter I

It was February 1968, and three months had passed since the tragedy in Williamsburg where Bob Beffort and Dr. Soblen had met their deaths. Of course, Smith Beffort and the American forces had managed to destroy Atomia Island, pulverizing the formidable power of Madame Atomos, but the sinister woman was still alive!

For three months Smith Beffort had concentrated on looking for his wife, Mie Azusa-Beffort, who had gone on the hunt for Madame Atomos in order to avenge her son with her own hands. But the two women were not to be found. Nevertheless, the FBI and the members of the Green Dragon Force spared no effort; they went over the entire country with a fine-toothed comb, meticulously checked the most absurd leads to the whereabouts of the two Japanese women, but all their efforts were in vain.

Of course, Beffort had his own idea about Madame Atomos. Hadn't the terrible woman told him that she would easily rebuild her fortune *taking money wherever she could find it*? Apparently they were not empty words because since November the country had seen a new wave of armed robberies and thefts of all kinds. Still, it was difficult, if not impossible to know for sure which crimes were committed by Madame Atomos and therefore to tell how fast she was amassing the money needed to muster a new army of crime that would be used against the United States.

It was troubling, but that was all. No matter what she did, Madame Atomos could never again acquire the extraordinary power that had made Americans tremble in fear for five years; nor would she terrorize crowds or dictate her conditions to the White House as she had tried. In brief, Madame Atomos was no longer Public Enemy No. 1 but an ordinary criminal who, sooner or later, would be captured by the police during a raid… Unless the sinister woman managed to accomplish a totally unexpected feat in the current state of affairs.

So, Beffort pretty much knew how Madame Atomos was spending her time. On the other hand, he had absolutely no idea what had become of his wife and this was much more important to him.

Today he was in the office of James Edward Evans, more of a friendly visit than for work, and he was listening to a report by one of the agents who was still making sure that the Atomos Organization had been dismantled for good.

"…the final proof we can give to the State Department is the total disappearance of the Boss' corpse. At the very second that Atomia Island was blown to smithereens, the guards saw the corpse literally melt inside its glass coffin. Well, he'd been there for a very long time, preserved in spite of everything, as if some miracle were going to bring him back to life."

J.E.E. nodded. "Okay, Blythe, you can go." The G-man waved to Beffort and left the room. When the door closed, J.E.E. said, "There you go, Smith! The United States is definitely rid of Madame Atomos…"

"Not Madame Atomos," Beffort corrected, "but her Organization. I'll admit that I'd prefer the contrary because the disappearance of the first would have automatically meant the disappearance of the second, but the inverse is not true."

J.E.E. waved it off, "After the dangers you lived through, you have to admit that we can breathe more easily now!"

"That's true, Evans, but don't forget that my son and poor Dr. Soblen paid for our victory with their lives. Personally, I still have a score to settle with Madame Atomos."

J.E.E. nodded. "I know, Smith, I know. But we have to find Mie first, don't we?"

Beffort gritted his teeth and slumped back in the armchair. He looked discouraged and really was. All of this had lasted too long. Whenever it looked like the game was over, new troubles and new problems sprang out of nowhere.

"How do you expect us to find her, Evans? She's imitated Madame Atomos to a tee in the hope of meeting up with her and beating her and she won't give up the chase until she's found her prey. She has money, a powerful weapon…"

"The paralyzing pistol?"

"Yes and she knows how to use it. I think that nothing can stop her."

J.E.E. raised his eyebrows, "Mie's been all worked up for three months. She's hiding from us while trying to get information about the woman who killed her son. And us with bigger and better means at our disposal are trying in vain to do the same thing. If you want my opinion, Smith, your wife will give up soon. It's impossible for her not to understand how useless her efforts are."

"She's a lioness whose cub was taken away from her, Evans."

"Could be, but she's a smart lioness... and she's got to be thinking of you, too. How could she forget that Madame Atomos swore to kill you?"

Beffort's smile had no joy in it. "Madame Atomos swore to kill the Befforts! Mie's in danger, too, and that's why we have to find her. In her battle against Madame Atomos, she's no match for her... especially since she wasn't completely healed when she ran away from the clinic in Williamsburg."

Evans looked up. "You mean her behavior is not completely normal?"

"Isn't that obvious?" Beffort mumbled. "Truthfully, it's surprising she hasn't totally lost her mind! Don't forget that Mie witnessed the gruesome scene of Bob..." He left the sentence unfinished and looked away. Evans understood how he felt. Little Bob had been eaten by a tiger in front of his mother who was paralyzed with horror.

After a long silence Beffort continued, "Besides, we can't forget that Mie underwent very delicate brain surgery in Atlanta when the surgeons removed her motor-brain."

Evans raised his arms to the sky. "Come on! After that operation Mie was totally normal! Don't get dramatic, Smith."

Beffort got out of his chair and went to stand in front of the window. He said, "I'm not being dramatic. I'm just trying to understand my wife's behavior and I'm having a hard time. Logically, after Bob's death, she should have got closer to me, needed comfort... instead of that she threw herself into a hopeless manhunt."

Evans drummed his fingers on his desk blotter. He, too, was starting to think that Mie had lost her mind. She had not given her husband any news since November, which was rather unusual.

"If she's not crazy," Beffort continued, "why hasn't she given us some sign that she's alive? A simple telephone call would reassure me and she knows very well that I'm not against her projects… Just the opposite! The two of us worked far better together! That's something she must know!" He turned to face Evans, "But I'm searching for an explanation when the truth is much more logical than we imagine."

"Which means?"

"Mie is chasing Madame Atomos who swore that she would kill her. We know that from square one both women have murder on their minds. Now, let's suppose that they meet up, that the battle takes place and one of them comes out the winner. In your opinion, who'll it be?"

J.E.E. did not answer. There was no point. Three months after her disappearance, Mie Azusa-Beffort might very well be dead.

"Don't you have an opinion?" Beffort asked.

"You have a way of putting it that can only have one answer, but after thinking about it, I don't think it happened like that."

"Why not?"

"Because Madame Atomos would let you about your wife's death right away! I'm sure she would've sent you her head. For Madame Atomos that would be the best way to put you down for the count and that's what she's trying to do, isn't it? You're her fiercest enemy. The most relentless adversary would abandon the duel now that she's been knocked down, but not you. She knows that you'll hunt her as long as you have breath in your lungs, an ounce of strength, and if she can't eliminate you directly, she'll take every opportunity to traumatize you. Therefore, I deduce that Mie is still alive."

Beffort nodded. "She's alive, but her days are numbered. I'm sure that Madame Atomos will manage to capture her if we don't stop her in time."

Evans stayed quiet. For three months he and Beffort were shaking things up every which way, but nothing had come of it. And these endless discussions were wearing him down. The FBI and the Green Dragon Force could not find the slightest trace of Mie…

All of a sudden the phone rang. Evans turned on the speaker and his secretary's voice said, "Sir, we've just received a message from the bureau in Billings, Montana, and it's about Mrs. Beffort."

"Mrs. Beffort! Good God, talk, where is she?"

"In a nursing home located about three miles from the city, not far from Acton."

"Since when?" Beffort asked.

"It seems that your wife's been there for more than a month," the secretary recognized the G-man's voice. "But she had no identification on her when she was found wandering around the countryside."

Evans and Beffort looked at each other. Evans spoke into the speaker-phone, "How is she?"

"Physically fine, sir…"

A pause, probably because Beffort was listening. Evans demanded, "Don't keep anything secret! Tell us what you know!"

"The report is brief, sir," the secretary sounded uncomfortable, "but it seems that Mrs. Beffort has really lost her mind. She couldn't give her name, didn't remember her past and appears to know absolutely nothing about what she's doing in Montana."

"Okay," Evans said, "give me the address of the clinic."

Beffort stared blankly at him as he wrote down the address. He was thinking of the trials and tribulations awaiting him there.

When the plane landed in the Billings Municipal Airport in the afternoon, Smith Beffort stepped off. He had wanted to come alone for several reasons, but mainly to avoid any annoying publicity that his hasty travel might cause. Unfortunately, as often happens in such cases, the journalists were not kind enough to abandon the inexhaustible source of sensational headlines that the dramatic operations of Madame Atomos periodically supplied.

Moreover, everyone in the press knew that Mie Azusa had disappeared and they were all lying in wait in the hope of getting the scoop on her whereabouts. Like the FBI and Green Dragon Force, the press had its investigators on the trail of Madame Atomos and Mie Azusa-Beffort.

As Beffort was leaving the main terminal, he passed by a bookstore and jumped when he saw the newspaper headline spread across six columns: *Mrs. Beffort, aka Mie Azusa, aka Miss Atomos, vanished after the Williamsburg affair, has been staying in our area for a month!*

Beffort bought the paper and winced when he read that the journalist knew as much as he did about the address of the nursing home and the circumstances surrounding Mie's admission. It was a disaster! In no time at all, the news would spread to the rest of the press all across the country and it would only be a matter of time before Madame Atomos would strike!

All tensed up now, Beffort took a taxi to the nursing home. It was on the road to Acton, in a very remote location, far from any houses and with a high wall surrounding it. Beffort paid his fare, sent the taxi on its way and rang at the gate. As the seconds ticked off, Beffort noticed the extraordinary silence in the area. Then a thin face appeared in the little window and said, "If you're a journalist, you can scram! Dr. Enright gave strict orders that..."

"I'm not a journalist," Beffort interrupted. "I've come to see my wife. Her name's Mie Azusa-Beffort."

"You have identification?"

Beffort showed his badge and the guard swung the gate open. "Excuse me," he said, "but Dr. Enright's been harassed by a bunch of guys wanting to take pictures. He had to call the police to get rid of them."

Beffort stepped through the gate and the guard closed it behind him, turning the locks and dropping the security bar.

"How did the newshounds learn that my wife was here?" Beffort asked.

"We couldn't help it. We had to contact the police to find out who she was."

"Why didn't she go the city hospital like she should have?"

"It was Dr. Enright himself who found her wandering on the road. It was wicked cold and your wife was on her last legs. He put her in his car and brought her here to care for her... but I think the doctor can tell you more than me. If you just follow me."

Beffort fell in behind him and the two men went down a long tree-lined walkway. The cold was, in fact, very bitter and patches of snow were still lying on the lawns. What the devil was Mie doing in this area?

At a turn in the lane, Beffort saw the nursing home. It was a square building, three stories high, and had a sloped roof of blue slates. All the shutters were wide open, but there were bars on the windows!

"What kind of people do you keep here?"

The guard shrugged. "Nervous breakdowns, for the most part."

"Why isn't anyone on the grounds?"

"It's nap time. Besides, it's much too cold right now for Dr. Enright to authorize walks."

He went up four steps, pushed a door open and let Beffort enter before closing it. "Wait here. I'll tell Dr. Enright."

After he had disappeared at the end of the corridor, Beffort sat in one of the armchairs in the waiting room. He felt unusually sad. The place had an air of melancholy, of weirdness and there was the faint smell of medication. It was too silent. Beffort spotted an ashtray and lit a cigarette. What condition would his wife be in?

"The doctor will be right with you."

Beffort jumped. The guard had shown up without being seen or heard. He nodded and the guy slipped away silently on his rubber soles. Beffort put out his half-smoked cigarette and paced across the room. He did not like this place or the guard and he already felt that he would not like Dr. Enright.

"Mr. Beffort?" Beffort turned around and saw a young man in a business suit. "Dr. Enright." He was smiling and looked nice.

Beffort held out his hand. "Nice to meet you. If I'm not mistaken, my wife owes you her life?"

"Don't exaggerate," Enright protested. "The road she was on is busy enough. If I hadn't passed by, someone else would have found her. Still, I appreciate that luck was on my side."

"That's what I meant. How is she?"

Enright smiled. "She's in good health."

"You don't have to beat around the bush."

"She's in good health," the doctor repeated, "and that's the important thing, even if you don't think so. Now, let's hope she'll snap out of it when she sees you. So far she hasn't even been able to remember her name, and she knows nothing about her past. Follow me."

Chapter II

The room was on the second floor, at the end of a long, badly lit corridor, room no. 6. A nurse was sitting in an office equipped with a bulletin board, a huge medicine cabinet and an interphone.

Enright stopped in front of her and murmured, "Miss Toohey, this is Mr. Beffort."

"Nice to meet you," the nurse said curtly.

"He came to see his wife," the doctor went on. "Is she awake?"

Miss Toohey looked at her big, man's watch, which she wore up near her elbow in a pretty eccentric way. "You have to wait a little. Mrs. Beffort usually sleeps until 4 p.m. and it's only 3:30."

"Okay," Enright decided, "We'll wait." He took Beffort's arm amiably and as he led him to the stairway said, "I guess you're not in a hurry, right? If you'd like, we could, of course, wake up your wife, but seeing that she's on tranquilizers, I wouldn't advise it. Come on, we can wait in my office."

Beffort followed him in silence. He was feeling completely helpless. Being used to action, it was a hard blow to him that he could do nothing for Mie and he fell into a predictable slump.

"Sit down," Enright offered. "Cigarette?"

Beffort accepted, struck his lighter and asked, "I understand that my wife has been with you for just over four weeks. How is it that you didn't discover her identity earlier?"

Enright spread out his hands. "You know, at the time, I didn't care who she was. I hospitalized her and that was it. Miss Toohey took care of contacting the police. And only because your wife had no identification on her and the particular circumstances…"

"Just a second," Beffort cut in. "When you saw her on the road, what made you think she needed help?"

Enright was surprised. "But I thought you knew. Mrs. Beffort was walking around at seven in the morning in the snowy countryside, 100 yards off the road, in heels and without a coat. Out of professional habit I always watch the people hanging around my clinic. In the past there were some patients who got over the wall during one of their fits and when I saw your wife, I immediately thought I was faced with such a case. I stopped my car and went to meet her. Naturally, I saw that your wife was not one of my residents, but her attitude was strange enough that I was concerned for her health. And she wouldn't answer my questions. I saw her shivering in the cold, looking completely dazed, so I brought her to my car…"

"She wasn't carrying a handbag?"

"Nothing, sir, nothing at all. And since she was in a pretty remote spot and not even on the road, I figured that she had strayed, maybe suffering from amnesia… In sum, I brought her here and Miss Toohey gave her lots of attention. Later I tried to question your wife again, but I didn't get much out of her. She knows she's being treated in a clinic, but doesn't try to find out when she'll leave or how she got here. For the moment it's clear that her memories go no farther back than waking up in room 6. She knows me and Miss Toohey as well, listens to the radio distractedly, reads the papers the same and doesn't say a word to the other patients when they meet on the grounds."

Enright ashed his cigarette, sat back comfortably in his chair and continued, "I don't know what to think of her condition. I'm thinking of all kinds of things. I was sure that she'd suffered some very violent emotional shock and after examining her, I figured that the scar she has on her head might be from some grave surgery, fairly recent, maybe one or two years ago, and it had left some after effects that just took a turn for the worse. That's what I was thinking when I found out that my patient was Mie Azusa, the ex-Miss Atomos."

"Conclusions?"

"For me, Mr. Beffort, there's no doubt at all that the tragedy in Williamsburg is the source of your wife's illness. In her place, others would have completely lost their mind. Mrs. Beffort just wiped out the past unconsciously."

Beffort nodded. He simply understood that Mie was no longer part of society and the rest of her life would probably be spent between the four walls of a nursing home. Thus, after an unreckoned amount of time, in spite of everything, Madame Atomos had reached her goal.

Dr. Enright said, "I think we can go up now. It's four o'clock."

Beffort followed him up to the second floor and in the corridor they met the nurse, who said, "Mrs. Beffort is awake. I told her that someone wanted to see her and she said she didn't want to, that she wasn't interested in talking to a stranger. She seemed pretty worked up, doctor."

Beffort looked at Enright and asked, "What do you think?"

"We have to try," he said firmly. "Psychologically speaking your wife has nothing to lose. Follow me."

He went down the corridor, knocked on door 6 and pushed it open without waiting for an answer. Beffort went in behind him and felt a little twinge finding himself face to face with Mie. She was sitting up in bed, her back supported by two pillows and she was calmly watching her two visitors. She was a little pale, the shut-in or invalid kind of pale, and her eyes looked veiled.

"Hello," Enright said. "This is Dr. Beffort." He quickly stepped aside, showing Beffort in full, but Mie did not react as expected. She leaned slightly forward and trained her attention on Enright, who said, "Don't you remember Dr. Beffort?"

Mie shook her head.

"He came to see you once or twice," Enright pretended. "He's come back today to ask you a few medical questions. Do you feel up to answering?"

Mie hesitated, but finally said, "Okay, but I have nothing special to say."

"It doesn't matter," Enright said cheerfully. "Dr. Beffort just wants to have a friendly chat with you."

"I don't want to chat."

"Please try," Enright pleaded gently.

"I won't talk," Mie assured him, staring at Smith Beffort.

Enright turned an embarrassed eye on the G-man and whispered, "Say something to her or else she'll clam up and we won't get anything out of her."

With a ball in his throat, Beffort went over to the bed. "If you don't want to talk," he said, "it's no problem. I can sit in the chair and we can listen to the radio without saying a thing."

Mie looked him up and down and smiled, "You seem nice, doctor. I'd like you to stay a while but only if you give me some cigarettes."

"Hold on!" Enright said. "You didn't tell me you smoked!"

Mie smiled thinly, blushed and said, "I didn't dare, see? Miss Toohey says that tobacco is bad poison and I didn't want to argue with her. She doesn't smoke and can't understand... Dr. Beffort's fingers are stained yellow from the nicotine, so he'll understand."

Enright glanced over at Beffort. "You can give her cigarettes, but if she doesn't want to talk, don't force her. I'll come back in a little while after I've looked in on the other residents." He headed for the door and left the room.

Smith Beffort sat down and took his cigarettes out of his pocket. Mie took one, lit it with her husband's lighter and blew smoke out hard toward the ceiling. Then she did it again... Beffort was very intrigued. Mie never used to smoke. Moreover, the sick woman's veiled eyes seemed to brighten up curiously after Dr. Enright left.

"You're not smoking, doctor."

Beffort lit a cigarette and caught Mie winking at him, which peeked his curiosity even further. The atmosphere had suddenly changed a great deal. If Mie was not totally insane, she was trying to make him understand something in secret, as if a third person was in the room.

Another wink, another puff of smoke and a little crook of her finger inviting him to come closer...

Beffort slowly moved his chair while asking, "You really don't want to talk?"

"No, smoke!"

When Beffort was just a few inches from his wife, she lowered her head and whispered, "Watch out, Smith! There's a mic here and they're certainly watching me

147

through a peephole. We have to make a lot of smoke, get it?"

Smith Beffort sat like a statue—he was totally stunned. Mie was not crazy. She was still on the trail of Madame Atomos and being in the clinic was obviously part of a carefully thought out plan. The details of this plan were beyond him, but he knew that from now on he could trust his wife. She had already set up a secret meeting by pretending not to want to talk with Dr. Beffort so that no one would be surprised at the complete silence in the room. Then she said she wanted to smoke, hoping that the smoke would form a kind of safety screen for them. The peephole was probably installed in the ceiling and that was where the smoke would accumulate first.

"It'll take too much time," Beffort whispered.

"No, just so that Miss Toohey can't see our lips moving... How are you, Smith?"

"A lot better now. Can you tell me what you've been doing for the last three months?"

"I've been following Madame Atomos," Mie's voice could barely be heard, "but I haven't caught her yet."

"How did you stay on her trail?"

"Madame Atomos committed a series of crimes on her trip across the United States. I think she's already amassed a considerable fortune because all her victims were rich. That's what led me from state to state, especially since I set off from the right place, in that antiques shop in Savannah, Georgia."

Beffort remembered. Madame Atomos had disintegrated on Atomia Island and reconstructed her human form in that shop after an extraordinary tele-transportation trip by means of electromagnetic signals.

"So," Mie kept whispering and blowing smoke, "I followed her trail because I was anticipating the crimes she would commit. Every one of them was an arrow pointing me in the right direction. The trip lasted almost five weeks before I ended up here in Billings. For three days nothing happened and then a jeweler couple were murdered in their apartment on Broadwater Avenue. A large sum of money was stolen from a chest where they'd kept their cash before taking it to the bank and the newspapers said the crimes, without a doubt, had been committed by someone familiar with the layout. This didn't match with the idea I had of Madame Atomos' new methods, but our enemy certainly was in Billings, I would've sworn to it. In a discreet investigation I found out very quickly that a certain Marie Toohey had worked for the jewelers. She was a nurse and occasionally gave the lady injections, but that was a couple of weeks before and the police had let Miss Toohey go after questioning her about her work schedule on the day of the double murder. But since Madame Atomos didn't have enough time to stake out the jewelers to know exactly where they hid their money, I figured that Marie Toohey and Madame Atomos were in on it together. Not being able to find the latter, I started watching the nurse. After her shift, she always went back home on 18th Street and never left until it was time to go back to the Enright clinic early in the morning. One evening, however, Marie Toohey went to a bar around Veterans Park and up to the second floor where I couldn't follow her. She stayed there around an hour before getting back in her car and going home. I stopped following her then, knowing I'd made a mistake by not trying to find out right away who she had met in that bar, so I went back to Veterans Park. The waiter there told me that the tall, skinny woman (that would describe Marie Toohey) had sat down at a table occupied by a middle-aged Asian woman. They had chatted for a while before the skinny woman left first through the front door. When I went back down I saw that the building did, in fact, have another exit and I knew that was how Madame Atomos had left."

"Hell," Beffort whispered, "you can't really be sure it was her."

Mie looked at him calmly. "I'm sure it was her, Smith. Since our son died, I feel I can sense her, like a dog sniffing its prey as long as it knows its smell. Besides, it all coincides perfectly with my verifications. Anyway, I had just missed Madame Atomos, but I knew she'd be in Billings for a while."

"How did you come up with that?"

"Because it was the first time since she left Savannah that she was working with someone else. I don't know how she picked Marie Toohey to be her new informant, but seeing that she wasn't killed, I had to believe that Madame Atomos was planning to use her on other occasions. To tell you the truth, I firmly believe that after one month Marie Toohey is now the oldest member of the new Atomos Organization!"

"Hush," Beffort hissed. "You're talking too loud, Mie."

They stayed silent for a moment. There was not a sound in the clinic, but Beffort felt like he was being watched. The curtain of smoke gathering on the ceiling was a pathetic cover. If Marie Toohey was spying on the couple through a peephole in the floor above, she would be much more hampered by her bird's eye view than by the cigarette smoke.

Mie stubbed out her butt, held out her hand and said loudly, "Give me another cigarette, doctor."

Beffort offered his pack, whispering, "Don't you think we should start a conversation."

"Why?" Mie whispered back. "Marie Toohey believes I've lost my memory and undoubtedly thinks my behavior is normal. Since I've been here I've forced myself to act like a fickle woman. I've even managed to fool Dr. Enright, so I have to keep going."

"Why did you come and get committed to this nursing home?"

Mie took a drag on her cigarette and smiled. "Marie Toohey was my only link to Madame Atomos. Living here was a good way not to lose her. Plus, I wanted to know how deep she was in with Madame Atomos, who seemed not to trust her completely because since I arrived here, Marie Toohey has treated me very kindly. I wasn't expecting this so I decided to telephone the newspapers and reveal my identity."

Beffort scowled. "I thought it was the police who…"

"I don't know what the police did, but I know the papers wrote about me thanks to my phone revelations the night before last. You see, Smith, the outside line is at the end of the corridor and nobody was paying attention to me because I was supposed to be asleep from the tranquilizers. No need to tell you that I haven't taken one of them. Since Dr. Enright's treatment doesn't require shots, I throw the pills in the toilet, empty the cups in the sink and keep my eyes and ears open. That's how I know Marie Toohey put a microphone under the table over there and dug a hole in the corner of the ceiling to install a wide-angle peephole. It all happened yesterday after the newspapers came out and it proves that Madame Atomos has finally decided to deal with me."

Beffort sighed. So, that was Mie's plan when she got admitted to Enright's clinic. "You're completely crazy! If Madame Atomos gives the order, Marie Toohey will pump you full of poison and send you directly into the great beyond."

"It's not that simple, Smith," Mie was still calm. "If I die, there'll be an investigation and the police will know right away that I was murdered. Miss Toohey will be questioned again and she'll be in a tough spot. Already suspected in the jeweler's murder, she won't be able to get out of it twice. Then her inevitable confession will also put Madame Atomos at risk."

"So, you think Madame Atomos will give up her vengeance out of fear of the police?"

"No, she'll try to kill me, but more subtly."

"How?"

"I don't know, but I hope I can strike before she does!"

Chapter III

Dr. Enright knocked and entered without waiting for an answer. He saw the cloud of smoke floating in the room and furrowed his brow. "This smoke den is unreasonable, Dr. Beffort," he scolded while opening the window. "You've been with my patient for almost an hour—have you had time to form an opinion about her condition?"

Beffort stood up. "She really has lost all her memory," he said softly, forcing himself to look dismayed. "She doesn't know who I am or what she's doing in Montana." He took a step toward the doctor and whispered, "She's even forgotten all about Madame Atomos."

Enright shook his head. Like all Americans, he knew everything about the battle that freed the Befforts of the sinister Japanese woman. Beffort added confidentially, "She doesn't remember her son or Dr. Soblen... It's hopeless."

"Did she say anything?"

"No, she just listened, but it obviously bored her. Frankly, I don't see how to snap her back to reality."

While talking, he got closer to the table where Miss Toohey had installed the microphone. Enright followed him automatically, thinking that Beffort did not want his wife to hear.

The G-man said, "Still, I can't leave her here forever. Nothing's preventing her from returning to Washington, right, doctor?"

Enright nodded. "I told you she's in good physical health and she can get up if she wants, but like a lot of patients suffering from a nervous breakdown, your wife feels safe in bed. She is free from all obligations here, from all responsibility, and she doesn't have to do anything."

Beffort pretended to think about it. If Mie was fooling Enright so easily about her condition, it was precisely because she had had a real breakdown in Williamsburg and her current behavior was mimicking what had forced her to stay in bed after the death of Bob and Soblen. If it worked on a man like Enright, there was no reason for Miss Toohey and Madame Atomos to suspect the truth. Mie wanted Madame Atomos to reveal herself in an attempted attack and the best way to hasten this attempt was to make her believe that Mie was going to be leaving soon, that she would be under FBI protection again and it would become practically impossible to reach her then.

"I'm not going to rush her," Beffort said. "With your help, I count on getting her to accept being moved to Washington by the stranger that I've become in her eyes. Taking little steps, we should manage to get her to see that she would be better cared for over there…"

Enright frowned. "It's not very nice for me, but I think we can do it pretty quickly. Keep playing doctor, try to gain her trust, even if it means making me look incompetent, and I bet she'll follow you without too much fuss. So, it would be good for you to come and see her a lot over the next few days." He looked over at Mie, who was pretending to read, and said, "The best thing would be for you to stay here, but unfortunately I have no rooms available."

"Too bad," Beffort was sorry for that as he thought of his wife's security. "I'll get a room in Billings. Can you recommend any hotels in town?"

"No, not really. But I know the owners of an inn, kind of a bed and breakfast, not too far from here. If you stayed there, you would be less than 15 minutes away on foot. And you can eat there, too."

"Sounds good. What's the name of this inn?"

"It has no name. If you came be car, you couldn't miss seeing it a few hundred yards before you turn onto the road leading here."

"I came by taxi and I have no means of transportation."

Enright waved it off. "That doesn't matter. I'll ask Miss Toohey to call and reserve a room and I'll drive you there myself on my way home. Stay with your wife and I'll come get you soon." He turned around and left the room.

Beffort heard footsteps scurrying in the room upstairs and knew that Miss Toohey was leaving her post in order to answer Enright's call. He went over to the bed. "Now, Mie, we can talk without worrying about being heard. I just had a conversation with Enright..."

"I heard most of your conversation, Smith. Enright's mighty cooperative, isn't he?"

Her tone surprised Beffort. "What do mean by that?"

"He wasn't telling the truth when he said he had no rooms available. This morning there was still one. Why didn't he want to give it to you?"

"Since this morning," Beffort said calmly, "he could have got a new patient. Don't paint everything black, Mie. The time's passed when Madame Atomos got everyone to serve her by sticking a motor-brain in their skull."

"That's true, Mie sighed, but I just can't believe that Madame Atomos has lost her power. Why did you

155

tell Enright that you were going to take me to Washington?"

"For Miss Toohey to hear it and for her to tell Madame Atomos. After that, probably by tonight, your life will be hanging by a thread. If they attack in your room, do you have anything to defend yourself?"

Mie opened the drawer of the nightstand and lifted up a hand towel in which Beffort could see the grooved handle of the famous paralyzing pistol.

"Damn! How did you manage to sneak that weapon into the clinic?"

Mie closed the drawer, saying, "Before getting saved by Dr. Enright, I had made my plans, Smith. I was carrying nothing when Miss Toohey undressed me, but the pistol was on the outer wall since the night before waiting for me. All I had to do was pick it up during my walk."

Beffort nodded. "You thought of everything, I admit, but you can't stay awake 24 hours a day! If I were Miss Toohey, I would enter your room during the night…"

"Miss Toohey has no reason to be in the clinic at night."

"Who replaces her?"

"A young nurse. She's mostly in charge of telephoning Enright when something goes wrong, but that hasn't happened since I got here."

Beffort pinched his lips. "I don't like this situation much, Mie. You're taking a terrible risk and I won't be able to protect you. In my opinion, we should give up your plan."

"Do you have another?"

"Yes. I'll arrest Miss Toohey, take her to FBI head-quarters in Billings and force her to tell me where Madame Atomos is hiding. It's simple and effective."

Mie took his hand. "Don't be stupid, Smith. Madame Atomos is too smart to have told Marie Toohey anything that might spell her ruin. Plus, if you arrest her, Madame Atomos will surely learn about it right away and disappear once again."

Beffort found nothing to say. Mie took the opportunity to add, "In this affair, our best chance rests in the fact that Madame Atomos doesn't know that we're on her trail. Of course, she learned I was hospitalized in Dr. Enright's clinic and therefore might deduce that I was after her, but since I've lost my memory…"

Beffort did not hide his skepticism. "It's impossible for a woman like her not to suspect a trap. There are too many coincidences in this adventure. It would have been much more likely that you got sick in Washington, for example. We would have done what was needed to keep the newspapers relatively quiet, as if we were revealing a secret, and the result would have been the same. Your presence here looks like a set-up. Madame Atomos can't…" He stopped because someone had screamed in the yard. He jumped to the window and opened it. When he stuck his head between the bars he saw a light shimmering on the ragged ground.

"What is it, Smith?"

Beffort smelled something burning, heard crackling and turned around. "Get out of bed, Mie, and get dressed. I have the feeling that Madame Atomos has just struck!"

Mie threw off the covers and ran to the closet where her clothes were kept. At the same time, Dr. Enright's voice shouted, "Fire! John, Miss Toohey, help the patients evacuate the building!"

There was a dull explosion somewhere on the first floor and a cloud of black smoke shot up to the window. Beffort closed it to keep out the draft and rushed to the door. The corridor and landing were already hidden behind the smoke. No one to be seen, but cries of alarm were coming from the upper floors. With their windows barred, the clinic was a prison where escape was difficult.

"Mie, hurry up!"

The young woman fastened her skirt, put on her shoes and joined her husband in the doorway. At that very second, a tongue of fire roared up the stairs and quickly ran down the corridor. The blaze was spreading with stunning speed, already consuming the walls and floorboards near the stairway, and it was growing every second, blowing foul-smelling smoke that would soon be unbreathable.

Beffort closed the door. "We can't get out that way!"

Mie bent down to feel the floor and then stood back up. "It's still cold, which means the fire hasn't reached this wing of the building."

Beffort knew what she was hinting at, so he looked around for something strong enough to pry up one of the floorboards. If Marie Toohey had been able to install a peephole in the ceiling so easily, that meant that the construction was not so solid. Then he swore, "We need at least a crowbar."

They looked at each other. Time was running out. The nursing home was cracking apart everywhere and smoke was starting to sneak under the door. Farther away the patients were screaming, but their cries were drowned out by the roar of the fire. Room 6 had still not been touched, but it was only a matter of minutes, a reprieve, a gift from fate that they had to use to their advantage at all costs…

Unfortunately the hospital room contained no object that looked in any way like a crowbar. Beffort quickly made up his mind that he would not find what he was looking for. He opened the door again, recoiled before the curtain of flames that was eating away the floor, and then slammed it shut. As often happens in such cases, the upper floors were burning before the first floor because of the draft from the stairwell, so they would have to expect a cave-in soon.

Up above, the patients had quieted down and even Dr. Enright had stopped calling out for help. Mie sat on the bed. She was pale. Her dilated eye stared at the peeling, cracking ceiling. The heat was becoming intolerable and the smoke was thickening in the room, stinging their eyes and choking their lungs.

"We won't get out of here, Smith!"

All of a sudden, the lights went out, flashing briefly from the short circuit just as the door burst open under the pressure of the flames. A spray of fire spattered the room and licked at the bed. Beffort and Mie ran toward the window; their hair and eyebrows were singed. Everything was getting too hot. The windows exploded while the ceiling continued its slow disintegration.

Beffort coughed and dried his eyes. Before him he saw the five bars that condemned them to death, then, suddenly, everything collapsed and Beffort saw nothing but a void around him. He felt himself sliding, gripping his wife's hand, jumping in a spray of sparks and an incredible din of raining debris. All at once, he found himself in a relatively clear space, running next to Mie while the building was crumbling behind them; and the sky seemed to melt.

Far away among the trees, they stopped, speechlessly dazed at seeing themselves unharmed, barely burned on their hands, but so exhausted that they had to lie down on the chilly ground. After taking their son and their best friend, fate must have owed them this miracle...

From the surrounding wall, Beffort and Mie watched the firemen arrive, along with the ambulances and a squad of police. The clinic was a smoking ruin and at first sight it looked like there would no survivors. Beffort dragged his wife to the gate and they slipped out unnoticed. Stopping at the intersection of the driveway and the road, they washed themselves in a little stream of icy water and brushed off their plaster-coated clothes. Under the little bridge they took stock of the situation as the first ambulances passed by overhead.

"Now," Beffort commented, "we know that Madame Atomos will stop at nothing to exterminate us. She might think we're dead, but I don't believe she'll be satisfied with half-certainties. Still, it'll be some time before she finds out that we escaped the flames. We have to use this time attack."

Mie leaned against him. She was worn out and suffering the nervous after-effects. "Right now," she said, "I can't go any farther, Smith. I'm dead tired and you're talking about attacking like it's as simple as that! Without Marie Toohey, we can never get to Madame Atomos."

Beffort hugged his wife and said, "For the moment there's no question of doing anything. We're going to go to Billings, get a hotel room under a false name and fix ourselves up."

"How are we going to get to Billings?"

"Farther down the road there's an inn where Dr. Enright was supposed to take me. Come on, it'll only take us ten minutes or so."

They climbed up onto the road and started walking, but dove into the ditch every time a car drove out of the clinic. When they finally reached the inn without incident, Beffort left his wife outside and went in to ask for a telephone. The room was full of journalists and nobody said a word to him. He shut himself inside the booth, called a taxi, paid for the call and went back to Mie, who was waiting patiently in the shadows.

"Everything's all right," he assured her. "No one saw you and no one paid any attention to me. Later, the taxi driver might say he picked up a couple, but only if someone questions him about it."

Mie stared at him. "You're going to let everyone believe that we died in the fire? Even J.E.E. and Owen Bernitz and Akamatsu?"

"Of course not! We'll call J.E.E. when we're in the hotel and ask him to inform Akamatsu and the Green Dragon Force. If Madame Atomos decided to set up in Billings, it's because she has a refuge here. Don't forget that the Atomos Organization dug thousands of underground shelters throughout the United States and we only know about a few. Madame Atomos certainly can't use her disintegrator ray or her electromagnetic shield now, so she'll hide whenever a threat appears, with nothing but traditional weapons at hand to counter our attack. From now on we can say that the battle will be more equal."

Headlights came shooting around the bend and Beffort raised a hand to hail the taxi. "Are you the person who called on the phone?" the driver asked. Beffort nodded and helped Mie inside.

Fifteen minutes later the couple got a room at the Morosco Hotel under a false name. To everyone now they would be Mr. and Mrs. Wynand from Fairbury, Nebraska.

A little later, Smith Beffort called Washington and revealed to James Edward Evans the outline of his plan.

Chapter IV

The next day, all the newspapers in the area were reporting the catastrophe at the Enright clinic and the deaths of Enright himself, the patients and the hospital personnel, adding that "in all likelihood" Mie Azusa and Smith Beffort had also perished in the blaze.

Marie Toohey was the only survivor. In a brief statement she confessed that Dr. Enright had let her go home at 6:30, a half hour before the fire, and she considered herself a living miracle. Strangely, no paper spoke of arson; they just said that a boiler had exploded in the basement, but before drawing any conclusions as to the origin of the catastrophe, they had to wait for the verdict of experts.

"Evans did a good job," Beffort said, "and the journalists must be kicking in their stalls. They must be wondering what it's all about since they don't know that Madame Atomos is in Billings…"

The telephone interrupted him. Mie picked up and heard Yosho Akamatsu on the line. "Hello, Mie," the Japanese policeman said, "I arrived in Billings this morning. So, it seems that Madame Atomos is in the neighborhood?"

"Exactly, Yosho, and don't forget that we're burned to a crisp."

"I know, Mrs. Wynand. I made sure to ask the operator for this name. Can I speak with your husband? Evans wasn't very talkative."

Smith got on the phone. "How are you, Yosho?"

"Fine," the Japanese said curtly. "I guess it's the same for you considering the attack you just escaped.

Anyway, it proves that Madame Atomos has absolutely no intention of hanging up her gloves. Evans told me that you had some work for me. What's it about?"

"A stakeout, Yosho. A certain Marie Toohey who lives at 316 18th St. If you've read the local paper, you should be up-to-date."

"I know who she is. Why watch her?"

"According to our conclusions, this woman should be the first member of the new Atomos Organization. She's apparently the one who sparked the fire at the clinic on the instructions of Madame Atomos."

"In short, you want me to trail this Marie Toohey in the hope that she'll lead me to her boss?"

"Affirmative."

"Okay, Smith, I'll get on the watch immediately. Should your hotel be considered HQ for this operation?"

Beffort hesitated before finally answering, "For the moment. We'll get things up and running soon and talk about it again when we're better organized. Call here if you have news. I won't move before Owen Bernitz gets in. Then, let's say around noon, someone will take your place. Is that okay with you?"

"Absolutely. I'll call back around noon."

Akamatsu hung up, hailed a cab on the street and went to 316 18th St. When he arrived, he paid his fare, crossed the sidewalk and went straight into the building. On one of the mailboxes he spotted Marie Toohey's name, saw that she lived on the 5th floor and gave himself a ride in the elevator. He was using the empirical method, but he was conscious that he was playing a game of poker. With Madame Atomos, you had to act fast or you would find yourself bound hand and foot before you had the chance to move your pinky.

Akamatsu rang at Marie Toohey's door, heard feet shuffling and then a voice asked, "Who are you and what do you want?"

The reaction of a cagey old girl, Yosho thought. But that would make things a lot easier for the Japanese policeman. He wanted to make sure the nurse was at home, even if it meant revealing himself, but without betraying himself.

"I would like to speak with Miss Toohey," he said through the door.

"What about?"

"I'm a journalist."

"Not interested!" the nurse barked. "I've already said what I know. Hit the road and don't come back and bother me or else I'll call the police."

Akamatsu smiled, turned around, got back in the elevator and slammed the door noisily. When he left the building, he stuck close to the walls so that the nurse would not see him if she was watching the exit. He turned the corner, crossed the street and when he was out of sight of the apartment, he came slowly back on the opposite sidewalk.

18th Street was very busy, with both pedestrians and cars, so there was little chance that Marie Toohey could notice him among the people milling around the stores. But what was true for the nurse was also true for Akamatsu. He had only a description of her and a photo from the newspaper. A tall, skinny woman with an equine profile who dressed pretty old-fashioned. At 10 a.m. a woman answering this description appeared at the front door. Akamatsu was immediately certain that it was Marie Toohey; she looked so much like her press photo. He gave her a little head start and then had a touch of panic when she climbed into a Chevrolet parked in a nearby lot. But he found another taxi right away and was able to keep on her tail when the Chevy took off.

One behind the other, the two vehicles crossed Billings and reached South Park, specifically 8th Avenue, where Marie Toohey parked her car. She got out and walked to a strange place called the Zag Zag: windowless and with a darkened sign that seemed to indicate that it was closed.

Akamatsu sent the taxi away and casually sauntered up. On closer inspection, he saw that the Zag Zag was a nightclub and Marie Toohey had gone in through the service entrance. He was flabbergasted. What was an old gal like her doing in a seamy place like this?

He glanced through the grill and saw pictures of nude girls. So, the Zag Zag was a strip club and their merchandise was top choice.

Akamatsu went and sat in the diner across the street, waiting for Marie Toohey to come out. At noon he was still there and the nurse had not finished her visit. He ordered something else, went into the glass phone booth where he could still keep an eye on the Zag Zag and called Beffort. "It's me, Smith. Toohey led me to a club on 8th Avenue and she's been in there for around 45 minutes."

"A club, huh?"

"The Zag Zag, strip club, pretty swanky clientele, drinks at five bucks, and so on. If Toohey isn't in cahoots with the management to give contraceptive shots to…"

"Pills," Beffort reminded him. "Marie Toohey is obviously not at the Zag Zag on business. On the other hand, doesn't it seem a little crazy that Madame Atomos would become the owner of a nightclub?"

Akamatsu snickered. He, too, did not see Madame Atomos in this role. Beffort continued, "Whatever the case, I'm going to send a guy to relieve you. Bernitz is in Billings with his teams and twenty or so cars with radios. Where are you?"

Akamatsu gave the address of the diner and hung up. For the next 15 minutes not a sign from the Zag Zag and things were no different when a man entered and headed for Akamatsu's table. "Hello, Simms," the Japanese said. "So, they put you on it?"

Lucky Simms shook his hand warmly and took a seat. "Beffort assigned me because Madame Atomos doesn't know me," he explained. "Where's the club in question?"

Akamatsu pointed to the nightclub on the other side of the street, described Marie Toohey in great detail, and left for the Morosco Hotel.

All afternoon, Beffort, Akamatsu, Mie, Owen Bernitz and the 300 men of the Green Dragon Force waited, arms at the ready, for a sign from Lucky Simms, but he only called to give them discouraging "Nothing To Report" reports. Marie Toohey was still in the Zag Zag, which, he had made sure, had no other exit but the one on 8th Ave. Finally, at 9 p.m., the nurse made an appearance. She got into her Chevrolet and went straight back home. Lucky hung around the nightclub, letting a car from the Green Dragon Force take care of watching the nurse. On the radio Owen Bernitz found out that Miss Toohey had just turned out her lights and was probably gone to bed. He phoned in the news to Beffort, who felt a little disappointed.

"Personally," Mie said, "it doesn't surprise me. Madame Atomos will act cautiously, lay low for a little while. We have to learn to be patient, Smith."

Beffort started biting his nails and stared at Akamatsu who was sprawled in an armchair. "What do you think, Yosho?"

"I'm not for patience. Someone has to get into the Zag Zag to find out what goes on there, what kind of clientele they have, and, if possible, who owns the place."

Beffort nodded. "We're on the same wavelength. A guy like Lucky Simms fits the bill."

At eleven o'clock Lucky Simms stopped his orange Cadillac right in front of the nightclub's door. He was in a tuxedo and held his chin up high, looking haughty and contemptuous. At first sight you could see that the young man was loaded and thought he was the bee's knees. The valet made no mistake about it. He hustled to the door, opened it wide and showed off an Ultrabrite smile. "The show's about to begin, sir, I..."

Lucky slipped him a dollar. "Shut up, boy! Park my boat and give a whistle if you smell a raid, okay?"

"Okay," the valet accepted, snapping up the dollar. He was not happy with himself, figuring that he was terribly wrong about the true identity of his client and in his business that was the kind of mistake that could be his last.

Lucky kind of overdid it by pulling on his holster strap as he entered the club. At the coat check, he threw off his hat and overcoat before sailing through the heavy, purple curtain. He was grabbed immediately by the headwaiter and brought to a free table next to the dance floor. Apparently the Zag Zag was exactly the same as all the other clubs. Asthmatic orchestra, filtered lights, sleepy bartenders, sophisticated girls hiding paper-mache skin under their makeup... However, the club seemed to have a good clientele: middle-aged, rather calm, drinking in moderation, waiting for who knows what.

It was this imperceptible tension that put Lucky Simms on the alert. Certainly, the strip show was supposed to start in a minute and a group of younger men were fussing around the bar, but the older couples were all looking toward the padded door with one word inscribed in it: Private.

A long-legged brunette came to sit at Lucky's table and crossed her legs high enough to show her panties. Snapping his fingers Lucky asked for another glass and then offered her a cigarette. It was the classic setup.

"My name's Myriam," the girl said.

"Pleased to meet ya."

"Are you from Billings?"

"Not really. I'm coming back from vacation. Wanna dance?"

On the dance floor nobody bumped into each other. The orchestra was playing the last song before the shows—a slow piece, well designed to urge the people back to their seats. Myriam stuck to her partner like a vacuum.

"Not much ambience, eh, Myriam?"

"It's a nice place here. At least until one in the morning. After that the old fogies go to bed and the others come and we can have fun. You've never been here before, have you?"

"Sure, but it was almost two years ago."

"Ah! When there was the old owner?"

"Right. Back then we had a good time here…"

Myriam backed off a little and stared at him. "A month back, I guess the Zag Zag was the funnest place in Montana, then Zagabelli died and this lady bought the lot of it. She chucked everyone out—the musicians, waiters, bar girls, all the way down to the strippers. After being closed for 15 days, she opened the doors and this is what it turned into."

Lucky Simms showed no expression. "What did Zagabelli die of?"

"Someone sent him a cobra in a box of cigars... It's not like he had nothing but friends in the business, but they were expecting machine gun fire or something like that."

"And the new owner, who is it?"

Myriam shrugged. "She doesn't come here. I've never seen her myself." Her hand slipped down a little and touched the hard metal of the .38 that Lucky carried under his arm. "Say, you're not a cop, are you?"

Lucky did not answer. It was the end of the dance and he shuffled back to his table without worrying about Myriam.

She watched him, then sat down and said, "I don't think you are. Would you excuse me for a minute?"

Silently, with a nod of his chin, Lucky allowed. Out of the corner of his eye he saw the girl go toward the bathroom but veer off toward the exit. She obviously wanted to talk to the valet.

Lucky forgot about her. He already knew that the Zag Zag had been taken over by a mysterious woman after the brutal death of Zagabelli, all the personnel had been replaced, and the nightclub was not a "fun" place before 1 a.m. All that remained was to find out how Toohey was mixed up in this mess.

They announced the shows, the lights went out and Myriam reappeared. She seemed more relaxed and right away put her head on Lucky's shoulder. The valet must have reassured her about her client's character. They turned on a spotlight and the girls started coming out. Striptease with no imagination. Lucky eyed the "old fogies" who used the darkness to get up, one by one, and head for the bathroom. Drugs?

Myriam's hand was massaging Lucky's neck. "You'll see, honey, the next one is little Deb…"

"Deb?"

"Deborah. She's super sexy."

In fact, she was. But that did not keep the old fogies from continuing to vanish. Myriam must have had a sweet spot for Deb because she was so excited that she turned red. Lucky left her to her ecstasy and went to the bathroom. At the door he ran into the cigarette girl. With her basket she became an imposing obstacle that took Lucky a little time to get around. When he finally got in, everyone had had the chance to straighten up, so there was nothing to see. Lucky finished, flushed and washed his hands. Nobody was moving and he knew that nothing would happen as long as he was in there.

When he got back into the room, halfway to his table, a huge rat showed up in the spotlight circle, almost under the legs of Deborah, who was finishing her striptease. The girl screamed and ran into the wings as the clients climbed up onto their chairs. The men were chuckling, but the headwaiter jumped forth, pulled an automatic out of his pocket and emptied the chamber into the beast, which had not moved.

At the same time, all the lights flooded the room and Lucky saw that the headwaiter was pale. Another waiter, also pale, brought out a bag and shovel. He scooped up the rodent's carcass and went off while the orchestra started in on a lively little number. Two minutes later a fat man came out and made excuses on

171

behalf of the management before little Deb restarted her number.

Lucky finished his trip back to the table and sat next to Myriam whose cheeks were just barely starting to get their color back. "All this stink for a lousy rat," Lucky said, "isn't that kind of overdoing it?"

Myriam did not answer. Her teeth were chattering.

Chapter V

The next morning, at the same time, Marie Toohey sat in her car and went back to the Zag Zag. Except, this time she was carrying her nurse's bag.

Art Baxter, who had replaced Lucky Simms, waited until 4 p.m. When, on his own initiative, he decided to take a tour of the nightclub. He went to the service entrance, tried the handle to no avail, made sure that no one was watching and put his picks in the lock. Before belonging to the Green Dragon Force, Baxter, just like his partners, was one of the tough guys whom Beffort had recruited from prison. Baxter knew locks like others knew stock prices.

In 30 seconds, the service door yawned open. Baxter entered, closed the door behind him and followed the corridor that was buried in darkness. He went silently down the deserted corridors, ended up behind the orchestra platform and snuck a peek into the room. Without a doubt, the Zag Zag was as empty as a nightclub could be at this hour.

Just to be sure, Baxter checked out the bathrooms, the bar and the backroom, the cloakroom and ended with the room marked Private, which was a luxuriously done up office, but that had obviously not been used for some time. A big accounts ledger and various papers were piled up on the desk. Baxter paid no heed. He was here to find out what mysterious work Toohey was doing while the place was closed, not to examine the books.

He went back into the main room, searched and finally found the trap door leading to the cellar, where he went down using the flame of his lighter. It was a normal, reasonably sized cellar with no secret exit, and with an army of bottles carefully lying in their racks against the walls. Baxter climbed back upstairs, closed the trap door and sat in a dark corner.

He had seen Marie Toohey enter the Zag Zag. She was still here, but he could not find the slightest trace of her coming or being here. Like all of Smith Beffort's partners, Baxter was up-to-date on Lucky Simms' report and the incident caused by the rat during little Deb's performance, especially the panic it had created and the head waiter's attitude, using a gun to get rid of a simple rat, all of which did not fail to pique the interest of Beffort and his men.

According to Lucky, the rat had arrived from the wings. Art Baxter left his corner, crossed the dance floor and went to check out the two rooms that might be used for headliners and then a bigger one where the strippers must have got ready. Costumes and makeup and their smells mixed with tobacco and sweat. No window, therefore no ventilation—the perfect place to become a customer in an asylum... A door opened and a metal object jangled. Art Baxter snuck a peek and saw a cleaning woman carrying a broom, a bucket and a mop. He let her pass by, slipped into the corridor and then out the service entrance, finding himself back on 8th Avenue.

Back in the diner, a stern Owen Bernitz was waiting for him. "Damn, where have you been, Art?" Baxter explained and Bernitz said, "And if Toohey was clearing out while you were messing around in the cellar?"

"I would've heard her, Owen. Hold on, look!"

Marie Toohey was calmly leaving the Zag Zag through the service door and heading for her car parked in a nearby lot.

"You're letting her get away?" Baxter asked.

"Stutton'll take care of her," big Bernitz answered, clamping his unlit cigar between his teeth. "So, you say she wasn't in the Zag Zag, huh?"

"She was there, but not anywhere that could be seen," Baxter confirmed matter-of-factly.

Bernitz knew him well enough to know that he was telling the truth. If Art did not find Toohey in the night-club, it was certainly because she was nowhere to be found. However, she had just left through the service door.

"Okay! Art, you stay here. Now I think it's high time the boss took control of things."

Owen left the diner, climbed into his car and drove to the Morosco Hotel. In the presence of Beffort, Mie and Akamatsu he recounted Baxter's failed attempt.

Smith Beffort said, "If Madame Atomos really is behind all this, it's likely that the club has an under-ground shelter whose entrance Baxter couldn't see. I wonder what she's cooking up?"

Since Mie and Akamatsu kept quiet, Bernitz spoke up, "Toohey could tell us loads about it. What if we put the screws to her a little?"

"Madame Atomos has changed her methods, Owen, and we have to go with the flow," Beffort said. "If we touch Marie Toohey, Madame Atomos will know right away that we're after her and she'll crawl back into her hole. No, we have to act discreetly, on tiptoes. So, let's try to find out who owns the Zag Zag and where the new employees came from after Zagabelli's death. When does Lucky Simms have his date with the bar girl?"

Lucky and Myriam entered an Italian restaurant in Pioneer Park and sat far from the door, in a relatively quiet booth. They were playing at being in love, but neither of them were. Myriam had been hoping for a long time to meet a man who could pull her out of her environment. She was thinking, without too much hope, that Lucky might fit the bill.

Lucky was here to wheedle secrets from the girl. Deep down inside, he thought she was nice, not really cut out for this role as bar girl that she had at the Zag Zag and he was not kidding himself about why she had accepted to meet him. To be sure, he also had the feeling that she was scared, but he could not be sure. He waited for the end of the meal to move on to more serious matters and asked, "Why didn't the new owner of the Zag Zag keep the old employees?"

Myriam shrugged her shoulders. "I don't know anything about it, but it's pretty common in nightclubs."

"As far as the show, sure," Lucky admitted, "but a new owner has to keep the same orchestra, the same headwaiter and his staff. They're the ones who know the clientele and so help to keep them loyal."

"The clientele isn't the same anymore," Myriam said, obviously getting bored with the conversation. "Are you coming to the club tonight?"

Lucky looked bored, too. "Why not... spend the night there or somewhere else... I've got nothing planned, see. In fact, I still wonder what I'm going to do for the next hour."

Myriam shot him a sidelong glance. "You're not working?"

"No," Lucky played with his fork.

"Well, aren't you the lucky one," the girl sighed. "If I were in your shoes, I wouldn't be bitter about it. You've got a big car, pockets full of dough..."

"Not so fast," Lucky cut in. "It's all just for show, sweetie! I rented the car and I'm blowing the last of my money. In eight days, I'll be broke as a tramp and have to find work…"

Myriam puckered her lips. "Oh! Didn't you tell me you were coming back from vacation?"

Lucky looked around, leaned forward and whispered, "Baltimore, State Prison… Three years at taxpayers' expense. Some vacation, huh?" He was playing his cards, a little offhand, and waiting anxiously for the girl's reaction.

Myriam become serious all of a sudden, put her elbows on the table and said, "I know what it's like. Before getting hired at the Zag Zag, I did a 12-month stint in Williston."

Lucky whistled softly. "Hey, hey, it looks like we were made for each other. How did you hook up a gig with your record?"

Myriam was rolling bread crumbs between her fingers. "I had almost given up when Mr. Joyce showed up and offered me this job at the Zag Zag, just in the nick of time. I accepted on the spot because I was thinking I might have to walk the streets to survive. But now I think I might have been better off with that." She stopped talking, stared hard at Lucky, and added, "If you came to the Zag Zag looking for work, you should've…"

Lucky raised his hand to interrupt. "Hold it a sec! I went back to the club to see Zagabelli and not this Mr. Joyce. With Zagabelli I could work. What kind of work could this Mr. Joyce offer me?"

"But that's exactly what I want to warn you about. If you talk with Joyce, he'll tell you that he's got nothing at the moment, but that a place will maybe open up in a week or two. After that, he'll get information about you, go through your background from top to bottom and inevitably find the crime you served time for. Get it?"

Lucky raised an eyebrow. "I see all right, but I don't understand what good it would do him. Some kind of blackmail?"

"Yes."

"How can you blackmail someone who's got nothing?"

Myriam impulsively grabbed his hand. "Listen, Lucky, I can't tell you anymore, but take my advice and don't step foot in the Zag Zag again if you want to remain free. Now I have to go. I start work in 30 minutes. Thanks for the dinner." And she snatched up her bag.

Lucky said, "Right! I won't go into the club, but I'll wait for you on the corner after it closes. Okay?" Myriam hesitated. Lucky quickly added, "Right now I'm not in top form and I'm tapped out. Still, I have connections that can help me when the time comes. If they get me back on my feet, I can do something for you."

"In spite of what Mr. Joyce knows about me?"

Lucky snapped his fingers. "Your Mr. Joyce won't matter a straw if everything happens as planned. So, okay for 3 a.m., Myriam?"

She smiled. "Okay, Lucky. See you then." She got up and left the restaurant.

Lucky waited for her to get away before going to the phone and calling the Morosco Hotel. He was quickly in touch with Beffort and summed up what he had just learned. Beffort said, "If I understand correctly, this Mr. Joyce is only hiring people who are getting out of prison and with a pretty shady past. He's the manager of the Zag Zag?"

"Apparently he's the one calling the shots," Lucky confirmed.

"What did you learn about the owner?"

"I didn't have time to talk to Myriam about it. Plus, it would've been kind of premature. The girl was scared, anyone could see that. She only fessed up to me because I came straight with her. Can you fix me up with a seriously messed up criminal background?"

"Your own will do."

"It would fit the bill if Madame Atomos wasn't behind Mr. Joyce. For the moment, no one knows for sure if she really is. But we have to figure that Myriam will be questioned about me, that she'll give him my name and say that I just ended a three-year stretch in Baltimore. From that Mr. Joyce just might take an interest in me and look for the chink in my armor to get me on his team."

"That's risky, Lucky!"

"Yes, but it's also the best way to find out what's going on in the nightclub."

"Okay!" Beffort suddenly made up his mind. "Starting right now you're Lucky Martin and you live at 65C Parkhill Road. Tomorrow morning you'll have your papers under this name and the Baltimore prison will know who you are."

"Who lives on Parkhill Road?" Lucky asked.

"Don't worry about it, it's one of our men. He'll verify that you've lived with him for a couple of weeks and you don't have a job."

"Great, but who's Lucky Martin?"

"Let's say that he was arrested for burglary, which earned him three years in Baltimore. Naturally, Martin was also suspected of drug trafficking, but nothing could be proved. I'll fix it so that Mr. Joyce finds out what the police couldn't. Figure that you were in cahoots with a certain O'Hara in New York. O'Hara just pulled 25 years. He could have gotten out of it with a reduced sentence if he'd agreed to reveal the name of his dealers. Mr. Joyce will find out that you were one of his dealers. How's that fit you, Lucky?"

"Like a glove. Before meeting Myriam, I have a little time. I'm going to pass by Parkhill Road to stake my claim."

"Go on. I'll tell the owner."

At three in the morning Lucky Simms turned at the corner of 8th Ave. and 30th St. and pulled his orange Cadillac up to the curb. After lighting a cigarette, he started watching the service entrance, which, during open hours, was also the performers' entrance. After his call with Beffort, he had taken his suitcase to 65C Parkhill Road, met the owner and pocketed the rental agreement. He was not yet entirely Lucky Martin, but it would not take long.

At 3:10 three bar girls and a couple of Mexican dancers left the club through the service door. A few minutes later a group of clients left through the main entrance and the valet immediately shut the gate and locked it. Soon afterward, the same valet, along with the coat check girl and the headwaiter filed out of the service door. The headwaiter waved and all the lights went out in the Zag Zag. After that, he closed the door, locked it and walked through the parking lot with the other two.

Lucky waited a while longer to keep his conscience clear, but he already knew that something had happened to Myriam. She usually left first with her colleagues and went directly home. At least, that's what she had told Lucky.

At 3:30, Lucky put the key in the ignition, turned on the headlights and started the engine. His role forbade him to take any unreasonable chances. He had a date with a girl and she had stood him up. For him, the matter was closed.

He shifted into to first and was just driving off when Myriam suddenly appeared on the sidewalk. She had slammed the service door and was waving frantically to Lucky, who stopped and pushed the car door open. The girl ran up, jumped in the car and slumped into her seat with a sigh of relief.

"Sorry, Lucky, but I had trouble with one of my heels."

She was pale and her tense smile did not hide her fear very well. Lucky sped away in the direction of Parkhill. The roads were deserted and it was very cold. When they were out of sight of the nightclub, Lucky asked, "Was the heel called Mr. Joyce, Myriam?"

She turned her big eyes to him. "Please, Lucky, don't ask me any questions."

He turned down a dark, little road, stopped the car and turned off the lights. In the shadows, Myriam's face was a white spot and her eyes and mouth just darkly hollowed holes. He took her by the shoulders and spoke softly, "How can I help you if you hide what's making you scared?"

She broke down right there and huddled up to him. For a month, that is since she was working at the Zag Zag, she must have been under a lot of stress. Now her nerves were snapping and sobs came from deep down, rising up out the depths of her terror, letting loose a torrent of tears.

Lucky waited for her to calm down and said, "Mr. Joyce asked you about me, didn't he?"

She nodded and whispered, "I didn't want to tell the truth, but you had talked with the valet and he already knew that you had trouble with the police. I tried to hide the fact that you were coming out of Baltimore…"

"But he didn't torture you, did he?"

She clung onto him, shivering. "It was worse, Lucky! He dragged me in front of the rat cage." She started crying again.

Lucky Simms lit a cigarette. What had Madame Atomos invented now?

Chapter VI

Myriam dried her tears with Lucky's handkerchief. He asked her, "There's a rat cage at the Zag Zag?"

"Yeah, in the cellar. It's a kind of cart with a metal cube on top divided into compartments by little grills. Each compartment has a huge rat, like the one you saw on the dance floor during Deb's number."

Baxter had not talked about a cage in his report. Therefore, it must usually be stored somewhere else.

"What's Mr. Joyce doing with rodents?" Lucky inquired, being pretty intrigued by the matter.

"I don't know," Myriam whined, "but everyone's scared. At first the cage only had a dozen or so animals. Now there's got to be a hundred, as ferocious as can be... They say a skinny woman comes to give them shots during the night after we're closed."

The picture of Marie Toohey popped into Lucky's mind. When she was working at the Enright clinic, she could only come to the Zag Zag at night. Now, however, she could spend hours taking care of Joyce's rats. What was all this about?

"Strange way to make people talk," Lucky remarked. "Did Mr. Joyce really want to know all about me?"

"As soon as I got there, he started questioning me about you. He already knew that we spent the evening together in the Italian restaurant and that you'd had trouble with the police. I pretended to know nothing, but Joyce kept on at me. Finally, a little before closing time, he asked me into his office where the headwaiter was waiting for us. Through a hidden stairway they led me into the cellar and I stayed alone with Joyce."

"The cage was already there?"

Myriam stared at him in astonishment. "Why do you ask that? I think the cage is always in the cellar."

"You think so, but you're not certain, right, Myriam? Like you obviously didn't know about that hidden stairs before you saw it?"

"That's right. What's all this to you, Lucky?"

Lucky shrugged. He could not tell the girl that he was working for Smith Beffort or that Madame Atomos was probably the owner of the Zag Zag. "According to what you just told me, it's obvious that Joyce is going to force me to join his team. So, I'm trying to understand what kind of work he'll be giving me. And you, Myriam, what kind of special work do you do?"

"Nothing at all! I have to be at the Zag Zag every night to make the clients dance and get them to drink. Mr. Joyce just demands that we don't talk to anyone about…"

"Drugs?" Lucky cut in.

"How'd you know" the girl was alarmed.

Lucky smiled and lied, "In Zagabelli's day that was already one of the place's main activities. Except, at that time, they didn't raise rats in a metal cage! See, sweetie, think about it and try to answer this question—since you've been at the Zag Zag, has Mr. Joyce ever asked you to do something out of the ordinary?"

Myriam furrowed her brow. "Once he asked me carry a package to Garden Avenue to a certain Mrs. Cameron, but it wasn't anything extraordinary. Then I found out that almost all the employees had also delivered packages to Mrs. Cameron."

"What was she like, this Mrs. Cameron," Lucky asked off the cuff.

"She was a very nice Japanese woman."

Lucky forced himself to stay calm. Mrs. Cameron might very well be Madame Atomos. "Is she young?" he asked casually.

"Hey! How should I know how old she is. Anyway, she's rich because her house is surrounded by lots of land that goes right up to the Yellowstone River. Plus, she has scads of servants and three cars in the garage."

"Where exactly does she live?"

"I don't remember. Why all these questions?'

"I told you, Myriam. If I'm going to be forced to accept Mr. Joyce's offer, I want to avoid getting mixed up in any shady deals. I don't want to end up back in Baltimore for twelve years! Drugs, rats, this mysterious Mrs. Cameron... Say, what if Mrs. Cameron was the new owner of the Zag Zag?" He dropped it like it was off the top of his head.

Myriam shook her head. "She's too good to go to places like that."

"Yeah? So, the little packages that Joyce delivers to her regularly contain what? Cubes of butter?"

"Oh! You think it's drugs?"

Lucky waved it off. He was telling himself that Myriam was kind of a patsy. She'd done 12 months in Williston and Joyce had still found enough dirt in her past to force her to work for him.

"Why so quiet, Lucky?"

"I was just thinking, doll. Mr. Joyce is a blackmailer, right?"

"Yeah."

"What's stopping us from doing the same to him? He deals drugs—that's more than enough to lock him up for the rest of his life. And if we find out what he plans to do with the rats, I think he'd give us anything we want! What do you think, doll?"

Myriam said nothing for a few seconds. It was a possibility that she had never thought of before. Lucky's proposition opened up new horizons for her, undreamed of horizons, and she had to soak it in.

"Mr. Joyce sends packages to Mrs. Cameron," Lucky continued, "and she's rolling in dough."

"It's not drugs," Myriam declared. "The packages are way too big. Deborah told me that she thought they contained sleeping rats."

Lucky was startled. "Sleeping rats? What could that be for?"

"How should I know? Maybe Mrs. Cameron does experiments on them?"

Lucky started up the Cadillac, made a U-turn and headed for Garden Avenue.

"Where are you going?" Myriam asked.

"To take a gander at Mrs. Cameron's house. You think you can recognize it?"

"Sure," Myriam unenthusiastically.

She was scared, he could feel it, but he pretended not to notice. More than anything, he wanted to know where Mrs. Cameron lived. Tomorrow Smith Beffort would find out the real identity of the woman and would act accordingly.

After 15 minutes, the Cadillac turned onto Garden Avenue. Lucky slowed down and took a sharp right turn. In the cold moonlight, he saw the river sparkling and could make out the distant greenery of Josephine Park.

"That's it," Myriam said suddenly.

Lucky stopped in front of the gate. It was low, like the surrounding wall, no more than 6 or 7 feet high. That meant that Mrs. Cameron had nothing to hide, that she was not afraid of being spied on... Nothing at all like the precautions usually taken by Madame Atomos. Lucky started to have doubts.

"You see," Myriam whispered, like someone might have been listening. "The property's so big that you can't even see the house from here. One day I was going by on the other side of the river and saw that Mrs. Cameron had a little dock with a boat. She's really loaded."

This way of setting up next to water, far from prying eyes, and having a boat at your disposal to escape in case of emergency was typical Atomos! Lucky became hopeful again.

"When you delivered the package, what did you see, Myriam?"

"Not much, since it was night."

"How's that? You were given the errand after the club closed?"

"Of course! Mr. Joyce called a taxi that does a lot of work for the Zag Zag and I came here. I rang at the gate while the taxi waited at the curb and they opened up right away. A man in a servant's uniform brought me up to the house and we went into a room where Mrs. Cameron was waiting, just sitting there, smiling. Two other servants and a maid were standing by the door..."

"At three in the morning?"

"3:30," Myriam corrected. "As you can see, it takes around 30 minutes to get there from the Zag Zag."

"Didn't you think it weird that all these people were still up so late?"

"Sure, but it was none of my business. I was there to deliver a package to Mrs. Cameron and that's what I did. She thanked me nicely, then the uniform brought me back to the gate. That's when I saw the three cars in the garage… and the taxi took me home. That's it."

"If you gave the package to Mrs. Cameron," Lucky pressed, "you had time to look at her."

Myriam sighed in boredom. "I didn't give the package to Mrs. Cameron, but a servant took it from me and gave it to her. Besides, her face was kind of in the shadows. I can't tell you anything else about the woman, Lucky."

She was starting to find it strange that her companion was asking all these questions. Lucky knew that he should not push any further if he did not want to look suspicious. Myriam was ready to collaborate with a guy who was coming out of a three-year stretch in Baltimore, but she would drop out if she learned that this same man was working indirectly for the FBI. Therefore, he had to cool it…

"Okay," he said. "We're going to wait for Joyce to contact me before making any decisions. Trying to make him sing might be too dangerous… I'll take you home now, Myriam."

The girl relaxed right away and slid over next to him. "You know, Lucky, I don't really want to go home."

She was not hard to understand. Lucky took her in his arms and leaned over her parted lips. He was just a man and Myriam was very desirable. The girl buckled under his embrace, groaned and wrapped her hands around his neck. Lucky felt a slight sting, but he paid no attention to it.

30 seconds later, he collapsed against the steering wheel.

Myriam got out, walked around the Cadillac, pushed her victim over and sat behind the wheel. She put back into her handbag the ring with a small, sharp needle that she had used to send Lucky into a deep sleep. After starting the engine she shifted into first and drove the Cadillac up to the gate. She flashed the headlights twice and the grill opened automatically. Then she entered Mrs. Cameron's property.

Lucky Simms had a hard time waking up. When he opened his eyes, the walls were turning like a merry-go-round. He tried to move, unsuccessfully, and lowered his eyelids to shut out the lurching walls and ceiling. It took him a minute to collect his thoughts, to remember—he was kissing Myriam… then everything went their natural way. He acted like a rookie and dove headfirst into the oldest trap in the world: woman.

A while later the door creaked. Lucky opened his eyes again and saw a dark, kimono-clad woman who was walking slowly toward the bed he was lying on. Two men in servant uniforms followed at a respectful distance. One of them pushed an armchair up to the bed where Lucky was tied up. The woman sat down, with a wicked smile on her face, and said, "Mr. Lucky Simms, fully fledged member of the Green Dragon Force, has the honor of being in the presence of Madame Atomos and of still being alive. Satisfied?"

Lucky stared at Madame Atomos. It was, in fact, impossible to tell her age. According to the information supplied by Yosho Akamatsu, she was at least 50 years old. In reality, she looked more like 30… He tried to talk, but could only blabber senselessly.

Madame Atomos smiled a little wider. "Thank you for your appreciation. I'm glad to finally have one of my enemies as an audience. Truthfully, I would have preferred to be with Smith Beffort or Mie Azusa, but how can we speak of the dead?"

Even though Lucky could not talk, at least he was completely lucid and could therefore take some pleasure in the fact that Madame Atomos believed wholeheartedly in the Befforts' death.

"It's obvious," Madame Atomos continued, "that Yosho Akamatsu and James Edward Evans have taken up the flame. Except, they don't have Beffort's intelligence. You were identified when you first showed up at the Zag Zag and we let you alone for 48 hours to see if you were really dangerous. When you started getting interested in "Mrs. Cameron", Myriam figured it necessary to eliminate you and here you are." Madame Atomos turned to one of her bodyguards. "Give him a shot. I'd like to hear him."

The man dug in his pockets, pulled out a kit and brandished a little syringe. He went up to Lucky, stuck the needle in his arm and injected the product. After backing away, he put the syringe back in his kit and the kit back in his pocket.

Madame Atomos said, "In a few minutes, you'll be able to talk, Mr. Simms. In the meantime, since you won't be leaving my house alive, I'll tell you how I'm planning to spread terror among the Americans again, taking into account the limited resources at my disposal now." She paused, crossed her arms and resumed, "Imagine, I learned that the United States has been literally invaded by rats! Recently the President even asked the Senate for a loan of 40 million dollars to fight the rodents, whose population they estimated at approximately 100 million. Naturally, since the operation wouldn't net a single dollar in profit, the senators rejected the request with outrage, which now results in one rat for every two people in the United States![4]"

Madame Atomos raised her hand. One of her servants opened a cigarette case, the other gave her a light. Madame Atomos blew a cloud of smoke toward the ceiling before continuing her story.

"Every day the newspapers report how a black child's ears or nose was devoured by rats during the night. The rodents have become bolder and bolder because they face no opposition. As a result, there are more and more of them and they're getting bigger and bigger, to the point that they're openly attacking the cats and dogs that are sent after them. After the racial battles and the Vietnam War, it's obviously a plague that the USA will pull through. Nevertheless, it's nothing compared with what I'm preparing! I dreamed up, my dear Mr. Simms, a plan to inoculate a certain number of rats with one of those old maladies that modern man is no longer used to, that can wreak havoc before he detects it. In a week, a thousand rodents, carriers of the Yersin bacterium, otherwise called the bubonic plague, will be let loose in the sewers of every major city in the country. At first this might not seem terribly effective, but I've calculated that it'll take less than 60 days for 100 million American rats to become contaminated. And as I told you, since the plague has practically disappeared from civilized countries, they won't suspect it. They generally think that the plague can be controlled now by an antiserum, especially the treatment of streptomycin, and by

[4] True. This funding [for the Rat Extermination and Control Bill] was requested in August 1967 by President Johnson, who also provided the above figures. Before the month was out, the Senate refused the $40 million loan.

191

preventative measures like surveying ships, destroying rats and vaccinations. Well, now the government doesn't destroy rats anymore. It's satisfied just watching ships and it has only a small stock of vaccine. How will it deal with an epidemic when it suddenly breaks out? Who will think it's the plague when the infected ganglia start showing up on the sick, the old buboes, those swellings that form around the bite or sting marks? Because fleas also spread the plague, Mr. Simms, and there are plenty of them in the poor districts, aren't there?"

Madame Atomos turned serious and regretful, "To think that I used to use monumental means to destroy the United States when it was so simple! Rats! Nothing but rats! In a country that is ready to conquer the moon and that dominates the world with its wealth! How ridiculous!"

Lucky struggled hard and managed to say, "You're a monster, a criminal!"

The Japanese woman shrugged. "Remember Hiroshima and Nagasaki, my friend, and you'll find it totally natural that the United States receive the plague—with compliments of Madame Atomos!

Chapter VII

Now Lucky Simms knew what role the rats played and understood the great panic that broke out when one of the rodents erupted onto the dance floor of the Zag Zag.

"In one week," Madame Atomos continued, "Mr. Joyce will take a trip carrying four rats in his bags. He'll go to Cleveland and let the beasts loose in the miserable black ghetto of Hough where 65,000 blacks live. The next day, a thousand Yersin germ carrying rats will be taken from their secret refuge under the nightclub and in groups of four go and spread the epidemic throughout the United States."

"How will you do it?" Lucky asked. "An operation like this requires at least 250 people."

Madame Atomos laughed merrily. "I know it surprises you. You would never have imagined that I could rebuild such a big organization in three months. But you forget that I'm not relying only on enemies in this country—I have lots of money! With money, anyone can move mountains!"

Madame Atomos pointed to her bodyguards. "That one's named Scarlett and he's wanted for murder. The other is Keating, he's a hired killer. The police are looking for him, too. In short, Mr. Simms, I've quite simply imitated Smith Beffort. He created the Green Dragon Force by recruiting thieves and murderers. By using the same methods I've just got together a new Atomos Organization. Everyone on my team has done something wrong, something to be avoided like the plague—pardon the expression—lest the police get on their trail again someday. Therefore, everyone is extremely disciplined, especially since disobedience among us is punished by death." Madame Atomos smiled when she added, "That explains why Myriam refused to collaborate with you, even after you promised to help her by guaranteeing that Mr. Joyce would be helpless if your friends got involved."

"Ah, she told you about our conversation?"

"There was no need. She's wearing a mic that transmitted your conversations to me. I'm organized, my dear Mr. Simms, and I leave nothing to chance. That's how I know that you can't escape and so I can tell you these things. Now do you want to know how you're going to die?"

Lucky did not answer. He already knew that he had no chance of survival and was frantically trying to figure out how to warn Smith Beffort that an unprecedented epidemic was about to decimate the United States. Because things would happen exactly as Madame Atomos had told him. Joyce would leave for Cleveland in one week.

"We're going to lock you in a cellar," Madame Atomos said, "in a hermetically sealed concrete closet. Then Scarlett here will slip a hose through the upper grate and the room will be filled, very slowly, with water. It will last approximately 12 hours, at the end of which you will drown. Maybe beforehand, after six hours, you won't be able to stand up..."

"I understand," Lucky interrupted, "don't tire yourself out. You want to make me die a slow death to punish me for taking part in the destruction of Atomia Island. And besides, you'll never find rest until all those responsible for your defeat have paid for it... I understand you very well. Because of us, you've become this

194

ridiculous muse of a pathetic bunch of bandits. Ah, the extraordinary Madame Atomos is long gone!"

"Shut up!" she ordered.

Lucky chuckled. "What's going to make me? Certainly not your gorillas or your threats. I'm already condemned and have nothing to fear."

Madame Atomos stood up and turned her back on Lucky. "Take him down to the cellar," she said, "and give him something to eat and drink. He can also have a pack of cigarettes. Goodbye, Mr. Simms."

She walked away, opened the door and disappeared into the hallway. Without a word, the two killers grabbed Lucky and took him to the basement where they untied him and pushed him into a dark little room with wet walls. A meager light filtered through an invisible window and the door's cracks were sealed with rubber to prevent it from leaking water. In fact, the room was a veritable tank with no possibility of escape.

Lucky gave the cell a quick look-over. The window, or rather grate was at the top of a narrow shaft. That was where the water would come in. On the floor was a metal circle around 10 inches round where the water would be emptied.

The man called Scarlett said, "You can have cigarettes and a glass of rum, boy. What's your pick?"

"A pack of Luckys and a bottle of Cutty Sark," Lucky asked, calculating the distance between him and the two killers. He pretended to sit down and then rushed at Scarlett as he was closing the door. The other man, Keating, was already in the hallway, far enough away from the cell. Lucky hit Scarlett on his chin, felt like he was hitting a brick wall, and then found himself on the floor before realizing that Scarlett had simply tossed him to the other side of the room.

Scarlett had a sneering laugh, closed the door and whistled off. Lucky got back on his feet. He had just lost his last chance...

Ten minutes later the two guards came back. They threw on the floor a metal tray full of food, a bottle of whisky, a pack of cigarettes and a box of matches. Then Scarlett said, "You'd best eat fast. The water's going to start flowing in five minutes."

"Thanks for the tip."

"I can give you another—it's useless to cry for help. You'll keep us from sleeping and nobody'll hear you anyway. So, goodbye!" He backed up and closed the door.

Lucky heard the locks being turned and then there was silence in the cell. He was alone in the dark. He checked out the tray, saw that no object could be used for an escape and turned to the shaft. He wondered where the light was coming from. In the middle of the night it was strange and he did not think that Madame Atomos was kind enough to leave the light on just for him.

He had still not solved this problem when the first gush of water started flowing down the shaft. Lucky stepped back and sat down near the door. He had 12 hours to find a way to warn Smith Beffort.

Lucky was up to his knees in water when he emptied the bottle of its contents. He took off his coat, tied it up to make a pocket and slipped the empty bottle inside. After that he rolled up his left sleeve, bit himself hard enough to bleed, ripped his shirt and used the blood to write a message on the white fabric, starting as follows: *Urgent! Please take this message to Mr. Smith Beffort, Morosco Hotel, Billings, Montana, for a $1,000 reward.*

Then, in spite of being terribly cold, Lucky managed to write: *I am prisoner of Madame Atomos. Will be dead when you get message. Atomos ready to release 1000 plague rats in US. Stop Joyce before departure for Cleveland and find contaminated rats in Zag Zag basement. Atomos hiding at 70 Garden Ave under name Mrs. Cameron. Good luck. Lucky Simms.*

Lucky rolled up the piece of cloth and stuffed it into the bottle with the writing visible. Then he corked it hard. He was hoping that the bottle would leave the cellar through the drainpipe and end up in Yellowstone River, after which he hoped that someone would find it and take it to Beffort quickly. But the bottle might get stuck in a corner of the cell or it might go down the drain but no one would find it for years...

Whatever might happen, Lucky had nothing else to do. He was already at the end of his rope. The cold was paralyzing and he knew that he would not live the full 12 hours predicted by Madame Atomos. Anyway, it was probably better this way. What was the use of fighting when death was waiting no matter what? Lucky let the drowsiness overcome him. He dropped down and sat on the floor. Now the water was up to his chest.

Owen Bernitz was sitting in the armchair that Beffort had pointed to. He cleared his throat and said, "Lucky Simms has disappeared now, for a little over 15 hours. The last time Stutton saw him was in front of the Zag Zag. That was at 3:30. The girl, that Myriam, got in his Cadillac and they took off toward downtown. Following your own instructions, Stutton waited a minute before going after them. He thought Lucky and Myriam would end up spending the night together. He first went to Lucky's new place, but the Caddy wasn't around.

Then Stutton headed for Myriam's, but the Caddy wasn't there either. Stutton hung out for a long time, not knowing what to do and then just when he was about to take off, Myriam showed up in a taxi. She paid the fare, entered her apartment and went to bed. Since then she hasn't budged and Lucky seems to have vanished into thin air. There you go, boss."

Smith Beffort scowled. "It's obvious that Lucky was the victim of some foul play somewhere."

"That's what I think, too," Akamatsu said. "Except, I wonder how they neutralized him? Lucky was fully aware that he was playing a dangerous game and must have been especially careful."

Beffort stood up. "I'm afraid that he underestimated Myriam," he said gravely. "What time is it?"

Mie looked at her watch. "Seven o'clock."

Beffort grabbed a stack of notes and recited, "At 3:30 Lucky and Myriam left the Zag Zag together. The girl is the last to leave the club after all the lights are turned off, but I see that Stutton didn't note down when Joyce left. So, we can assume that the guy left earlier or that he lives somewhere in the club or that he got out through a private exit we don't know about. A little later Stutton scribbles Myriam's arrival back home…"

"At 4:30," Bernitz points out.

"Thanks. After that, nothing happens until 10 a.m. when Baxter sees Marie Toohey enter the Zag Zag with her medical kit tucked under her arm. She's there until 5 p.m., goes back home and stays put. At 6 p.m. Joyce takes his turn to leave the club and Baxter sees him carrying a wicker basket, like the ones used to transport cats, but as big as a suitcase. Baxter stays at his post and Sammy tails Joyce. Now, he crosses half of Billings in his car, stops at the end of Belknap Avenue and takes a short walk through the paths of Josephine Park. Unfortunately, Sammy lost sight of him for a few minutes. When he sees him again, Joyce doesn't have the basket anymore. Then the guy heads back to his car and Sammy hears an engine backfire on Yellowstone River. Since no one else is visible, Sammy thinks logically that Joyce gave his basket to a third party who was waiting in a boat on the river shore in Josephine Park... Now it's 7 p.m. Sammy is still following Joyce, Baxter's watching the Zag Zag and Stutton is waiting for Myriam to leave her house. Even if Lucky is in danger of death, we can't help him!"

Akamatsu smiled and said softly, "You and Mie certainly can't help him in any way whatsoever, since you're officially dead. It's great to fool Madame Atomos, Smith, but if we paralyze ourselves at the same time, where's it getting us?"

Beffort returned his smile. "We're acting like this, Yosho, to build up Madame Atomos' confidence by letting her believe that she's minus two enemies. But don't think that we're going to stay here doing nothing! Tonight, Mie and I are going out to the Zag Zag and..."

"You're crazy!" Akamatsu interjected. "If Lucky was spotted by Madame Atomos' people, you've got to know that you'll be instantly identified."

Beffort nodded. "You're right, but false moustaches, wigs and disguises weren't made for dogs."

"Mie is Japanese! How are you going to make her look like a white woman?"

"There are Japanese women in the USA," Beffort answered calmly. "Besides, Mie is thought to have died in the fire at the Enright clinic. By aging her a little, I'm sure she won't be noticed."

"Okay, but what do you expect to find at the Zag Zag?"

Beffort shrugged. "To tell you the truth, Yosho, I don't know, but the club is obviously the center of the affair. How do you explain that we can't find the name of the owner?"

"Because we haven't had time. Still, we know that Joyce runs the place and the Chamber of Commerce says the club belongs to a company whose initials are A.O.F.M.A. Moreover, we know that Zagabelli, the former owner, sold it before he died. That's nothing to sneeze at. By going to the Zag Zag, you won't learn anything we don't already know and you're taking a big risk!"

Beffort went back to sit across from Akamatsu. "Listen, Yosho, I know you mean well, but I also know we can't wait any longer. If, by chance, Lucky Simms fell into the hands of Madame Atomos, she now knows that the Green Dragon Force and the FBI are aware of her presence in Billings, which cancels out any hope of surprise we might have been counting on. So, we have to do something before Madame Atomos disappears again. Mie and I are starting tonight, even if it means stirring things up. They're trafficking drugs at the Zag Zag, but they also shoot rats with guns. Have you ever seen a simple rodent cause such panic?"

Akamatsu shook his head. He knew that the disappearance of Simms, one of the veterans of the Green Dragon Force, had affected Beffort a lot more than his dignity would allow him to admit. It was the straw that broke the already staggering camel's back after the death of little Bob and Dr. Soblen.

"For your part," the G-man continued, "you're going to find out what's behind that enigmatic abbreviation of the company running the Zag Zag. A.O.F.M.A.! What exactly does that mean?"

Owen Bernitz raised his hand. "I'm not sure, boss, but I have the feeling that I've heard of that thingy before."

"Yeah?" Beffort was surprised. "Where's that?"

Bernitz chewed his unlit cigar stub even harder. He narrowed his eyes and said, "I think it's the name of a movement created in San Francisco after the fake death of Madame Atomos...[5]"

Mie sat up straight, very pale, and reeled off in one breath, "The American Organization of the Friends of Madame Atomos."

"No!" Akamatsu shouted. "It can't be!"

"Goddamn!" Beffort swore. "Mie's right! Now I remember that an organization was busy erecting a monument in San Francisco to the memory of Madame Atomos, whom they believed was dead. At the time, there was an office in San Francisco for the Preservation of the Memory of Kanoto Yoshimuta and incredible amounts of money were sent to the headquarters in San Francisco. Well, Kanoto Yoshimuta, aka Madame Atomos, has friends in the United States! It's mind-blowing, but let's not forget that our country is stricken by Nazis, the KKK, and many other secret societies of the same sort that the government is very careful not to disband."

Akamatsu shook his head again. "It's crazy! Unbelievable, but certainly true. Otherwise Madame Atomos would have been unable to rebuild a team in three months like she seems to have done in Billings." He swept up his hat and marched to the door, grabbing his

---

[5] See *Madame Atomos Strikes at the Head* in *Miss Atomos.*

coat off the rack on his way out. "I'm going back to the Chamber of Commerce, Smith. By this time tomorrow I'll have all the names of the Zag Zag's owners."

Beffort called out, "Okay, Yosho. But watch where you're stepping because the ground is probably riddled with mines!"

The Japanese policeman smiled. "I'll give you a tip, Smith. Tonight, at the club, don't do anything foolish." Then he quietly closed the door behind him.

Chapter VIII

At 11 p.m. Mie Azusa-Beffort stepped out a taxi and entered the Zag Zag. She left her fur coat in the cloakroom and sat at a table between the dance floor and the bathroom. Mie was hardly recognizable. The local FBI make-up artist had transformed her into an older woman, of serious appearance, if not severe, who looked like she was used to spending her nights in clubs. The impression was only in the details, in her rather bored attitude, but the personnel had the feeling that this woman must certainly work in the arts and was there through professional obligations, which, by the way, was nothing out of the ordinary. It often happened that agents came to check out a show in order to bring it to other nightclubs.

Mie sat and got comfortable, put a notebook and pencil on the round table and refused the champagne that the headwaiter offered her, ordering a whisky soda instead and lighting a cigarette with practiced indifference.

Ten minutes went by before Smith Beffort took his turn to enter the Zag Zag. At first sight, he looked like he had come straight off his ranch, that he was hard set on having a good time and he was not there to sip lemonade. Beffort made a noisy entrance as he sat at the bar, ordered a double bourbon, Old Crow, and started ogling the bargirls. He, also, had spent two hours in make-up. He was wearing a thick, ill-kept moustache, two warts on his right cheek, long sideburns and a very bushy wig, all sandy blonde, which heightened the effect. Beffort had a limp as well, in his right leg, like a guy who had fallen off a horse, and he sported a vest and tie that stank of Texas to high heaven.

While Mie was calmly, attentively watching the different Mexican dancers, Beffort gulped down his drink, motioned to the bartender for a refill, and winked at one of the girls to come join him. Myriam peeled off her chair and swished over to him.

"Evening, doll," Beffort said, forcing a Texan accent, "what can I get you?"

Myriam settled on a stool. After what had happened the night before, she was not in the best of shape. She figured that Lucky had paid for his curiosity with his life and wondered if her turn might not be next. Mrs. Cameron was not playing around; she punished the slightest mistake with severity.

"Say," Beffort scolded, "are you in mourning or what?"

Myriam caught a hard look from Mr. Joyce who was standing behind the counter and forced herself to smile. "Sorry, I have a run in my stocking. Champagne for me... On a binge in Billings, cowboy?"

"Damn straight, doll!" Beffort guffawed. I'm from Denver City. You know it?"

"No, but I guess it's not next door. Ranching?"

"Yeah! Shall we dance?"

Myriam accepted, fluttering her eyelids. She slid gracefully off the stool and headed for the dance floor that was just being cleared of dancers. Beffort followed her, a little tipsy, remembering to limp, which was not easy.

Myriam hugged him close right away. She was pretty and provocative and Beffort started to understand why Lucky Simms was not able to put up much resistance.

"What's your name, cowboy?"

"John. And you?"

"Myriam to my friends. Texas is a long way from Montana, isn't' it?"

"Sure, but I've had my fill of the south. Truthfully, Myriam, I came to Billings to stake my claim."

"Oh? You want to start over again? Cattle aren't as exciting as before? Well, a guy like you makes me think of open skies, campfires, horses... Don't tell me you're going to quit everything to come and hole up in a little apartment in Billings!"

Beffort hugged her a little closer. "You know," his voice was mushy, "stuff like that only works in the movies. No one's ever got rich staying a cowboy. Me, I broke my foot and my spine's all messed up from being on a horse. So, I'm dropping it before I start traipsing around on a cane. Gotta see the big picture, right?"

"Do you have a job here?" Myriam asked casually. None of this interested her. She simply wanted to sit this guy down at a table and bring him a bunch of bottles to drink. Since she was working on commission, the evening just might turn out all right.

"No job," Beffort laughed, "but plenty of money!"

"Hey, I thought a cowboy didn't have a cent?"

"I got by."

His tone let it be understood that he had not got by in a very orthodox manner, that he thought he was pretty clever and proud of it. Myriam pricked up her ears. Was it by pure chance that she had hooked onto a guy on the run?

At that moment the dance finished and Myriam said, "My feet are aching. Why don't we go sit at a table?"

"Okay," Beffort said. "You choose."

Myriam sat at the first free table, right next to where Mie was sitting, and discreetly waved to the headwaiter. Beffort's eyes met his wife's as she glanced over at the bathrooms. He turned and saw that a lot of customers were going in there. When they left, they were heading straight for the cloakroom. Obviously one of the signs of drug trafficking noticed by Lucky.

"So," Myriam asked, "You got by?"

She wasted no time. The bottle of champagne was already in place, the glasses filled and the flower and cigarette girls were swooping down on them. Beffort offered her a rose, bought two packs of cigarettes and paid right away, pulling out his wallet stuffed with bills.

"Thanks," Myriam smiled. Then, with an eye on the wallet, "I see you brought plenty of bread when you left Texas."

Beffort's chest swelled, a stupid smile crossed his face and he raised his glass. "To your health, doll! I hope we can become good friends!"

Myriam rubbed her thigh against his and leaned over to show off her cleavage. She was interested now and could feel that this big idiot might become a juicy fruit if squeezed just right. "If you don't know anybody in Billings," she whispered, full of promises, "why won't we become friends?"

She was telling herself that in Denver City this cowboy must not have had much chance to see many girls like her. If she could make him drink, he would be telling her his whole life in no time at all.

A little while after this, the water had just finished draining out of the cellar where Lucky Simms had died. Scarlett and Keating unlocked the waterproof door and entered the room. Lucky's corpse was huddled up in a corner and the soaked food, which he had not touched, was spread over the floor in the large puddles. The neck of a bottle was sticking out of the drainpipe, which had a filter that Lucky had known nothing about.

Scarlett pulled it out and said, "No wonder it took so long to drain with this bottle stuck in there…" He stopped talking all of a sudden. "Come here and look at this, Keating!'

"Damn! It's a message! We gotta bring it to Madame Atomos right now." When Scarlett shot him a hard look, he corrected, "Sorry, I meant Mrs. Cameron."

"You take care of this guy," Scarlett pointed to Lucky's remains, "and I'll go up to Mrs. Cameron. You know what you have to do?"

"I'll take it in the boat maybe two or three miles down the river and drop with a rock tied around its neck…"

"Idiot!" Scarlett barked, "I knew you didn't understand a thing! The police have to think it's an accident. You're going to put all his stuff back in his pockets and throw him in the river like that. Now hurry, I'm going upstairs."

He left the cellar, climbed up to the first floor, took the other staircase and continued up to the second floor where he pushed open a door to enter a small vestibule. He rang the interphone and two seconds later the voice of Madame Atomos asked, "What do you want, Scarlett?"

This was the kind of thing that always surprised the killer. It was almost midnight and Madame Atomos was still awake and without a word being said she knew exactly who was in the vestibule. "Madame," he spoke respectfully, "I just found a message written by Lucky Simms before he died."

"How did he write it," she asked severely, "if you took away all his things?"

He cut himself and used his own blood to write the message on a piece of his shirt. Then he sealed it in the bottle of whisky. I think he was hoping it would go down the drainpipe and…"

"Okay," Madame Atomos cut him off. "Leave it on the table."

Scarlett did what she asked and Madame Atomos said, "Go back down and help Keating make the body disappear."

"Disappear?"

"Yes. I changed my mind. Now it'd be better if Lucky Simms were never found. Turn up the boiler and throw the body in the fire. When it's done, come back and get my orders."

Scarlett turned around and went back to the stairs. Madame Atomos waited until he was far away before entering the vestibule. She uncorked the bottle, read the message and her face froze in surprise and rage. So, Smith Beffort and his wife had escaped the fire!

Madame Atomos stood there petrified for an instant and then she picked up the phone and dialed a number. It rang four times before a voice said, "Marie Toohey here."

"Mrs. Cameron," Madame Atomos said softly. "Can you go to the club immediately? Something very important has just happened and you're needed at the Zag Zag."

"Should I bring my kit?'

"No," Madame Atomos ordered. "You'll only be passing through. No need to drive there. Take a taxi and Joyce will bring you back home. I can count on you, can't I?"

"I'm on my way, Madame." She hung up.

Madame Atomos did likewise and picked up again to call the Zag Zag.

"The Zag Zag," a girl's voice said.

"Can you tell Mr. Joyce that Mrs. Cameron wants to talk to him urgently? I'll wait." 30 seconds ticked off before Joyce's panting voice came on the line.

"Is everything okay over there?" Madame Atomos asked.

"Yes, the room is full and the take is good."

"I'm not talking about that, Joyce!" the terrible woman roared. "I've just received some last minute information that Smith Beffort and Mie Azusa are alive! They're staying at the Morosco Hotel and are obviously giving the orders!"

"But," Joyce objected, "Marie Toohey confirmed that…"

"She was wrong!" Madame Atomos jumped in. "You know what that means? She'll be at the club in a minute. She can't leave, understand?"

Joyce gulped noisily and said, "Understood, Madame."

"While you're at it," Madame Atomos said coldly, "include little Myriam in the package. She was the last one to see Lucky Simms and Beffort will find out if he hasn't already. I don't want him to question her. Fix it so that Myriam and Marie Toohey are gone for good before 12:30. Got it, Joyce?"

"Got it, Madame," Joyce squawked.

"Moreover," Madame Atomos continued, "you'd better watch your customers very closely. I wouldn't be surprised if there were a member of the Green Dragon Force at your club tonight."

"Certainly not!" Joyce protested.

"Before swearing to anything, you'd better check new faces with the photographs you have. Go on, Joyce, look around and tell me if there's someone in the room who looks more or less like Smith Beffort or Mie Azusa?"

Joyce scrutinized the faces of the new customers. From the telephone, he saw everyone lit up as bright as day—it was the dance time before the strip-tease shows. A few minutes from now and the room would be plunged in darkness.

"Well?" Madame Atomos pressed him.

"I don't see anyone," Joyce stammered. "There is an Asian woman, but she's pretty old and…"

"How big is she?" Madame Atomos interjected.

"Hard to say. She's been sitting at the same table since the start of the evening and writing down the names of the dancers. I think she's around five feet five. If she weren't wearing glasses, she might look younger…"

"How didn't you recognize Mie Azusa earlier!" Madame Atomos thundered.

"Like you, I thought she was dead," Joyce defended himself. "Plus, I wouldn't swear that it's really her."

"We'll talk about it later, Joyce. Now look at the men. Smith Beffort is very tall and solid. He looks like a man of action, an adventurer. Is there anyone in the room that answers to that description?"

Joyce automatically spotted Myriam's client and he was jolted. The guy looked exactly like Madame Atomos' description. "Damn! I see the guy in question!"

"What's he doing?"

"He's talking with Myriam…"

Madame Atomos grunted. "You're an idiot, Joyce. After Simms' disappearance, you should have known that one of his friends would try to question the girl."

"I'm sorry," Joyce was humiliated. "But the guy looks like a cowboy and seems drunk. Plus, he limps, has a moustache and is blond. It's funny but…"

"No, Joyce, it's not funny! It's serious, very serious! Smith Beffort and his wife are on our trail. And behind them are the FBI and the Green Dragon Force. We have to act fast."

Joyce felt a shock. "Act? The nightclub's packed and Beffort probably left some of his men outside. And Marie Toohey's going to get here pretty soon. Under such circumstances, don't you think Beffort's had the nurse under surveillance since the fire at the clinic? Madame, maybe you haven't time to think about it, but it's clear that Mie Azusa got herself admitted to Dr. Enright's care because she already suspected Marie Toohey."

Madame Atomos winced. Joyce was right. Not very long ago, the Great Brain was thinking instead of Madame Atomos. It no longer existed and from now on the sinister woman had to make all the decisions herself. It was a kind of re-education. Madame Atomos felt discouraged for an instant. She used to have servants by the thousands, mountains of money and extraordinary weapons. Now she had only 100 assistants, a relatively large amount of money, and only one paralyzing pistol taken off of Lucky Simms.

"Madame?" Joyce asked timidly. He was afraid of her. Everyone was afraid of her.

Madame Atomos pulled herself together. Instead of hiding or fleeing, she was going to attack with ferocity. Maybe all her people would be killed in the battle, but it was absolutely necessary that Beffort and Mie Azusa also give up their lives! "Joyce, here's what you're going to do. As I ordered, kill Myriam and Marie Toohey. At the same time, offer Beffort and Mie a round on the house. Of course you'll drug their drinks. But don't kill them. Before that, I want them to know that I am responsible for their deaths."

"And if someone comes to help them?" Joyce asked flatly.

"Don't worry about it. I'm sending Scarlett and Keating as backup."

"It'll turn into a massacre!"

"Doesn't matter. Nothing can keep us from releasing the rats in the United States. Do it, Joyce! Afterward you call me and tell me how it went. I won't move from here. Good night."

Chapter IX

Joyce hung up the phone and walked away. His legs were wobbly and he felt sweat trickling down his back. The Befforts were formidable, powerful enemies, who had come to scout out the Zag Zag, but not without covering their backs beforehand. Joyce was perfectly aware that Madame Atomos had just given him a grueling task. Trying to neutralize the Befforts was like trying to chain up the FBI and the Green Dragon Force at the same time.

Joyce marched across the noisy room. When he entered his office, he flopped into an armchair. If he were not so scared of Madame Atomos, he would have taken off that very second, went to spend the rest of his days in a lost little town in his native Vermont. But, obviously, that was out of the question. For Madame Atomos, a man's life had no value. With a wave of her hand, a killer unknown to Joyce would be turned loose to hunt him down and execute him as matter-of-factly as he was going to kill Myriam and Marie Toohey.

Joyce sighed, turned on the interphone and got the headwaiter on the line. "Bird," he began wearily, "Mrs. Cameron just called me. She wants us to eliminate Marie Toohey and Myriam."

Bird scowled, but made no comment. He was as wary of Joyce as Joyce was of him. Maybe that was where Madame Atomos had proved to be most skillful. No one knew how freely the others were working for her or for how long. They continually wondered if the next guy were not the boss' eyes and ears. Divide and conquer. It was nothing new...

"Plus," Joyce went on, "you've got to know that tonight, in the club, we are welcoming Smith Beffort and his wife."

This time Bird swore and then said, "You're joking!"

"I wish I was. But if you look at table 12 and 13, you'll realized that I'm right."

"What? That Japanese lady and the cowboy might…"

"No doubt about it, Bird. Warn the personnel and do whatever's necessary to keep Marie Toohey from entering the club through the front door… get her to use the service entrance. Then quietly get Myriam away from Beffort without him becoming suspicious. When they're both in the basement, give the customers free drinks."

"On what grounds?" Bird inquired.

"Let's say that the management of the Zag Zag wants to mark this special night of its first month in business. I'll make an announcement in a minute to explain everything. You know, Bird, it's really just to make Beffort drink a Mickey to put him to sleep for a good long while. You see what I'm saying?"

"Yes, but I'm not totally sure about it."

"No one is asking for your opinion," Joyce said softly. "Mrs. Cameron gave instructions and it's better not to discuss them. Where's the show at?"

"Deborah just started her strip…"

"Good. You cut in when she's done and I'll get on the floor to make a little speech. In the meantime, get those Mickeys ready for the Befforts and take care of Myriam and the nurse. Quietly, Bird, very quietly! If Beffort thinks something weird is happening, he'll be on his guard and we'll lose our edge, don't forget!"

"I've got nothing else on my mind," Bird reassured him in a shaky voice. "Stay calm. If anyone plays around, it won't be me!" He hung up. Joyce took a big handkerchief out of his pocket and wiped his forehead. Right now he was feeling like the nightclub was turning into a powder keg.

While Smith Beffort continued playing cowboy with Myriam, Mie kept watching very carefully what was happening around her. First of all she noticed the headwaiter's long interphone conversation with Joyce and she saw him glance over at her a few times. After that, Joyce came out of his office. A minute went by before the lights went out. A spotlight focused on a young blonde who announced that the show would begin with the international number of Deborah Lange. The girl went off as the orchestra started in on a lazy, slow tune, and Deborah swished out.

In the darkness, Mie could make out the headwaiter holding a conference with the waiters at the end of the bar. Then he disappeared and one of the waiters threaded his way through the tables, leaned over Myriam and whispered something in her ear. The young woman nodded and the waiter left.

Smith asked, "What's all this hush-hush about, doll?" Mushy voice and glazed eyes, he seemed completely drunk.

Myriam gave him a strained smile. "I have to leave you alone for a minute, cowboy, my mommy wants me at the door. Behave yourself and try to finish the bottle. Soon…"

She got up, but Smith grabbed her dress, "You don't have to go, Myriam. When a mommy visits her daughter at a nightclub, it's almost always to give her bad news."

"Let me go, will you?"

Smith tugged harder. The dress started ripping and Myriam was forced to sit down. In a totally different voice, but with the same stupid smile, Beffort whispered, "I'm not a cowboy, Myriam. I work for the FBI and Lucky Simms was my friend. Joyce has probably just found out my real identity and wants to keep you from telling me the truth. How do you think he'll keep you quiet?"

At the next table, Mie tipped her hat, mentally. At no time had Smith seemed to notice the comings and goings of Joyce, the headwaiter or the waiters, but in reality he had not missed any of the fuss that had just been stirred up.

In her seat, Myriam was pale and at a loss for words. She had just been knocked out cold and was having trouble getting back on her feet. Still smiling, Beffort added, "The club is under surveillance right now by a group of guys belonging to the Green Dragon Force and I can guarantee you that nobody's leaving the Zag Zag except in handcuffs. So, there's no need to go and get yourself killed now, is there?"

Myriam looked like a hunted beast. "You got yourself caught in a damn trap, G-man! You're the one who won't be getting out of here alive."

"We'll talk about that later," Beffort lost his smile. "For now, you're going to tell me what happened to Lucky Simms. In exchange I promise you impunity, however guilty you are in the matter."

"Who are you?"

"Smith Beffort. And the Japanese lady next to us is my wife."

Myriam's eyes popped out. "The fire at the Enright clinic?"

"There really was a fire, but we escaped the flames by a miracle. For a while, Madame Atomos believed we were dead and she tipped her hand when she used you to capture Lucky. Come on, Myriam, talk before it's too late!"

At that very second Deborah finished her striptease. Under a shower of applause she hustled into the wings, the spotlight went out and all the lights came back on in the room. Out of the corner of his eye, Beffort saw Myriam being watched by the headwaiter—his eyes were not smiling. Two waiters were standing near the purple curtain that separated the room from the cloakroom. Then Joyce appeared on the dance floor and said, "Ladies and gentlemen, tonight I have the pleasure to inform you that the management of the Zag Zag is celebrating its first month in business. So, the next round of drinks is on the house!"

50 or so real night birds who had come for no other reason but to have fun welcomed the announcement with roaring applause. Joyce raised his arms to ask for silence, smiled and said, "Order whatever you want. The Zag Zag's paying! And now, the show must go on!" He disappeared in the wings and the waiters started taking orders from the tables.

Beffort turned back to Myriam and started, "Last night Lucky Simms left here with you and we haven't seen him since. Where did you take him?"

Beffort was making a mistake by forgetting the terror that Madame Atomos inspired in her servants. Myriam was not set on talking. She only had to look up to see Bird and the waiters eyeing her and she knew with certainty what would happen to her if she revealed anything about Mrs. Cameron's rats. She said, "I don't

217

know anything. Put on the handcuffs and go and interrogate Joyce. He can give you information."

She had spoken loud enough, unconsciously, and her words reached the ear of a waiter who was taking the order from a nearby table. The man immediately stopped serving and dashed back to the headwaiter. His action was natural in the confused crowd so neither Beffort nor Mie noticed him. However, Beffort was wary. They had asked for Myriam. He had held her back and Joyce must have been boiling his blood in the wings. Very soon someone would do something surprising, unexpected. Something Atomos-style...

He was expecting it but was still taken off-guard.

All of a sudden the lights went out, the orchestra started playing a hellish noise and a thunderous voice shouted, "Fire! Every man for himself!"

In the dark shadows, the message was like an electric shock on the customers. The women screamed and the men ran toward the exit like a stampeding herd, overturning everything in their way. Smith Beffort was forced to fight against it so as not to be carried away by the turbulent waves. Nevertheless, he was thrown to the ground. As he crawled toward the bar he took his paralyzing pistol out of the shoulder holster and then managed to stand up at the precise moment when the orchestra stopped playing. Once on his feet, he forced his way toward the dance floor so he could sneak into the wings to look for the master switch for the electricity. He figured that Joyce had turned out the lights to escape.

Beffort shoved someone out of his way, reached the dance floor and was suddenly out of the crowd. He moved forward, got tangled up in the curtain, bumped against a stool and then finally pulled out his lighter. The small, flickering flame instantly lit up the control panel of the stage manager. Every switch was labeled: *Dance floor. Front Spot. Yard Spot. Court Spot. All Lights…* Beffort switch the last one and the room, dance floor and wings were all lit up abruptly.

Tables and chairs turned over, dresses torn, suits ripped and the 50 or so customers blocked at the doorway of the cloakroom by Owen Bernitz and his men. Beffort came out and with a quick glance saw that all the Zag Zag personnel had disappeared, as well as Myriam… and Mie!

"No one left, Owen?"

"No one, boss. The club's been surrounded for more than half an hour."

A customer came up to Beffort. "Can you tell us what's happening?"

Beffort flashed his badge and ordered, "Everyone go back to your seats and get your IDs ready! Owen, get three of your men to check this little mob while we go search the club."

Bernitz appointed a team and joined Beffort with a dozen men. There were Baxter, Stutton, Sammy and other members of the Green Dragon Force who had battled for years against Madame Atomos. They were all armed with paralyzing pistols and did not need instructions on how to do their job. In less than five minutes the club and its property had been gone over with a fine-toothed comb. Then the team regrouped on the dance floor.

"Nada," Bernitz groaned.

Beffort clenched his jaws. They had evacuated in 60 seconds with diabolical precision, taking advantage of the customers' panic. The musicians had abandoned their instruments, the striptease dancers had left in their costumes, the waiters in their uniforms, the flower and cigarette girls in fishnet stockings and miniskirts... At least 20 people in weird get-ups who would not go unnoticed on the streets of Billings as dawn approached.

Beffort ran to the telephone booth and dialed the number of the FBI Headquarters. He was instantly put in contact with Eddy Witter. "Beffort here. Eddy, organize some patrols right away and lock up the city. Madame Atomos' people have gotten away and taken Mie and Myriam with them."

"How'd they do that?" Witter was alarmed.

"Secret passage. If you act fast, there's no way they can get across the city and Madame Atomos will be stuck in her hole. No need to tell you how much I'm counting on you, right? Get going! I'll call you back soon."

The two men hung up at the same time. Beffort went back to his team. He was doing his best to keep a calm face, but he was extremely worried about Mie's fate. "Owen," he said, "now we have to find the secret passage Joyce and his gang used to give us the slip. Have you checked the identity of the customers?"

Bernitz nodded. "They're on the up and up, but that doesn't mean a thing. To be absolutely sure, it needs an interrogation at FBI headquarters. In all this mess, there's probably more than one who's working for Madame Atomos. No one can make me believe that the people who come to the Zag Zag are white as snow. And speaking of "snow", I have the feeling that two or three couples have been taking coke recently."

Beffort waved it off. "There's no time to worry about that, Owen. Give a call to the Federal Bureau of Narcotics if you want, but before that get us some pickaxes. We have to find that exit even if it means tearing the Zag Zag down to the ground. Meet me in the basement. I'll take Stutton and Baxter with me."

While Bernitz was carrying out his orders, Smith Beffort and the two tough guys from the Green Dragon Force took the stairs behind the bar down to the basement. Baxter, who had already been there incognito, knew the place. He showed them the rack of bottles and said, "If this place has a secret door, it's probably stuck behind these crates."

Beffort did not answer. Maybe Baxter was right because the rack stretched from the floor to the ceiling and completely hid the walls. But Beffort was not losing sight of the fact that Madame Atomos had not had time to build tunnels near the nightclub. Therefore, she no doubt had to use existing installations that she had not created. For, and this must be kept in mind, Madame Atomos—at the height of her power—hated to build shelters in the middle of cities. Instead she chose remote areas either in the countryside or in the mountains and generally near a lake or river…

"What're we doing, boss?" Stutton asked, surprised by Beffort's introspection at such a moment.

The G-man shook himself out of it and said, "Let's start by moving this rack. We'll get onto more serious things when Bernitz gets here with the tools."

They got to work, but the job was not easy. The rack contained around 300 bottles. Before thinking of moving it, they had to lighten the weight. Facing such a difficulty, Baxter went to get reinforcements from the first floor and was soon back with a dozen men to help the task. The rack as rapidly emptied and then taken down, but the wall it was hiding sounded solid and had no suspicious abnormalities.

A little while later, Beffort and his men attacked a second rack that refused to budge in spite of all their efforts. At that moment Owen Bernitz came down with six pickaxes and Beffort asked them to tear down the stubborn rack. The men went at the wood and then the wall and ended up punching a hole through what turned out to be what else but a swinging door. When they opened it, the bottle rack pivoted with it, but the construction, on the whole, was very basic.

Beffort and Bernitz slipped through the hole, climbed a flight of stairs, pushed open another swinging panel and found themselves in Joyce's office.

Beffort wiped his forehead and said, "All that for nothing."

Big Owen looked at his watch and added, "For Madame Atomos, it was for something. It's been almost 30 minutes since Joyce and his gang took to their heels."

Beffort nodded. The affair was starting out badly.

Chapter X

Eddy Witter, with the help of Charles Hyde and the head of the Billings FBI bureau, organized the patrols and blocked off the city as far as they could. Unfortunately, it was a long-term project. Billings had a pretty large population in a small area, but its police force was proportional to these two demands and Witter knew that he could not accomplish his mission using only the municipal resources at hand. Since Beffort had thrown off his mask and the war against Madame Atomos had officially been given the green light. Witter decided to fall back on proven methods and bring in the armed forces. Through James Edward Evans, he made a request for reinforcements that was instantly accepted and several convoys headed to the Billings, which was fast becoming a hotspot.

From Joyce's office Beffort gave a call to his partner. Witter told him very succinctly about the measures he had taken. Beffort asked, "When do you think the blockade will be up?'

"Not before 4 or 5 a.m.," the federal agent answered without hesitating. "But a wide net is already closing in on Madame Atomos and her gang. For the moment she can still slip through, but her chances are narrowing as the minutes tick off and they'll be practically zero when the sun rises. I would have liked to go faster, but it wasn't possible."

"Your patrols haven't indicated anything suspicious?"

"Nothing. The streets are empty and everything's calm. It's like the Zag Zag manager is buried somewhere with his acolytes. Anything new on your front?"

"No," Beffort's voice was grave. "The Green Dragon Force is surrounding the place and Bernitz tore apart the basement with pickaxes, but for now our efforts are fruitless. Any news from Yosho Akamatsu?"

"Nothing at all. I think he's still looking at the Chamber of Commerce records. How can I get in touch with you in case of an emergency?"

Beffort frowned. He had no idea what the coming hours would bring and was completely ignorant of where the hunt for Joyce would take him. "If you need me," he finally said, "spread the word. One of Bernitz' radio-cars will inevitably hear the message and get it to me. Anyway, unless I run into some major obstacle, I'll call you every 30 minutes. Talk to you soon, Eddy."

Beffort hung up and got rid of his disguise at last before going back down to the basement where the sound of pickaxes was echoing. Bernitz and his men were not sparing their energy. The bottles and racks were taken apart and the bare walls were gutted so that they looked like they had been bombarded. In some places, the picks were attacking the floor directly and sprays of dirt were starting to burst out of the gaping wounds.

Big Owen straightened up when Beffort arrived. "We can quit," he huffed. "The walls down here aren't hiding any secret passages."

Beffort responded coldly, "There's still the ceiling and the floor. Give me a pickaxe, Owen. If there's an exit, and there has to be, here's where we'll find it."

With Stutton and Baxter he swung away at the concrete floor. Its surface was grainy, uneven and full of bumps and holes.

"The guy who did this work didn't kill himself over it," Baxter commented between strikes, "but it's still concrete, eh?"

The metal heads had difficulties biting into the floor; they struck dully. Beffort's pickaxe suddenly bounced off some strange obstacle. He leaned over, examined the thin line he had barely made and straightened up again, furrowing his brow. "A steel plate! Have you ever seen that in a basement floor, Owen?"

Bernitz spit out his cigar stub and got on his knees, inspecting the floor inch by inch up close. "The light's not good enough," he groaned. "Sammy, go and see if you can find a portable lamp. I feel like there's a crack here."

The floor was covered in dust and rubble, which did not make things easier. Sammy had dug up an oil lamp in the kitchen and put it on the floor. They could have used more light, but the glow, even if it only lit up a small patch, at least had the advantage of revealing some details. After clearing away the area, Bernitz ran his finger along the line that he was the only one to see and declared, "An armored trapdoor. It's around six feet by ten. Baxter, hunt up some explosives! Boys, let's get to work! We've got to dig here!"

It took around 20 minutes to make a diagonal hole next to the armor. Bernitz stuff it with explosives, set the detonator and everyone ran up and around the corner of the stairs. A few seconds went by and then the explosion shook up the Zag Zag's basement, sending thousands of concrete shards in every direction and unfolding the steel plate like a cardboard box.

Beffort grabbed the oil lamp. "We'll need flash-lights, Owen."

Under the basement was another one, but much bigger. It contained Myriam's corpse, and Marie Toohey's, a big, empty cage and a large table with laboratory equipment, hypodermic needles and bottles full of a yellow liquid. At the end of the room there was a door. Beffort opened it easily and aimed the beam of his flashlight. He discovered the long path of a tunnel, flanked by a narrow walkway all along a canal of putrid water.

"Damn!" Owen swore. "A sewer!"

"A storm drain," Beffort corrected. "Madame Atomos didn't have the time or means to dig, so she used what was already here. Let's go back up, Owen. When we get a map of the sewers, it'll make it a lot easier for us to hunt down Joyce in this maze."

As was to be expected, the storm drain emptied into the Yellowstone River at Garden Avenue, a little over a mile downstream from Josephine Park. Except, the walkway that went along it stopped long before that, under a manhole located on Sugar Avenue where there was a city control station under constant surveillance, which ruled out the possibility of Joyce and his group having left the sewers through this exit.

"Maybe they headed downtown?" Eddy Witter suggested.

Beffort shook his head. "I don't think so. When he left the Zag Zag, Joyce knew he'd never come back and he and his gang would be hunted from now on by the Anti-Atomos forces of the United States and particularly by those in Montana. So, his goal was to get away from Billings before any roadblocks could be set up. In my opinion, Joyce's group continued to the river on a boat."

Witter grinned. "In that case, they won't get far. My experience taught me that Madame Atomos loves to use water in her escapes. Therefore, my first precaution was to close off the river upstream and downstream from Billings, inside the roadblocks that—I am happy to tell you, Smith—have just been set up. Right now more than 20,000 men are surrounding the city and its suburbs, watching the roads, railways, footpaths and taking up strategic positions. Likewise, they're patrolling the streets and checking identities. Since no suspect has been arrested yet, I assume that Madame Atomos has picked up Joyce and your wife and they're all waiting in some safe house for things to quiet down."

Beffort nodded. "That's what I think, too, Eddy. Unless the whole gang, with Madame Atomos at their head, was able to leave the city before the roadblock was set up. Whatever the case, we have no choice. If we look at this map, we can see that the storm drain comes out in the river near Josephine Park. Now, if my memory serves me correctly, I think Josephine Park has already come into play. Joyce went there and delivered a mysterious package to a third party whom Sammy couldn't see because they took off in a boat."

Just then Akamatsu burst into the office. "Hello!" he said. "I have some news for you, Smith."

"You're like a ray of sunshine in winter, Yosho! Mie's been kidnapped by Madame Atomos' people and I have to admit that I have no idea which way to turn."

Akamatsu allowed a moment of silence. He was coming directly from the Chamber of Commerce and was not up-to-date on anything about the course of events since the start of the evening. "So," he said a little critically, "you got caught in a trap at the Zag Zag?"

"We were counting on a surprise attack," Beffort admitted, "but we were the ones surprised. Even with the very limited means at Madame Atomos' disposal, she's still a very dangerous enemy. But let's talk about that later. Tell us what you learned?"

Akamatsu pulled out a piece of paper. "Here," he said, "I have a complete list of the stockholders of the A.O.F.M.A., which stands for Artists' Organization For More Appreciation. Amazing, isn't it?"

"We're obviously far from the American Organization of Friends of Madame Atomos! But it doesn't matter."

"Probably not, seeing that, among others, Joyce and Mrs. Cameron run the group. We know that Joyce is in it up to his neck. Now we have to see if it's the same for this Mrs. Cameron. She lives on Garden Avenue on the river shore, near Josephine Park—and she's Japanese!"

Beffort threw on his coat, picked up his hat and rushed to the door. If Mrs. Cameron was not Madame Atomos, he would lock himself up for the rest of his life.

While Beffort and Akamatsu were asking to see Mrs. Cameron, Eddy Witter and Charles Hyde used the police to cordon off the area between the river and the property. It was close to 3 a.m. Joyce and his group had still not been found, but Mrs. Cameron could not, in any way, escape.

The sleepy servant who answered the door asked the two men to wait a minute and disappeared up the stairs. Very quickly he came back down and said that Mrs. Cameron was on her way. After that he stood in front of the door and did not move.

"Weird," Akamatsu whispered anxiously. "If this woman really is Madame Atomos, why is she seeing us?" He kept a hand on the butt of his paralyzing pistol and watched the grounds with a very suspicious eye.

"I'm wondering the same thing," Beffort whispered back. He was feeling nervous and had a vague hunch that the terrible woman was primed to play one of her tricks. Certainly she was holding Mie's life in her hands, but she knew that this advantage would not be enough to pull her out of this. By killing little Bob and Dr. Soblen, Madame Atomos had gone too far and had no hope of negotiating with her enemies. What was she hoping for by welcoming Smith Beffort?

The G-man stopped asking himself questions because a woman in a kimono had just appeared at the top of the stairs. Right away Beffort and Akamatsu knew that it was not Madame Atomos. The woman came slowly down the stairs and stopped a few feet from the two men. She looked very surprised, a little bothered, but was obviously very sure of herself. "Gentlemen?"

In front of the door, the servant was not moving. The house was calm, silent. No threat in sight...

Beffort stepped forward and showed his badge. "Mrs. Cameron, is it?" The Japanese woman bowed her head. Beffort continued, "I have orders to search your house and grounds. Do you have any problems with that?"

"No. But it's a very unpleasant surprise. May I know the reasons for this search?"

"You're one of the managing directors of the A.O.F.M.A. and it so happens that Mr. Joyce, the manager of the Zag Zag, is currently wanted for murder, kidnapping and drug trafficking."

Mrs. Cameron staggered to the nearest armchair and flopped down. Either she had just suffered a serious shock or she was a wonderful actress. That was still to be determined.

"The news is stunning," she grumbled. "Mr. Joyce always gave me the impression of being a balanced, perfectly honest man. How could he have lost his mind to commit such dreadful crimes?"

"Joyce works for Madame Atomos," Beffort reeled off, watching the woman closely, "and some of his recent activities lead us to believe that you may be in on it, too. I'm talking about his collaboration with Madame Atomos, of course."

Mrs. Cameron opened her frightened eyes. "Are you joking, sir? I am, in fact, one of the stockholders of the A.O.F.M.A., but I swear to you that I have never stepped foot inside that nightclub, the Zag Zag! I can't even tell you exactly where it is or…"

"However," Beffort cut her off, "you know Joyce?"

"For years. Before running the club, he worked with my husband in the import-export business. After the fatal accident of Mr. Cameron, I sold our business and Mr. Joyce must have went looking for another job."

"When did your husband die and what were the circumstances?"

The Japanese woman lowered her eyes. "It was three years ago. He disappeared during a research trip in Florida and no one's heard from him since. The investigators concluded that he drowned while swimming in Palm Beach…"

Akamatsu and Beffort glanced at each other. At that time, Florida was suffering one of the most terrible attacks Madame Atomos had ever delivered against the United States. Beffort had the sudden feeling that Mrs. Cameron, too, was a victim of the sinister ploys of Madame Atomos. He approached the armchair, put his hand on the back and whispered so as not to be heard by the servant, "Mrs. Cameron, I think it's time for you to…"

He was meaning to convince the woman that it would be in her best interest to change sides, but he stopped himself. Although he had not done it on purpose, Beffort was standing directly over Mrs. Cameron and in a split second he noticed two details that instantly changed his plans. First, the woman was wearing a brooch that, seen from above, turned out to be a cleverly disguised microphone. Second, in her carefully combed, but thin black hair Beffort saw the famous half-moon scar, the undeniable mark of the old servants of the Great Brain!

It was unbelievable, but it seemed that this woman had succeeded alone, and for some time, in escaping from the Atomos Organization. Where, when and by whom could she have had her surgery? Had she gone to Atlanta incognito to remove the frightful motor-brain that made her a slave? In that case, how was it possible that Beffort was never informed?

"You were saying that it was high time for me to…" She was watching him and there was untold terror in her eyes.

Beffort sighed and finished, "For you to come along with us in our search." He was speaking now only for Madame Atomos' ears. He was sure that the sinister Japanese woman was listening to their conversation through the micro-brooch and Mrs. Cameron was just a toy in her hands. More than anything, he had to avoid setting off any alarms.

Mrs. Cameron struggled to her feet. She was no longer young and she breathed heavily when she walked. But maybe the shortness of breath was the result of her emotions? She had certainly guessed that Beffort was ready to offer her a deal after understanding the role she was being forced to play and was no doubt wondering, for a few seconds, what would be the good answer.

"Where would you like to start?" she asked.

Beffort smiled gently. "With the basement, please."

And while Mrs. Cameron led the way, he quickly wrote on a page in his notebook: *Mrs. Cameron has a mic transmitting on a specific wavelength! Get a direction finder on it immediately! Atomos is probably listening!*

Then he gave the paper to Akamatsu and followed Mrs. Cameron to the stairs down to the basement.

Chapter XI

Mie Azusa-Beffort regained consciousness very slowly. She felt a pain in her neck and swallowed her saliva, which tasted horribly bitter. They must have knocked her out before drugging her.

She opened her eyes and looked at the things and people around her. Right away she knew that she was in an upper-story apartment downtown because she saw the steeple of Saint George Church at eye level through the window. She was sitting in an armchair. Pretty much everywhere, sprawled across the sofas, chairs and in the corners of the room, the personnel from the Zag Zag were sleeping, except, near the door, Joyce and the headwaiter, who were watching the television and chain smoking, but speaking not a word.

Mie closed her eyes and kept absolutely still. Her last memory was from the nightclub. Smith was talking to Myriam when the lights went out. Then someone yelled "Fire!" Mie stood up, hit something hard, and collapsed...

Through her half-closed eyelids, the young woman stared at the sleepers and was relieved to see that neither Smith nor Myriam were among them. Without moving, she looked at her watch. It was 3 a.m. So, since midnight she had been lifeless, out of circulation, and probably still alive because she could eventually be used in bargaining.

She made sure that Joyce and the headwaiter were looking away and slipped her hand against her thigh where, under her dress, she kept her paralyzing pistol, but of course it was no longer there. "And now," she asked aloud, "what's going to happen?"

Joyce and Bird jumped. Their nerves must have been on edge. Joyce scowled and pointed the barrel of his automatic at her. "Be quiet," he ordered, "and don't move or we'll have to put you to sleep again."

"Sorry," Mie said, "but I have to go to the bathroom badly."

The two men looked at each other, annoyed. They had killed Myriam and Marie Toohey in cold blood and were wondering why Madame Atomos was sparing this prisoner. Being there among them, she could bring nothing but trouble. In the next few hours they would certainly have to leave Billings by getting through the police and army checkpoints. How would they do this if they were dragging around a prisoner who could call out for help at any minute?

"The bathroom?" Mie asked.

Joyce stood up and motioned to her to do the same. "Follow me. I'll show you where it is, but I'm warning you—if you don't behave, I'll knock you over the head. Got it, Mrs. Beffort?"

Mie nodded. Basically she wanted to see the layout of the place and maybe take advantage of a moment alone to try to escape or cry out for help after locking the door to the bathroom.

Joyce led her down a dark hallway, holding her arm tightly, thus showing that he planned to leave her no chances. He said, "Here, Mrs. Beffort, we're on the 16th floor of a downtown office building. If you yell, no one will hear you, but I will punish you severely because I hate when people torture my eardrums. No need to tell you that it would hurt me a lot to have to get violent with such a pretty girl as you, but since I've already killed

Myriam, it wouldn't be too hard. Cruelty is a habit that you easily acquire when you work for Madame Atomos."

He pushed open the door, squeezed in with Mie and turned on the light after closing the door behind him. The room was tight; it had only a sink, a shower and a small toilet in the corner. Joyce leaned against the door with a libidinous smile on his face and said, "Go on, you won't bother me."

Mie's face was stone. She took a step toward Joyce, saying, "You're getting out of here immediately! The circumstances have probably made you forget who I am, but I swear that you will remember when you go before the court… if my husband doesn't kill you first. You're big and strong, Joyce, but in this narrow space, you're at mercy, in a way."

Joyce's smile disappeared. He had, indeed, forgotten that this young woman had been Miss Atomos and then battled for years against Madame Atomos and being her cruel enemy she had more than one trick in her bag.

"Your weapon won't do you any good," Mie continued, impressively calm, "because your boss gave you instructions to keep me alive until all danger has passed. You're just a small-time crook, a murderer of weak and helpless women, but if I put my hypnotic powers to work on you, you'll stick to that door…"

She took another step forward, stretched out her hands toward the man's face, and staring him straight in the eyes said, "Sleep, Joyce, sleep…"

It was a brazen bluff, but Joyce fell for it. Mie's slanting eyes suddenly looked disturbing and very likely to start giving off pacifying rays. He slapped down her threatening hands, open the door and jumped out. Mie slammed the door shut, locked it on the inside and leaned against the wall. It was not much, but if they came to get her, they would have to break down the door, which would make plenty of noise. As much as was in her power, she was continuing to fight Madame Atomos and her new Organization!

Mrs. Cameron led Smith Beffort slowly into the different rooms of the huge basement. The G-man kept the conversation to small talk, waiting patiently for an opportunity to talk freely with the Japanese woman. At last, Mrs. Cameron opened a heavy door and flipped a switch to reveal an empty room, all in concrete, instantly bathed in soft light. Beffort followed Mrs. Cameron into the strange room. He felt like he was in a tank. The door was waterproofed, the walls wet and the floor had a weird plug that could easily be hiding a drainpipe.

"Here," the woman's voice trembled, "my husband cultivated aquatic plants."

It was unlikely, but Beffort did not argue. He put his hand on the woman's shoulder and said, "Mrs. Cameron, we can talk freely. The transmission from your microphone can't go through these concrete walls. But we only have a little time, so just answer my questions."

The woman looked around, terrified, but in spite of everything nodded in acceptance.

Beffort whispered, "Did you belong to the Atomos Organization?"

"Yes."

"How did you get rid of your motor-brain?"

"I went to the clinic in Atlanta after Yuri Belof's told me about it[6]. The surgeons operated on me, then I fled from the clinic before the end of my recovery. At

---

[6] See *The Return of Madame Atomos*.

the time, you were dealing with a new attack by Madame Atomos, which is why my operation and disappearance went unnoticed."

"Your husband's death?"

"He, too, belonged to the Organization. He died during the operation in Florida. On the streets of Palm Beach he was killed by soldiers armed with flamethrowers."

Beffort remembered the details she called up. This woman had suffered through terrible experiences, but was only one of the many victims of Madame Atomos. "After you came to hide in this house," Beffort whispered, "your old boss found you again?"

"That's right. In fact, the initials A.O.F.M.A. stands for the American Organization of the Friends of Madame Atomos. The Artists Organization For More Appreciation doesn't exist." She turned her tortured face to Beffort. "I also have to tell you that Madame Atomos is going to release plague-infested rats throughout the United States."

Beffort was shocked. Mrs. Cameron continued, "She's usually here. Last night when she found out that you were at the Zag Zag, she knew you would come here and she ordered me to take her place."

"Do you know where she's hiding?"

"No. Nobody knows. But I'm sure the contaminated rats are with her. I…"

She was cut off by the door slamming shut. Beffort ran to it, but it was too late. On the other side of the thick door, the bolts were turned and someone spun the wheel lock. Beffort turned to the woman. His face was hard. "It was a trap, wasn't it?"

Mrs. Cameron shook her head. "I don't know anything about it, I swear. It's the servant or Scarlett or

Keating. We're done for. This is where Madame Atomos drowned your friend Lucky Simms."

A gurgling sound drew Beffort's attention. Against the opposite wall, under the tall shaft that he had not noticed, a stream of water was starting to flow in. "This is ridiculous," he said to reassure her, "my men know that I'm in the house. They'll free us in no time."

Mrs. Cameron, pale-faced, leaned against the wall. "This room is soundproof, the walls are reinforced concrete, the door is armored... Even if your friends find where we are, how do you think they'll get us out before the water drowns us?"

Beffort furrowed his brow and suddenly felt less optimistic. Lucky Simms had died here. That meant that no one could escape without help from the outside.

The communications van drove slowly toward Yellowstone River. Unlike ordinary detecting missions, this was not about locating the transmitting device but about finding the receiver. For this the FBI men were using a new method based on infrared rays, which was only possible because of the late hour, the lack of traffic and the semi-certitude that Mrs. Cameron's mini-transistor could not have a range of much more than a mile.

The method was based on the fact that all warm bodies emit heat, thus infrared rays, and on the possibility of detecting a ray emitted by a device, such as a receiver, which is really just a hot engine. Nevertheless, the search was laborious, delicate, maybe made easier than usual by the fact that only one receiver was capturing Mrs. Cameron's transmission and so leading the searchers to a fixed point that would be reached no matter what if the transmission lasted long enough.

This was exactly what Akamatsu was hoping for when the waves abruptly stopped. The operator played with the controls, then stared at the blank screen, disgusted. "It's shot."

Witter eyed Akamatsu, "What's happening, Yosho?"

"I don't know," the Japanese said in ignorance. "But Smith was well aware that the transmission had to last a certain time to get a positive fix. Let's wait, maybe it'll start up again."

They waited 15 minutes, then 30. Finally Akamatsu decided, "Let's go back to Mrs. Cameron's property. Smith will explain why it stopped."

The van turned around and rushed back along Garden Avenue. When it pulled up quickly in front of the gate, Charles Hyde came running up to his colleagues. "Is there a problem?"

Witter shrugged. "A disappointment. Mrs. Cameron's mic went quiet. Did anyone try to leave the property, Charlie?"

"No, everything's calm here."

Witter told Akamatsu to follow him as he pushed open the gate. The two men hustled down the walkway and climbed the front stairs.

"Ah!" Witter exclaimed.

The body of the servant was lying in the middle of the sitting room. Akamatsu bent down to feel the man's chest. He stood back up saying, "He's dead and not for a long time. See the flask, Eddy."

Witter picked up a glass tube that had rolled over the waxed floor. He sniffed it and concluded, "Strychnine. The guy was poisoned, but maybe not as recently as you think. He swallowed this junk right after we left."

Akamatsu looked at his watch. "That was 40 minutes ago. Why hasn't Smith been around here?"

Witter pulled out his paralyzing pistol. "I think we'd better take a little tour of the house. None of this makes sense to me."

Akamatsu nodded and followed him. They climbed up the stairs, did not meet a living soul, went back down to the first floor with the eerie feeling that they were playing a game whose rules were being kept secret from them.

Pensively, Akamatsu examined the grounds through the bay windows. He turned around and said, "Before sending me on the mission, Smith was preparing to visit the basement with Mrs. Cameron. Do you think they're still there?"

Witter flipped back his hat. "That would surprise me, but if the basement is miles long underground, why not?"

Akamatsu nodded again and headed for the stairs. After dashing down, he turned on the light and saw a row of doors flanking a long, straight hallway.

"I don't mean to press it," Witter groaned, "but I don't see Beffort playing hide and go seek with us."

That went without saying. Akamatsu turned off the light and went back upstairs with Witter, who said, "In my opinion, we should be searching the grounds, especially on the river side. I wouldn't be surprised if there's a boat mixed up in this story."

Akamatsu did not answer. He had no idea how Beffort and Mrs. Cameron had not managed to see the corpse lying in the sitting room.

In the tank, the water was slowly but surely rising. Beffort and the Japanese woman were already soaked up to their ankles. They heard only the gargling water running in through the shaft and this sound like a mountain torrent was actually sinister.

For the 20th time, Beffort walked around the tank, found nothing new and came back to Mrs. Cameron. "How long before it's all over?"

"In six hours we'll be swimming," the woman said bluntly.

"In five and a half," Beffort corrected. "Tell me, Mrs. Cameron, where does the water come from?"

She stared at him in astonishment. "From a watering hose connected to a faucet behind the house. Why?"

"Because that means that this tank is not totally soundproof. If the hose is just sticking through some kind of opening, our voices should reach outside. In fact, what is the opening?"

"A grate. If you lean over, you can see the bars at the top of the shaft."

Beffort squeezed into the narrow duct. That was where the water and light was coming in, but it was impossible to see the bulb or the end of the hose. He cupped his hands and yelled loudly. Like hitting an invisible obstacle, his cry came echoing back, almost as clear as his voice.

"See," the Japanese woman said, "the sound won't get out. It's obviously due to the fact that the window is located in a ditch between the house and the protective wall around the lawn.

Beffort stepped back. His jaws were clenched. If Akamatsu did not figure out that he could be nowhere but in the basement, Mie would soon be digging another grave... As long as she were still alive!

Chapter XII

At 4 a.m. the telephone finally rang. Joyce reached out, picked it up and right away heard the nasty voice of Madame Atomos. "In ten minutes a truck is going to stop in front of your building, Joyce. Everyone will get on board, except you and Mrs. Beffort. The truck will leave Billings by a route that the driver knows and that the police are not watching. As for you, do what's necessary to control your prisoner. Afterward, you'll take the elevator to the basement and go to the garage where you'll find a gray Chrysler. The key's in the ignition. You'll cross the city and go directly to the place called Thoeny on the left bank of the Yellowstone River. You know it?"

"Yes," Joyce answered, "but what'll I do if the police stop me?"

Madame Atomos laughed. "Make sure you're not stopped, my friend!"

"Easier said than done! Smith Beffort..."

"He won't be bothering you, Joyce. Right now he's watching the water rise in the cellar of Mrs. Cameron's house and his friends are looking for him in Josephine Park. It's because the police are focused on that sector that you'll be able to take your little jaunt in peace. By the way, I hope that Mrs. Beffort is still in good health."

"She's fine," Joyce said. Nothing in the world could make him confess that Mie was locked up in the bathroom and he had no way of getting her out without breaking down the door.

"In that case, Joyce, everything's perfect. Follow my instructions to the letter. I'll be waiting for you in

Thoeny on the dock. You'll see a little red light. That'll be my boat. See you soon." Madame Atomos hung up.

Joyce put the receiver down and scratched his nose, preoccupied. Bird asked, "What did she say?"

Joyce repeated Madame Atomos' instructions. Bird puffed up his cheeks and tilted his head, saying, "I'm not at all thrilled by this truck drive."

Joyce sighed. "The trip in the car doesn't thrill me either, but outside of being stuck here, I don't see how we can escape the cops. Wake up this bunch of knuckle-heads. The truck will be here any minute."

Bird did not move. "And the night watchman?" he said softly. "Maybe he's going to tip his hat when he sees us filing out in front of him?"

Joyce looked at him scornfully. "If he wasn't dead at the start of the evening, do you seriously think we could have entered the building?"

Bird could not stop himself from shuddering. Madame Atomos had a way of getting rid of troublesome people that froze his blood.

"Wake up your team!" Joyce was getting impatient.

Bird stood up, went around kicking people, shook those who were still nodding off, and pretty easily managed to get everyone ready in the given time. Without Myriam, Joyce and Mie Azusa-Beffort, he found himself at the head of only 17 people. But the members of this group could be spotted miles away. If a policeman stopped the truck, he would instantly know who the cargo was.

When he heard a rumbling engine on the street, Joyce leaned out the window. From the 16th floor the truck looked like a toy and inspired no confidence in Bird. "Once inside," he mumbled, "we'll be at the mercy of the driver... Who is it?"

"I've got no idea," Joyce growled, "but don't worry about it. Get down there quick. A patrol car might think it strange that a truck is parked in the business district at this hour."

As Bird turned around, Joyce grabbed his arm. "Before leaving, give me Mrs. Beffort's paralyzing pistol."

Bird hesitated, having hoped that Joyce would not ask for the weapon, but Joyce bared his teeth and slipped his hand inside his jacket. "Let's go, Bird. Who's in charge here?"

Bird gave him the pistol, turned round and headed for the door. The musicians, bargirls and strippers followed him, filing out through the half-open door and disappearing into the hallway. Joyce went to the window. A few minutes later the whole group was climbing into the truck. The driver closed the back door, locked it and went back to start the engine.

After closing the window, Joyce crossed the apartment and stood in front of the bathroom door. "Mrs. Beffort?"

"I hear you," Mie answered.

"We have to leave and I'm asking you nicely to come out of your hole. If you refuse, I'll use the paralyzing pistol to make you behave, then I'll break down the door and the end result will be the same. What's your choice?"

Mie immediately decided to give in. If Joyce paralyzed her, she would be completely frozen for 60 minutes and therefore unable to take advantage of any possible opportunity to escape. She turned the lock and opened the door. Joyce grinned while pointing to the hallway with the barrel of his gun.

"You're being reasonable and I like that better. The idea of carrying you all the way to the garage did not put a smile on my face. Now go on and don't look at me."

He had taken the young lady's threat seriously and did not want to be hypnotized in a flash! Even if he did not really believe it, he had heard enough about her to take no risks. Mie walked on, left the apartment and headed for the elevator. When Joyce pressed the button their eyes crossed.

"Turn around," he ordered, "I don't like the way you're staring at me."

Mie obeyed and when the elevator arrived at the 16th floor, Joyce stepped in, pulling his prisoner after him. He pressed the button for the basement and the car plunged down fast before coming to a halt.

"Open up," he ordered again.

Mie pulled the metal door open and was pushed forward into the middle lane of the garage. During the day there were the cars of the people who worked in the offices, but at this hour there was only a big, gray Chrysler sitting there, thanks to Madame Atomos.

"You drive," Joyce barked, "but I'm warning you that I'll open fire if you try anything."

Mie did not reply. She sat behind the wheel while Joyce climbed into the passenger seat.

"Where are we going?" Mie asked, starting the car.

Joyce leaned back, "Leave the garage and then I'll give you directions."

Mie pulled out, took the ramp and came out on a street that she did not recognize. She had purposefully not turned on the headlights in the hope that a car driving without lights might eventually attract the attention of the police.

"Hey," Joyce roared, "do you take me for an idiot? Turn on the lights!" He was not terribly smart, but he was clever enough and wily—it was going to be tough to trick him. Mie obediently turned on the lights.

"Now," Joyce indicated, "turn right. We're going to the river. That's where Madame Atomos is waiting for us."

Over the next 15 minutes Mie tried desperately to find a way to catch Joyce off his guard, but found nothing and decided that she would have to take a big risk, knowing the fate that Madame Atomos held in store for her.

"Left," Joyce said. He had the situation under control, was no longer afraid of being stopped by the police, but did not fear the consequences unduly. The paralyzing pistol was an effective weapon. With a flick of his finger Joyce could freeze anyone in range of the formidable ray. Exhilarating sensation... especially for a crook.

Joyce was keeping a close eye on things but letting himself slip into dreams of grandeur. Like: how much would the government of the United States give to capture Madame Atomos alive? Or: who could stop him from cleaning out the safes of Bank of America if he paralyzed the guards?

All of a sudden the scenery toppled over and Joyce caught a glimpse of a wall coming straight at the car. Then he felt a shock and heard a loud noise of crushed metal. He was ejected from his seat, struck the windshield and was out for good among the wreckage of the Chrysler, which was already going up in flames.

30 feet away, Mie scrambled to her feet. She had jumped before the crash and only got a scratch on her elbow. As the car caught fire, she ran to a telephone

booth. With a little luck the police could get to the river before Madame Atomos figured out that Joyce was no longer one of the living.

In the truck, Bird felt his anxiety rising steadily as time went on. From the start the truck had given him the impression of taking a tortuous route with no end in sight. Bird had inspected the dark shell using his lighter. The fact that he and the Zag Zag personnel were locked in with no possible means of escape bode no good ahead. Moreover, he had no way of communicating with the driver. Bird had never seen a truck as hermetically sealed as this one!

"I wonder where we're going?" one of the bargirls asked.

"You'll find out, Dolly," one of her friends answered nervously. "In the meantime, you'd better get some sleep."

Someone else piped up and then everyone was giving their opinion. Bird said not a word. He was listening to the sounds from the outside and heard a distant bellowing. It sounded like a ship's foghorn. He listened more closely, but the voices around him were too loud.

"Shut up for a second," he yelled. "You're like sheep being led to the slaughter."

The others stopped talking and Bird wondered why he had made that comparison. Then he heard the lowing again and changed his mind. It was not a foghorn, but actually a train whistle muffled by distance or by the walls of a tunnel. Just then the truck stopped, waited a few seconds and then started moving again.

"I think we've arrived," someone said.

A rumbling could be heard in the distance, coming closer fast... it passed by making the truck shudder and went off. A train. Bird could not understand what the truck was doing near a train track.

He was still thinking about this when the truck stopped again. This time the driver did not restart, but another sound echoed in the big vehicle. It was like another engine, totally different from the one sitting under the hood, just starting up.

"The floor's moving!" a woman screamed.

It was true. The truck was slowly rising, like the bed of those trucks that load and unload construction equipment, and Bird could not stop from sliding toward the rear gate. With one hand—it was a tenuous hold—he grabbed onto a metal hook, while the women screamed and the men swore, piling up on top of one another against the gate, which was very soon going to be the only horizontal part of the truck. He was just about to let go when the gate suddenly opened, dropping its human load into a vat of dark liquid. Bird heard the awful howls and saw his companions struggling with inexpressible pain written all over their faces. But these people were not drowning.

In terror, Bird hung desperately onto the hook, but his hand opened nonetheless and he plunged into the death tub, disappearing after only a few seconds. Then the truck got under way again before the bed was back in position, passing by a sign that read: *Beware! Danger! Sulfuric Acid!*

It was Akamatsu who discovered the secret in the form of a water meter that was strangely ticking off numbers although no faucet was on in the house.

"That doesn't tell us where Smith is," Witter complained, hiding his worry under a grouchy veneer.

Akamatsu tapped the counter and prophesized, "If we find the open faucet, Smith won't be far away. Let's look around outside."

The grounds were swarming with cops searching the bushes. Akamatsu and Witter walked around the front of the house and found the faucet with a watering hose connected to it. Akamatsu turned off the water, followed the hose and discovered the grate stuck between the house and the garden wall. He put his mouth up to the opening and yelled out Beffort's name. There was silence and then a voice came up, faraway and feeble, but perfectly recognizable.

"Damn!" Witter swore. "He's at least 150 feet underground!"

"In any case," Akamatsu said, "he's locked up in the basement." Then he yelled down, "Smith! We're coming!"

In front of the armored door, crammed with locks, bolts, security bars and a flywheel, the two men knew that freeing Beffort would not be as easy as they had imagined. They sent word to bring in a team of specialists, who, when they showed up with all their tools, went at the door until around 5 a.m. When it finally gave in, it emptied a torrent of water that flooded the hallway. Stuck against the wall, soaked up to his thighs and shivering with cold, Smith Beffort was supporting Mrs. Cameron's unmoving body. Witter and Akamatsu helped him out of the tank while the policemen put the unconscious woman on a stretcher.

Beffort said, "It's about time you got here. We would've died of the cold before the water could do us in. Eddy, hand me a cigarette."

In the sitting room he warmed up very quickly and told his colleagues how Madame Atomos was preparing

249

to attack the USA by letting loose the plague-bearing rats across the country. Then he took Mrs. Cameron's microphone clip out of his pocket. "I turned it off just in case. I didn't know how long it would work and anyway it was better like that. If Mrs. Cameron puts it back on fast and if Madame Atomos is still listening, we can pull off a trick that will inevitably flush her out of hole."

Witter frowned. "That's an awful lot of ifs, Smith. Personally I don't think Mrs. Cameron's going to be on her feet for a while. Maybe you didn't realize it, but it's already 5 a.m. Pretty soon the folks in Billings are going to hit the streets and it'll be impossible for us to screen the hundreds of them. Plus, the infrared won't be any use…"

Beffort nodded. He had lost all notion of time while in the basement, concentrated as he was on not passing out or dropping Mrs. Cameron's limp body. He thought about Lucky Simms, wondered how long he had held out, he who had no hope of being saved.

Akamatsu understood that Beffort had not yet recovered all his physical and mental faculties. He put a friendly hand on his shoulder and advised, "Before anything, Smith, you have to get better. You're drenched, exhausted…"

"Come on, Yosho," Beffort cut him off, "do you really think I'm going to lie down when Mie's in danger of death? Not to mention the hundreds of rats that Madame Atomos can let out of their cages at any second." He jumped up and walked toward the door. "Take me to a radio. I have to contact Owen Bernitz, Baxter and Stutton. I know that you haven't had time to think about them, but they've probably made some headway in their investigation."

There were several radio-equipped cars parked on the grounds. Beffort climbed into one of them, turned on the radio and unhooked the microphone. "Beffort calling Green Dragon... Beffort calling Green Dragon..."

Bernitz' voice boomed through the speaker, "Owen here, boss. Your wife's with us."

"Good God, you found her!"

"She found us. She got rid of Joyce by letting him fry in a burning car and she thinks she knows where Mama Atomos is hiding out. If you come right now to the intersection of Sugar Avenue and Garden, you'll arrive in time to direct the final act."

Beffort smiled, "Don't move, Owen! I'll be there in three minutes, max!"

Chapter XIII

The car carrying Beffort, Akamatsu and Witter reached the intersection in the allotted time. Mie ran into her husband's arms. Then big Owen Bernitz said, "My boys are standing ready to take action and the boats of the River Police have started searching the river. You just have to give the green light, boss!"

Beffort glanced around. Bernitz and Hyde had gathered a large armed force there. The two avenues were packed with police cars and vans. The cops were carrying rifles and tear gas grenades and they had just installed a 50-caliber machine gun on a fire engine.

"Where are your men, Owen?"

"Up and down both sides of the river where Madame Atomos is supposed to be hanging out. They're armed with paralyzing pistols and have orders to put down anything that moves."

"How did you find out that Madame Atomos was here?"

Mie ran through what she had learned during her short drive. "Joyce," she finished up, "said that Madame Atomos was waiting for us on the river and given the direction the car was headed, we concluded that she could not be far from the Cameron house."

"Okay," Witter jumped in, "this location fits with the start of our stakeout. Mrs. Cameron's micro-emitter had a range of just over a mile. Therefore, there's no point in searching beyond this distance."

Mie hung on tightly to her husband's arm. "We have to act quickly, Smith! When we left the building where I was being kept prisoner, Joyce was supposed to bring me straight to Madame Atomos. When we don't show up, she'll know that something happened. You know how brilliant she is at keeping herself informed at all times."

Beffort nodded and decided, "Okay, let's go. Let your troops loose!'

He climbed into the car with Mie, Akamatsu and Witter and headed directly to the river. From their own car, Bernitz and Hyde gave their orders and the other cars and vans scattered on the spot. A few minutes later the Yellowstone River was bombarded with hundreds of beams from spotlights and teams of armed men lined up along its banks. Likewise, the boats from the River Police came up inspecting closely all the boats docked against the pontoons. It was a perfect encirclement, a steel trap whose jaws were slowly but surely closing tight.

Fifteen minutes passed before everyone found themselves surrounding a loading dock in a placed called Thoeny where there was a small pleasure craft snuggled up against the dock. There was nothing special about it, but Beffort was interested because a weak red light was shining on board. Besides, it was the only inhabited boat in the entire sector.

Using a megaphone, a police officer asked the occupants of the boat to come out and a little man climbed onto the deck. He was obviously frightened by the unusual display of force. He blinked his eyes in the spotlights, but made no movement to lead them to believe that he was afraid of them boarding his craft.

Beffort stepped to the edge of the dock and jumped on board. Behind him was almost an entire regiment of police, the whole Green Dragon Force, rifles, paralyzing pistols, a machine gun... In front of him, nothing but a little old man floating in his oversized coat. Ridiculous!

With a bitter taste in his mouth and in his heart the half-certainty that Madame Atomos was far away, he asked, "What are you doing on this boat?"

"Well, it's mine, ain't it?" the old man answered logically. "If you think I stole it..."

"It's not that. It's 5:30 in the morning, there's a light on in your cabin, you're dressed and seem ready to lift anchor. Why?"

Beffort was aware that he was asking stupid questions. The old man could very well lift anchor whenever he wanted and go sailing wherever he pleased. The boat belonged to him and he was a free man.

"I'm waiting for passengers," the old man answered. "When you came driving up, I thought you was them."

Beffort hid his excitement. Madame Atomos was not at this meeting. She had paid the old man to pick up Joyce and Mie...

"You got an interest in them?" the old man asked.

"Yes. I would like to know where you're supposed to take them."

The man's arm stretched out toward Josephine Park. "Over there to the last pontoon. Just between me and you, they could just have easily got there by car. Say, can you tell your boys to turn out their flashlights? My eyes are sensitive."

Beffort relayed his request to Hyde, who waved and all the spotlights went off. The old man whistled in admiration. "You really got them marching to your baton, eh? Me, when I was in the navy..."

"Who hired you for this job?" Beffort interrupted.

"A woman. She gave me 50 bucks, telling me that it was real important that I be on time. She wanted to surprise her daughter and son-in-law. Seems they's newlyweds."

"What was the woman like?"

"Real tan, with eyes kind of slanty. And dressed real nice to boot. Like she wasn't waiting for payday to eat her porterhouse... Do I have to give it to you, the 50 bucks?"

Beffort shook his head. "Keep the money. But do exactly what you would have done if the young couple showed up. Good night." He climbed back onto the dock while the old man started his motor and cast off.

Akamatsu pursed his lips. "Why this last ditch effort, Smith? It's obvious that Madame Atomos cleared out when she saw all the spotlights sweeping the river."

"She cleared out for sure," Beffort admitted, "but she's still in Billings."

"Probably, but you can't believe that she's still waiting for Joyce and Mie on the pontoon the old man was talking about."

Beffort watched the boat careening slowly toward Josephine Park. The current was not very strong, but the motor must have been as old as its owner, coughing and spluttering at each turn of the propeller.

"Josephine Park again," Mie said, after she came up to them. "That's what intrigues you, isn't it, Smith?"

"Yes. At first we thought the Zag Zag was Madame Atomos' refuge in Billings. Then everything pointed to her hiding out at Mrs. Cameron's. Finally this meeting looked like she'd chosen to stay on a boat. Now, none of this is true! Unless she's completely changed her methods, it's clear that Madame Atomos has a shelter in this city and we have to find it!"

"And fast!" Witter added, being the pessimist. "It's already 5:45. Any minute now the patrols are going to have their hands full."

Beffort gritted his teeth. He did not have much time. When the inhabitants of Billings spilled out into the streets to go to work, Madame Atomos could get lost in the crowd and find a way to sneak through the control posts set up around the perimeter. Beforehand, she would not hesitate to release the plague-infested rats. "Put the city under siege, Witter!"

"What?"

"It's too late," Hyde objected.

Beffort sliced his hand through the air. "It's our only chance! Spread the news using every means at our disposal. Use the radio, the newspapers, cars with loud speakers. Stop the public transportation and the taxis. Close down the streets and the shops. From 6 a.m. to noon, not a single person in Billings can step outside. Go on, Eddy, do it!"

Witter swung around and rushed away. Beffort turned to face Charles Hyde and Owen Bernitz. "Hyde, you go and contact J.E.E. in Washington and get more reinforcements. Before noon I want Billings to be surrounded by an impassable net. Tell him that the situation is far more serious than we thought and we made a mistake by underestimating her because she lost her power. If she manages to slip by us, everything will start over again exactly like before the destruction of Atomia Island. First she'll spread the plague among us, then while we're fighting against this scourge, she'll use her connections to set up a laboratory and workshops to rebuild her paralyzing weapons and the horrifying disintegrator ray, the electromagnetic shield and maybe, if she has the time, an armada of flying saucers. Make sure you tell

J.E.E. that nothing will ever end as long as she's alive! This woman is the devil personified!"

A terrible explosion highlighted his words. On reaching the pontoon at Josephine Park, the old man and his boat had just touched some infernal device. The river was boiling, debris flew through the air and the pontoon, the boat and the old man were now just memories.

Instinctively, Mie clung onto Beffort.

"Damn!" Bernitz swore. "You see what would've happened if Joyce had done his job? Mama What's-her-face is cleaning house. You can be sure that she won't leave a single witness behind her."

His comment made Beffort jump. "Mrs. Cameron? Which hospital is she in?"

"City Hospital," Hyde informed him. "Why?"

"She knows a lot of things about the A.O.F.M.A. If Madame Atomos learns that she's not dead, she'll do whatever she can to kill her. Call telephone J.E.E., Hyde. We're going to the hospital."

Owen Bernitz had predicted rightly. In spite of the two G-men standing guard before the door of her room, Mrs. Cameron was dead when Beffort leaned over her. The handle of the dagger was sticking out of her chest and the window was wide open, one of the panes cut out, leaving no doubt about how the killer had got into the room.

Beffort closed the woman's eyes and turned around. He looked stern. "Now nobody will be able to tell us about the A.O.F.M.A."

"Excuse me," Akamatsu said, "I have other names on the list."

Beffort raised his eyebrows. "When we visit them, they'll be dead or on the run. No false hopes, Yosho,

Madame Atomos prepared her return with great care. In three months she did monstrous work. In the next three months just try to imagine what she'll be able to accomplish."

His statement left everyone cold and they all suddenly felt that Madame Atomos, in one way or another, would get out of Billings safe and sound.

At seven in the morning, Billings became a ghost town. Eddy Witter was not twiddling his thumbs. He had performed miracles considering the time frame he was given. The stores were closed, not a single civilian was on the sidewalks and the buses and taxis were still in their yards. Police were patrolling the streets, entering buildings to check identifications, crawling through the sewers, searching public parks, etc.

At eight, things had not changed and Smith Beffort was pacing like a caged lion in the FBI office.

At nine a telephone call from the laboratory confirmed that the bottles found in the hidden basement of the Zag Zag contained a preparation saturated with plague bacillus, which only increased the tension among Beffort and his friends.

At ten another telephone call sent Beffort and his team into the east side of Billings, just near Rocky Mountain College. In the middle of a vacant piece of land, in a hangar that was thought abandoned, a patrol had just found a truck containing ten cages with about 100 rats each.

"Finally!" Mie exclaimed with relief. "There's one weapon that Madame Atomos won't be using!'

"This proves that she's in dire straits," Akamatsu judged. "You don't look very happy, Smith?"

"I'll only gloat when the laboratory gives us confirmation that these rodents are really carrying the Yersin bacterium. Can you give me some light, Owen, I see something in the back of the truck."

Bernitz switch the light on. Smith Beffort climbed into the truck, squeezed between the cages in which the rats were squealing wildly, and picked up a woman's shoe whose heel had stuck in a crack in the floor.

"Look at this, Mie."

The young lady took the shoe and examined it. "It's a showgirl's shoe. No woman would wear this kind of pump on the street." She looked up and stared at her husband. "The Zag Zag girls had the same… This truck was probably used to bring them to a safe place along with the musicians, waiters and Bird, the headwaiter."

Akamatsu leaned over and pointed out the gate. "Did you see this, Smith? Looks like the wood got splashed with corrosive acid."

"What's so surprising? A vehicle like this makes all kinds of hauls, doesn't it?"

"Sure," Akamatsu agreed, "but I'd point out the fact that this damage is very recent. The paint's gone and the holes dug by the acid are not even dusty. If they search hard enough, the patrols could certainly find where this truck was parked before being hidden here."

"That's an idea," Beffort admitted. "Sergeant! Drive this truck and its contents to the laboratory. I'll call in 30 minutes to find out if the rats are really contaminated and what kind of acid splattered the gate."

At the sergeant's orders, one of his men sat behind the wheel of the heavy vehicle, another closed the gate and the truck took off for the police laboratory. Just then the light flickered and went out.

"Did you turn it off, Owen?"

"No, I didn't touch a thing."

Beffort and his group left the hangar. Outside, in spite of the timid sunshine, the air was still very cold. Beffort told Bernitz, "Owen, you're going to make a list of the factories and workshops that are currently using acids. After that, send your men around to each of them…"

"Mr. Beffort!"

Smith turned around and saw a radio operator running toward him. "What's going on?"

"HQ just sent an urgent message. The main transformer in Rimrock has been put out of service by some explosion and Billings will be blacked out for several hours!"

"It's Madame Atomos striking," Bernitz threw out.

"Without a doubt, but what for?" Mie asked. "It's barely 10:30 and a long way until nightfall. In the meantime the transformer will surely be repaired."

Akamatsu and Beffort remained silent. If Madame Atomos had taken the trouble to deprive Billings of light, there was certainly a specific reason for it. The sinister woman never did anything for nothing. All her actions were calculated with respect to an overall plan and if they seemed harmless at first, they would usually turn out to be strokes of genius that took her enemies by surprise.

"How could Billings being without light in the middle of the day be of any use to her?" Beffort wrinkled his brow in contemplation.

Akamatsu sat on the hood of the car. "It's a problem that she's put to us," he said dreamily. "Until we find the solution, it'll be useless for us to act."

Beffort nodded.

Mie climbed in the car and got comfortable. She knew that the two men would not budge an inch until they had discovered the reason for this apparently senseless action.

Chapter XIV

For 30 minutes after the sabotage of the main transformer in Rimrock, all of the clinics and hospitals in Billings reported that their emergency systems were not working. In each case, the breakdown was due to malicious acts and even though the damage was nothing compared with that caused by the transformer, they still had to figure on another two or three hours before repairs could be made.

As for the emergency surgeries, it was a disaster.

Naturally this created some chaos in all the departments of the city hospital so that no one paid any attention to the man who slipped into the office of Dr. Bogart who was desperately trying to forge through the operation he had started at the moment of the breakdown, working uneasily in the light of a few flashlights they had hastily dug up.

In the office the intruder was searching methodically through the drawers and file cabinets with such calm as proved that he was not afraid of being disturbed any time soon. When he finally found the papers he was looking for, he put them down on the doctor's desk. There were a discharge form, a transfer order to the city hospital in Roundup and a letterhead from Dr. Bogart's department. With this, the man picked up the telephone and asked the operator for an outside number. It took the operator a few minutes to get it, but as soon as it started ringing, someone picked up.

The man said, "Scarlett here. Everything's gone as planned, Madame."

"Great," Madame Atomos answered. "Get the doctor's signature no matter what it takes. I think they're going to order an evacuation very soon. What's Keating doing?"

"He's taking care of the ambulance, Madame. In all the confusion here, he shouldn't have any problems."

"Don't be so sure," she responded dryly, "Beffort knows how to do his job well and fast. I've just learned that he found the truck and its load. For us, nothing will happen if the evacuation isn't accepted by the FBI."

"Sure, but that's got nothing to do with me," Scarlett said shyly.

"I know perfectly well what you are capable of," Madame Atomos said ironically. "So, do your best and don't forget the bonus that's waiting for you if you succeed. Call me back when the doctor's filled out the transfer. Goodbye." She hung up before Scarlett did.

Pretty much at the same time, Dr. Wallace was pointing an accusatory finger at the man across from him. "If you refuse to let the patients leave the city, you'll be responsible for their deaths at the same time! The surgeons in the operating rooms can't work and right now we have 25 emergencies!"

"The breakdown isn't going to last," the local FBI director said softly.

Furious now, Wallace slammed his fist down on the arm of his chair. "They're not going to last either! If they aren't transported to Roundup in the next hour, I guarantee you that you'll have 25 corpses on your conscience! No event, however serious, should prevent us from saving a human life!"

"I'm damn well aware of that," the director barked, "but it just so happens that I can't make the decision by myself. Give me 15 minutes. That's how long it'll take to get Smith Beffort's endorsement."

Wallace swallowed his anger, stood up and put his hands on the desk, saying, "If you take 15 minutes to authorize 25 patients to leave Billings, they'll get to Roundup too late. They'll die on the road, I can assure you. Do your job and I'll do mine."

"Which means?"

"Every patient will be carefully verified on leaving the hospital, as well as the personnel with them and the ambulances. Furthermore, nothing's stopping you from checking them all again when they reach the hospital in Roundup." Wallace looked anxiously at the clock on the wall. "Please, make up your mind. Time's running out. We've already lost five minutes in useless conversation."

The director gritted his teeth, took a blank sheet of paper, sign it, stamped it and said, "You fill it out. Clearly indicate the names of the patients, the staff and the license plates of the ambulances. I'm warning you that the convoy will be checked on leaving Billings, somewhere on the way and when they arrive in Roundup."

"Thanks!" Wallace grabbed the paper and dashed out of the room. The lives of 25 patients depended on his speed.

Dr. Bogart was solemn. He had just lost a battle on the operating table and, although he knew that he was not responsible, he still harbored a terrible feeling of guilt. He was on his way back to his office when they came to tell him that Dr. Wallace had finally won his case and he, Bogart, had to draw up a list of patients who needed to be transferred to Roundup.

"Wallace already has the list," he said.

"He knows that you have four leaving, but wants their identities and all the staff going with them. He also needs the license plates of the ambulances."

Bogart went down to the administration desk to get all the information he needed and then climbed back up to the second floor. He figured he could telephone Wallace from his office. On the way, he grabbed the files of the four patients from the nurses' station, stopped by the cafeteria to swallow a coffee and went down the dark corridor. The lack of light complicated everything, created disorder; the elevators were not working and the corridors were full of gurneys and bustling nurses. Bogart hated the confusion and noise, but he knew that everyone was doing their best under the unusual circumstances, considering that improvisation is always a source of anxiety in a hospital.

When he closed the office door behind him, he found himself standing before a man who was sticking a strange looking gun in his face.

"Dr. Bogart, is it?"

"Yes, what do you want? I'm telling you, I don't have a cent…"

"I don't want your money," Scarlett scowled. "I just want you to add someone to the list you have to give to Dr. Wallace." He had just got the tip from Keating who was dressed as an attendant and roaming around the hospital with his ears pricked up. He knew that this news would modify Madame Atomos' plans, at least in the details because the big picture could not and would not ever change.

Bogart looked hard at the man. "If your request is justified, there's no need to threaten me. I'm ready to do what you ask. What's it about?" He was calm, figured he was dealing with a panicky man who probably had a relative in the hospital. As he sat behind his desk he added, "Besides, you don't even know whether the person might not already be on my list."

"She's not," Scarlett assured him, "and my demand is not justified. Take your pen and write. Go on! Do what I tell you!"

The glint in his eye and the tone of his voice made Bogart understand that he was not joking. He felt no fear for himself, but he was worried that this man would delay his call to Wallace and therefore put the lives of four patients at risk. "You can tell me your story in a minute," he said firmly, reaching for the telephone.

Scarlett whacked the hand with the butt of his pistol. "You're going to do exactly what I tell you," he said coldly. "You won't be calling Wallace until you do."

Bogart put his aching hand on the desk. Scarlett smiled cruelly. "Now, you can't use that hand for a little while, right? So play nice, otherwise I'll break your fingers. For a surgeon, that's pretty serious isn't it? Pick up your pen and write. Here's the names you're going to add to your list and give Wallace: Patient—Mrs. Sonia Singleton. Attendants: Scarlett and Keating."

Bogart tamely wrote down the names along with the ambulance plate lifted by Keating in the hospital parking lot and then, on Scarlett's order, he picked up the phone, called Wallace and gave him the new list.

"Hold on!" Wallace was surprised. "You have an extra patient?"

"Car accident," Bogart said laconically.

Scarlett was listening in. The doctor did not want to take any risks. He just told himself that he would alert the police as soon as he could. This man must be a maniac.

"Okay," Wallace said, "I'll add your 5th ambulance. We'll all meet together in 10 minutes before the North Park entrance. From there the convoy will take Highway 87 where it'll be checked. Then everything will go fast as lightning. Good luck, Bogart."

"You, too." Bogart hung up and Scarlett emptied a shot from his paralyzing pistol—the one taken from Lucky Simms. The doctor would pose no problem for 60 minutes. By then, Madame Atomos, aka Sonia Singleton, and her two bodyguards would have put a lot of distance between them and Billings.

Scarlett threw on the white coat and cap that Keating had acquired, grabbed the list drawn up by Bogart and went down to the first floor. At the administration desk, he pretended that he was sent by Wallace in order to take charge of the hospital convoy. No one doubted him so they gave him the papers to leave. Five minutes later, the ambulance driven by Keating was leaving the hospital with four others in its wake.

"Do you have the oxygen tent?" Scarlett asked.

"It's all set up," Keating confirmed.

"Okay. Now all we have to do is pick up Madame Atomos."

A little over a mile later, the head ambulance broke down in front of an underground parking lot on 24th Street. The other drivers offered to help, but Scarlett assured them that he could fix it quickly and be back on the road in no time.

When the four ambulances were out of sight, Keating drove into the deserted parking lot and pulled in next to a van in which Madame Atomos was waiting. The sinister woman climbed into the ambulance, lay down under the covers and Scarlett closed the oxygen tent around her. Inside, Madame Atomos could not be recognized and barring some unexpected accident, she would be leaving Billings with a minimum of risk.

The factory was located beside a railroad track at the end of a private road. Beffort's car rolled up to the vats where Owen Bernitz and his men were waiting. It drove around the platform and under the huge roof that protected the acids from the rain and dust.

"It's here," Bernitz said.

Beffort and his group got out of the car. The vats were half-buried and the visible part was no more than a few feet above ground. Bernitz showed the tire tracks in the loose dirt. "The truck came in backwards and then lifted its bed. That's all that's left of Joyce's employees."

A nauseating heap was stuck to the ground. Everything the acid had not yet eaten away was there. Even though it was not much, they could still count the number of victims by certain details. Mie turned on her heels and ran to the car. She had just seen a hand clutching the rim of the vat.

"It's a woman," Bernitz explained. "She hung on trying to pull herself out and then died. The acid ate her body all the way up to her arm there, but the hand kept its grip on the edge. Which means that all the victims were alive when the truck was emptied here. Signed Madame Atomos, no doubt."

"She gave the order," Beffort murmured, "but I'd really like to know who was driving the truck."

Akamatsu shrugged. "What's amazing is that no one will be able to swear before a jury that Madame Atomos is a criminal. As far as I can remember, she has never killed anyone with her own hands. If she did, who could prove it?"

"I know you're right, Yosho, but it doesn't matter. Without her, none of this would have happened. You'll never be able to convince me that she's not responsible."

"I don't want to," Akamatsu protested. "I was just saying, that's all."

Right then Mie stuck her head out the car window. "Smith!" she called. "FBI headquarters wants to talk to you."

Beffort walked to the car, grabbed the mic, identified himself and heard the local director. "Mr. Beffort, I'm calling to tell you about a decision that I had to make without you because of an emergency."

"I'm sure you did the right thing," Beffort said. "What's it about?"

"I don't know if you're aware, but soon after the sabotage of the transformer in Rimrock, the emergency power in the Billings hospitals were also damaged and…"

"Wait a second," Beffort cut in. "You mean that the hospital generators were sabotaged?"

"Exactly."

Beffort's stomach turned. "Well, what connection does that have with the decision you made?"

"A direct connection seeing that the breakdowns made the operating rooms unusable in our city. Dr. Wallace asked me for a pass so the urgent patients could be taken to Roundup to have surgery. That's the authorization I gave before being able to consult you because time was short. I hope I didn't go too far…"

"How many patients are on the way to Roundup?" Beffort was very stressed.

"Wallace gave me a list of 26 patients and 52 staff members all belonging to…"

"Okay," Beffort interrupted again. "Only the women interest me, friend. Especially Asian women. Don't tell me that you've got one there."

The local director snickered. "That's ridiculous. If you think that Madame Atomos could have been admitted into a hospital, pretended to be sick and then loaded into a convoy of emergencies, you're on the wrong track."

It was Beffort's turn to laugh. "With Madame Atomos, everything is possible. Nothing unusual in the list?"

"No, not really."

"Did you call the hospitals to see if the patients were really patients?"

"What for? The hospitals gave me the lists. It was just the city hospital that had to add an extra name to the original."

"Yeah? Who?"

"A Sonia Singleton."

"Great," Beffort lied. "I think everything's in order. No one will blame you for this." He hung up the mic and wave Bernitz over. "Owen, get to the nearest telephone. Call the city hospital and ask how long Sonia Singleton had been there."

Bernitz jumped in his car and shot off like a rocket.

"What's happening, Smith?" Akamatsu came up to inquire.

"Maybe nothing!" Beffort exploded. "Or else Madame Atomos is right now slipping through our fingers by the authorization of the local FBI director!"

Chapter XV

Owen Bernitz came back in record time, jumped out of his car and said, "Sonia Singleton has been in the hospital for three weeks. She's being treated for heart failure."

"False alarm, no luck."

"Wait, boss, something's screwy here because the woman is still in her bed. So, whoever's going to Roundup right now is someone else."

Akamatsu asked, "Someone else has taken the place of Mrs. Singleton?"

"No," Bernitz answered, "Sonia Singleton didn't need a transfer. Plus, there's something else weird in all this. Dr. Bogart..."

"Who's he?" Beffort asked.

"The one who gave the list of emergencies to Wallace. So, for around 45 minutes he's been unconscious. One of his colleagues diagnosed a sudden attack of paralysis."

Akamatsu and Beffort had the same shock. Bernitz lit his cigar, eyed the two men and said, "If you remember that Lucky had a paralyzing pistol on him..."

Beffort jumped into his car, grabbed the microphone and called the FBI bureau, "Beffort here. I've just learned that the last patient put on the list by Dr. Bogart has not left her bed in the city hospital. Can you at least tell me where the convoy is right now?"

The director gulped. "Are you sure?"

"I'm sure. Now answer my question—how far from Roundup are the ambulances?"

"I don't know, but I can tell you that it was halfway there at the second checkpoint. That was 15 minutes ago. All the ambulances were present and all the papers were in order. Listen, Beffort, maybe I was wrong to sign that transfer paper, but I'm no babe in the woods. The convoy isn't traveling alone through the country. There's a highway patrol in front and back of it. If there's a black sheep in there, it won't be slipping away without us knowing."

"Can you contact your men?"

"Nothing easier."

"Okay, tell them that Madame Atomos is traveling under the name of Sonia Singleton and her companions probably belong to her Organization."

"Okay. They're going to arrest her."

"No!" Beffort barked. "One of the two men has a paralyzing pistol. If your G-men make any kind of move, they'll be put down for the count. Moreover, they can't open fire on the ambulance without us making sure beforehand that it really is Madame Atomos inside."

"But you just told me…"

"I know! There's a 50/50 chance that Madame Atomos is actually traveling in the ambulance. It's just as likely a trick meant to throw us off her trail."

"Damn!" the director swore. "What are we supposed to do under such conditions?"

"Your boys have to watch that vehicle like hawks, follow it if it leaves the convoy, but never get within 500 yards or else they'll be paralyzed. They can stay in contact by radio with the HQ and give you a minute-to-minute update. I'll get a helicopter, catch up to the convoy before Roundup and see for myself what it's all about. Call your men. For now, let them play sheepdog."

26 ambulances, each measuring 20 feet long and keeping the legal distance of 100 feet between them, spelled a convoy stretching out for more than half a mile. There was no way to be precise because of the accordion effect, but whatever the distance, it was unavoidable that the federal car at the back lost sight of some of the vehicles when the highway became curvy. And what was true for the rear was likewise true for the head car, so that a dozen of the ambulances disappeared from its sight in the long and winding curves of the road.

It was precisely when the highway was passing through a forest that Madame Atomos decided that the time had come to part company with the feds. Everything was calm and there was no hurry, but Dr. Bogart would be waking up and telling his story in 15 minutes or so, which would naturally trigger an alarm and a swarm of police with Smith Beffort at their head would be after her.

Madame Atomos pushed back the covers, climbed out of the tent and said to Scarlett, "We're in a forest on a twisting highway. Is it possible to clear out?"

Scarlett looked at the map and spotted a blue line that represented a secondary road. He said, "In just over a mile, we can make a run for it, Madame. This road can't be well known, but it'll take us to Highway 12 where we can get hold of a less conspicuous car."

Madame Atomos smiled. "Very well. Tell Keating to get ready."

Scarlett passed the word to his partner who was driving and the ambulance reduced its speed. It took the curves slowly, braking, and then speeding up again. In this way, a hole was quickly made between it and the ambulance in front, but the one behind was judging its speed and following closely so the distance remained the same.

"Now," Scarlett said, "you can go!"

Keating floored the accelerator and the ambulance literally flew off. The ambulance behind it was so surprised that it did not react immediately and Madame Atomos was soon alone on a short stretch of road. When Keating made a sharp turn off the highway, the other ambulance had not yet caught up and the one in front was still not in sight. The turn was made as they were coming out of the woods so that when the ambulance finally did catch up to the one in front, it did not notice that it was different from the one it had been following since Billings.

Four minutes later, the two vehicles with federal agents got the message from the local director. The car in the back sped through the convoy, counted just 25 ambulances and immediately contacted Billings by radio.

"We didn't do anything rash, sir, but it seems that Mrs. Singleton's ambulance is missing!"

"Good God! Look again! And try to find out when her ambulance left the convoy. I'll be waiting."

The message reached Beffort as his helicopter was flying over the imaginary line separating Yellowstone and Musselshell counties.

"No one knows exactly when the ambulance left the convoy," the director told him in a shaky voice. "They only know that it was still there at the checkpoint…"

"Doesn't matter!" Beffort interrupted. "Do whatever's necessary to close the roads between Billings and Lewistown and between Bozeman and Miles City. The ambulance hasn't had time to get out of that area."

"It will by the time the roadblocks are up. All the available forces from Montana are tied up around Billings. It'll take at least an hour before they can get in position."

Beffort's knuckles on the microphone turned white. He was solely responsible for the operations in this affair. Thousands of men were surrounding Billings on his order, but Madame Atomos had just breached the iron circle with her usual ease and there was no one left to chase her. The Green Dragon Force and Eddy Witter's men were still searching in Billings. How pathetic!

"Do what you can," Beffort said, "and cordon off the state if you have to! An ambulance can be spotted for god's sake! I'm going to fly over the area until I run out of gas. Over."

While this conversation was going on, the helicopter had continued toward Roundup. Beffort was sitting next to the pilot. Akamatsu and Mie were in the back seats. Akamatsu tapped Beffort on the shoulder, showed him the map he was examining and said, "Look at his, Smith, and tell me what you think. Between Billings and Roundup, Highway 87, which we're flying over, has almost no side roads in this sector. I see only this blue line that hooks up with Highway 12."

"Interesting," Beffort said. "Especially since it's just after the point where they noticed the ambulance had disappeared." He turned to the pilot and said, "Follow this side road, Helms, 87 can't tell us anything new."

The pilot changed his course and the machine headed northeast. At 300 feet altitude, every detail was perfectly visible and there was no difficulty in identifying vehicles. After ten minutes of flying, the helicopter arrived at the intersection of the two roads and Beffort had to choose between veering off toward Roundup or going on to Bascom. In fact, there was no choice: How could Madame Atomos ever think of going to Roundup when she had done everything in her power to avoid it? Moreover, the road to Bascom went on to Miles City, Baker and the border of North Dakota. Once in North Dakota, Madame Atomos could take advantage of the lack of coordination between the police of the different states and would have little to fear from the FBI.

"Straight ahead, Helms," Beffort ordered.

At nearly 200 miles an hour, the helicopter sped through Bascom and onto Sumatra without seeing anything auspicious.

"We're going the wrong way," Akamatsu said. "If the ambulance took this direction, we would have spotted it a long time ago."

"I agree with you, Yosho. Helms, turn around!'

Beffort looked grim. He felt like his chances of catching up with Madame Atomos were diminishing by the second. The terrible woman had obviously cooked up an impeccably planned scenario to throw Beffort to the wind. She was about to win another round. Beffort was deeply convinced of this and the semi-victory of capturing the plague-ridden rats was not enough to console him.

As the helicopter was flying over Bascom again on its way to Roundup, Mie suddenly leaned over. She had very good eyes. "There!" she shouted. "It's an ambulance!"

Beffort grabbed his binoculars. He cursed. It was, in fact, the ambulance from the Billings city hospital. It was driving fast, curtains drawn and its rotating beacon was on. The siren was probably screaming, but Beffort was too far, too high up and too deafened by the whirling helicopter blades to know for sure.

"Down, Helms! We have to stop it!"

All at the same time, he, Akamatsu and Mie pulled out their paralyzing pistols. Then he called the FBI HQ in Billings. "Beffort here. We've just found the ambulance! It's heading toward Roundup. Make sure you stop it in case we can't!'

"Got it! You can count on us!"

Helms brought the helicopter down and skimmed the roof of the ambulance.

"Okay!" Beffort shouted. "Set her down across the road to force it to stop."

The helicopter sped ahead, hovered at the top of a slope and set down. Beffort, Mie and Akamatsu instantly jumped out and dove into the ditch, aiming their weapons at the slowing ambulance. The sun reflected off its windshield, preventing them from seeing the occupants. It finally came to a halt about 15 feet from the helicopter. The door opened and a tall, skinny man in overalls stepped out.

"Hands in the air!" Beffort ordered. The man might be one of Madame Atomos' companions.

The guy raised his hands and stepped forward nervously. "Who are you?"

"Federal police!"

The guy laughed and stuck his hands in his pocket. "In that case," he said, "you'd better get after my Chevy instead of playing Cowboys and Indians with me. Two guys and some yellow doll swiped it off me 10 minutes ago. I was just going to the police station…"

The Chevrolet was found in a parking lot in Bascom with a little note stuck under the windshield wiper on the driver's side: *Well, Smith, what do you have to say?*

Of course it was Madame Atomos' writing. Beffort held back the rage that wanted to explode out of him, balled up the paper and felt the hood of the Chevrolet. "The engine's still warm," he said. "So warm that I would swear it only stopped here a few seconds ago."

Akamatsu opened the rear door and found a tape recorder on the back seat. Right next to it was an envelope addressed to Smith Beffort and Mie Azusa. Beffort tore it open and took out a piece of paper on which was written: *Turn on the tape recorder. There's a recording for you.*

Beffort was already reaching for the play button when Mie abruptly grabbed his hand. "Don't, Smith!"

"Why not?"

Mie clung onto his arm with savage force. "I'm sure it's a trap. That miserable woman lost this round and here is without a doubt her final act, her final attempt to kill you." Beffort gently lifted the device and found it unusually heavy.

In the laboratory in Bascom, the specialists defused the infernal bomb inside the tape recorder's shell. Strangely, the bomb was not set to go off when the recording started to play: the play button would have set off a detonator timed to explode between 7 and 8 minutes later—a rough guess, it was hard to say.

"Now," one of the specialists said, "you can listen to the recording if you want. Should I start the track?"

"Go ahead," Beffort accepted.

The tape started rolling. There were five or six seconds of silence before they heard the voice of Madame Atomos:

"Mr. Beffort, I'm going to escape from you again, but we shall meet again soon. Now you know that I have friends and money and that I'm going to do everything I can to rebuild an Organization worthy of my name. Thanks to Lucky Simms, I've got a paralyzing pistol that will serve as a model for a whole new line. When I manage to get a few scientists on my team, I'll be able to rebuild my disintegrator ray. And when I do that, there's no need to tell you that I'll stop playing cat and mouse with the USA! This time, I'll strike hard, very hard…"

There was a pause. The specialist said, "That's when it was supposed to explode."

Then Madame Atomos resumed, "You're very clever, Mr. Beffort, seeing that you're still alive and listening to the rest of my message. But I was kind of expecting that… So, to wrap up, let's make a date for three months from now in Cincinnati, Ohio. There I'll show you that Madame Atomos is not dead! See you soon, Mr. Beffort and take good care of your wife…"

Beffort stopped the recording. Akamatsu said, "In three months in Cincinnati, huh?"

"We'll be there, Yosho. In the meantime, let's try keep trying to capture her before she gets out of Montana. Inspector! Tell your patrols to close the roads…"

Beffort gave his orders, but it was more to set his mind at rest than anything else. He knew perfectly well that he would hear nothing more from his enemy before this so-called date in Cincinnati…

Michel Stéphan:
The Red Silk Scarf

London and Japan, 1933

What seems a long time ago, I shared a number of extraordinary adventures with an extraordinary man— Harry Dickson. His reputation as one of the world's best detectives was widespread; he was as respected by his peers as he was feared by his enemies.

Everyone still remembers Harry Dickson. Everyone is still familiar with his exploits. They were so fantastic that one might almost believe he was a superman—and he was indeed gifted with prodigious talents. But his aura of fearless avenger hid another side of his personality. Now that many years have passed, I can tell a story that will illuminate another facet of that wonderful man. And if his reputation as a crime fighter suffers somewhat, he will only appear more human. Don't be too concerned: his legend won't be tarnished.

It was the year 1933, a troubled time in Europe, as the rise in nationalism foreshadowed a somber future. London was, more than ever, the prey to some fantastic villains. Mr. Dickson and I had little time to rest between our cases, but I learned a lot from him and got a great deal of job satisfaction. We had just dealt with the notorious gang of the Spider and needed a break, when my Guv received an invitation from one of his correspondents, Dr. Daisuke Serizawa, to come and spend a few weeks in the Empire of the Rising Sun.

Dr. Serizawa lived in the northern section of the town of Nagasaki. He was a physicist interested in all kinds of subjects, which made him a wonderfully erudite host. He had turned his house into a laboratory, except for the sitting room which remained an island of tranquility where we could discuss at length every topic, such as the similarities between scientific research and criminal investigation.

A fourth person soon joined us: Dr. Serizawa's research assistant, who came twice a week to help him in the laboratory, a young girl named Kanoto Yoshimuta. Miss Yoshimuta wasn't only beautiful, she was also prodigiously gifted for her age—or so Dr. Serizawa proudly told us. After we arrived, she increased the frequency of her visits and took part in our conversations, contributing her opinion on every subject, impressing us greatly with her charm and erudition. I have to confess that I wasn't in the same intellectual league as these three exceptional minds, so, when the discussions became too complex for me, I often took refuge in a game of patience.

Mr. Dickson, however, became fascinated by this extraordinary young woman. But what I initially deemed to be a purely intellectual attraction soon turned into something more powerful. Dr. Serizawa took some pains to keep me entertained and out of the way of the newly-formed couple.

Holidays don't last forever. The villains haunting the East End and the moors of Devon don't take vacations. England needed Harry Dickson back. We spent our last few days in Japan visiting various sites. I was surprised by the changes in Mr. Dickson. At that time, I had already shared many adventures with the "American Sherlock Holmes" and I thought I knew him well. But now, I was discovering a heretofore unknown side of him. Even Dr. Serizawa seemed somewhat puzzled by his transformation. He wasn't behaving like a schoolboy madly in love with his flame! No, his relationship with Miss Toshimuta was more like a mentor and his protégée. But Mr. Dickson's normally stern expression had been replace by one of happiness, and I only had to see the light burning in his eyes when he talked to the young Japanese to understand that a door had opened in his mind, leading to rooms he had never visited before.

Miss Yoshimuta was, as I mentioned, very beautiful. Her long jet-black hair cascaded down her shoulders all the way to her lower back. Her face showed a remarkable mixture purity of features, illuminated by her genius and pride. She had the most entrancing eyes I have ever seen, before or since.

One day, as Mr. Dickson and Miss Yoshimuta were returning from a stroll near Mount Unzen, I saw my master blush lightly when I noticed a small wild flower, a *kyushu*, delicately pinned on his jacket lapel. It was the only outward sign that enabled me to understand how close they had become.

The night before we left, we were all tired, having spent the day walking around the Fugen Drake Mountains. Dr. Serizawa wished us all good night; I wasn't quite ready to go to bed.

Miss Yoshimuta took advantage of that time to ask Mr. Dickson to follow her into a large storage room attached to the laboratory where they kept all kinds of scientific equipment. She said she wanted to show him a new tattooing process she had devised. My master hadn't wanted to say no, but I could tell he was tired. He sat in the only chair in the room and quickly fell asleep.

When he woke up, it was dark. He realized that he couldn't move his arms. He looked down and saw that his wrists had been tied with a red silk scarf. He had barely time to open his mouth to inquire about what was happening when he felt her lips pressing against his and her young, lithe body wrapping itself around him...

Mr. Dickson was ever a private man, but I needed no detective license the next day, as we were about to return to England, to figure out what had taken place between the two of them. The light bruises around his wrists made me think that he couldn't have tried very hard to free himself. All he told me was that he had promised to return to see Miss Yoshimuta exactly a year from now.

Even though I worked by Mr. Dickson's side constantly, we rarely had time to talk about personal matters. One night, several months later, as we enjoyed a quiet evening by the fireplace which Mrs. Crown had had swept before winter came, I seized the opportunity to remind my master of his promise to Miss Yoshimuta.

"Aren't you supposed to be in Nagasaki next month?" I asked. "Have you heard from the young lady?"

"Yes, Tom. I received two letters, which I answered, of course. She is a fascinating woman. We had some wonderful exchanges on the slopes of the Fugen Drake, but I confess that there's something inside her that I do not understand. I'm still haunted by her eyes, which could go from soft and dreamy to hard as steel and frightening when I mentioned certain topics such as America. I *am* an American, Tom, and in those moments, I couldn't suppress a small shiver. She actually scared me. Just as puzzling was her fanatical obedience to her Emperor and the Military Caste which rules Japan. It is all very strange to us, westerners, and even stranger in the mouth of such a beautiful girl. You know that I've always believed, like Rabelais, that 'science without conscience is but the ruin of the soul.' …But now it's time for dinner! I believe Mrs. Crown has prepared another of her specialties…"

"One last thing, Guv… Perhaps you should go alone this time."

"We'll talk about that later, Tom. I decided to postpone my trip anyway. Scotland Yard needs us to look into that "Iron Temple" business. I plan to write to Miss Yoshimuta to inform her of the delay and offer my apologies. I won't do that lightly, because I know that such an action is considered very impolite in her culture, and I do care a great deal about her opinions, but I can't leave my duties behind."

About a month later, when Mr. Dickson came home, one late evening after having spent most of the day at the Yard, he showed me the evening paper he'd just bought.

"More bad news from Asia. Not content to foment trouble in Manchukuo and seeking to become the sole leaders in East Asia, Japan has now resigned from the League of Nations. Well-informed sources expect they might even invade China…"

"If you don't mind my saying so, Guv, they wouldn't get away trying those sort of shenanigans with true-blooded British soldiers—God Save the King! Americans soldiers too, sorry, Guv!"

At that moment, Mr. Dickson collapsed on the floor, like a tree felled by lightning.

"My legs, Tom! I can't move them!"

I pulled him up and helped him into an armchair. We pulled up one leg of his trousers and with a pin, determined that his lower body no longer reacted to such stimuli; what's more, his skin had taken a slight, unnatural bluish color.

Mr. Dickson was taken to Kensington Hospital at once, where he was examined, poked and probed by the greatest specialists in the Kingdom. All hinds of experts in tropical and other rare diseases analyzed his blood, took skin samples, but none one could figure the nature of his ailment—even less cure him.

That is until a letter arrived for him from Japan. It was from Miss Yoshimuta and here is what it said:

Dearest Harry,

You know my feelings towards you, and I can but hope that they are reciprocated; but there are times when I'm filled with doubts. You belong to a people who are acting increasingly hostile towards my own and whom I understand less and less every day. When we met, I thought you might be different. You promised me to return a year hence; but I kept telling myself, what if you are not different? What if you break your word to me? So the last night of your visit, when you fell asleep—a condition for which I was responsible, since I had drugged you earlier—I made a small injection in your right wrist, in the radial artery, large enough to inject a miniature capsule of my invention that was carried by the bloodstream to lodge itself into your heart, which is said to be the seat of love—an irony I couldn't miss.

A year and a day from tonight, very exactly, the capsule will release a toxin of my design which will paralyze your legs. If you have returned to me, I will have secretly administered an antidote and you will never learn what I did. If, on the other hand, you broke your word, you will become paralyzed and eventually die as the poison works its way through your body. If that occurs, I have arranged for this letter to de delivered to you in England. May you reflect during the days you have left to live on the price paid by those who fail to keep their promises.

Kanoto Yoshimuta

After reading that letter, we knew that no one in England or America could save Mr. Dickson.

"She's mad," said Mr. Dickson. "It's true that I didn't keep our appointment, but I write to her. My feelings for her were never in doubt!"

"It seemed as if she'd planned it all from the start," I said. "Frankly, if she wanted to test your love, she should have injected herself with her devilish poison. Knowing you as I do, Guv, you'd have crossed the Earth and not stopped for anything to go and rescue her!"

The only possible course of action was to appeal to Miss Yoshimuta. A friend of Mr. Dickson's, an American doctor named Francis Ardan, had immediately sent to Kensington a special blood-recycling machine of his invention that had succeeded in slowing somewhat the course of the toxin. A special medical plane was chartered and, a few hours later, we were in the air.

In addition to the two RAF pilots, the crew consisted of one military intelligence officer, four soldiers and one doctor to watch over the patient. I was, of course, part of this hastily-improvised mission.

Mr. Dickson was strapped to a medical bed, connected to Dr. Ardan's machine which kept pumping new blood into his veins. His was deathly pale and very weak. I joked that he was sicker from having been tricked by that Japanese girl than from her deadly toxin.

The weather throughout the journey was horrible; we were buffeted by storms and pelted by incessant rains. Everyone aboard was on edge, prepared for the worst.

The officer in charge of the mission, a well-read man named John Ashenden, delivered final warnings about what might happen when we got to Japan.

"This may be something of a wild goose chase, old boy. We have made every effort to contact Miss Yoshimuta through diplomatic and scientific channels, but relations between our two countries have deteriorated a lot in the last 12 months. We have been granted permission to land at a small military airport near Nagasaki, but we won't be able to disembark. If your Japanese dragon-lady doesn't show up, after two hours, we'll have no choice but fly out. That's the deal."

Mr. Dickson looked at Mr. Ashenden and in a wan voice said:

"She'll be there. I know she will."

Then he fell back on his bed, exhausted.

The weather over Japan wasn't any better and the landing was one of the worst I ever experienced. The sound of the engines was drowned by the roar of the storm, and several times, I feared that our plane would be carried away like a straw in the wind.

Finally, we touched ground and rolled unsteadily over the tarmac towards a single building located at the end of the strip. Inside the plain, Mr. Dickson's health had taken a turn for the worst and Dr. Leicester had applied an oxygen mask to the detective's face and was massaging his temples, as if somehow he could add his life to my master's.

When the plane came to a stop, and the door opened, Mr. Ashenden and I rushed out in the pouring rain. The small building was nothing more than a bare waiting room, furnished only with a few benches, illuminated by a weak electric light.

It was empty.

"She's not here!" I cried. "There's no one here! Mr. Dickson's going to die!"

Still, following the instructions we had received, the four soldiers, under Dr. Leicester's supervision, brought Mr. Dickson down from the plane and into the barracks.

The task was barely over when a black automobile silently drove out of darkness. I was still screaming as if I'd been on a ship going down in the ocean. The car parked next to the building and Kanoto Yoshimuta got out of the back seat. I couldn't see who her driver was.

"Go back into the plane!" she ordered to our men. "You have no right to set foot on Japanese soil!"

"Mr. Dickson's going to die," I repeated, numb to anything else.

"You brought him here so I could save him. Your task is done. All of you, return to your plane. I will take care of Harry. Then you can have him back because Japan doesn't need foreigners like him."

The rain had stopped, but I no longer cared. Only Dr. Leicester and I were allowed to remain at Mr. Dickson's side as Miss Yoshimuta pulled out a syringe from a small black handbag.

"Americans' word can't be trusted," she whispered, "but you, Harry, can always trust mine."

After injecting Mr. Dickson with a crimson-colored liquid, she applied a silver disk to his chest, on the exact location of his heart, and pressed twice. We saw Mr. Dickson's body shake twice, as if he had received a powerful electroshock. Dr, Leicester was fascinated by the operation.

Miss Yoshimuta them pulled a pin from her hair and lightly stabbed Mr. Dickson on the foot. From the twitching of his toes, we could tell that he was cured.

"The discoloration of the skin will vanish in a few days," said the deadly Japanese. "Now go back to your plane. I must speak with him alone."

Mr. Dickson later reported the essence of their conversation to me in order to satisfy my curiosity, and perhaps, as I realize now, as a kind of warning.

"You'll be fine now, Harry," said Miss Yoshimuta.

"What did you do to me?"

"Nothing you can even remotely understand. If I were to explain it to you, it would seem... supernatural. You still find it difficult to believe that other people can be superior to you, Americans."

"I never doubted your intelligence," said Mr. Dickson.

"Don't be condescending, Harry. It doesn't become you."

"You have changed, Kanoto. I barely recognize you."

"I have learned to see England's and America's lies for what they were, Harry. Your world is one where the rules are set by and for the white man. You pillage and plunder at will. But let Japan try to claim what is rightly hers, and suddenly the rules change. You lied to me too, Harry."

"I didn't. I fully intended to return. My duty..."

"I know. I did receive your letter. And that's why I came tonight. But never attempt to see me again. I wouldn't be so merciful a second time."

Harry Dickson never knew if he or Miss Yoshimuta leaned forward for a brief and last kiss.

When the black car had gone, and Dr. Leicester and I helped Mr. Dickson back to the plane, his face showed no more emotion than a living, ghastly waxwork.

As I write this in the later years of my life, America is struggling against the deadly threat of Madame Atomos.

Mr. Dickson lived a well-filled life, but I am happy that he didn't live long enough to see the carnage that Kanoto Yoshimuta has wreaked on the land of his birth, for I recognized her hand right away beneath that hideous sobriquet.

It seems incredible that my Guv was once in love with that terrible woman. I was too young at the time to fully understand what brought these two exceptional beings together. However, their respective paths and obsessions could only drive them apart. The name of Harry Dickson came to symbolize order and justice, as that of Madame Atomos represents death and destruction.

Still, during his entire life, in a discreet corner of his Baker Street flat, Mr. Dickson kept a small *kyushu* flower neatly stuck between the yellow pages of his favorite book.

Tom Wills, 1969

(English adaptation by Jean-Marc & Randy Lofficier)

Matthew Dennion:
The Most Dreadful Monster

Los Alamos, 1963

A single ray of sunlight cast a small modicum of illumination in the dark abandoned bunker. Madame Atomos sat in one of the two chairs in the former shelter as she awaited the delivery of the "package." She smiled as she mused how this location was the official birth place of the weapon that had ravaged her country and propelled her towards her destiny. The damage the Americans had wrought on Japan with their atomic bombs was unbelievable—and unforgivable.

The explosions themselves had killed tens of thousands, but the blast was only the first stage of the death the Americans had wrought on her homeland. The next two stages were by far the worst. The people who had died initially were the lucky ones; those just outside the blast range had died a slow, painful death from radiation burns and poisoning. Their bodies betrayed them and decayed like some form of advanced leprosy as their inside tore themselves apart. Yet, even these people were fortunate compared to the people who suffered under the third consequence of the nuclear attacks; the rise of the *daikajiu*.

Atomic mutant beasts had awakened, changed by the radioactive fallout, and ravaged Japan for years. Madame Atomos had watched as Gojira, Rodan, and beast after beast rose from the bottom of the sea and the bowels of the Earth to prolong the effects of the Americans attack. Her fury continued to build as she recalled these events. She stood and shouted: "The *Dakaiju* are not the most terrible monsters created by radiations; I, Madame Atomos, am the most terrible monster born of the nuclear fire, and soon, I shall bring pain and suffering onto America far beyond that of any monster!"

Outside the bunker, she could hear the sound of a car screeching to a halt. A door was pulled open as one her men shouted orders. She composed herself, as she realized her guest had arrived. The door flew open and several of her henchmen dragged a man into the room. He had a black sack over his head and was still in his pajamas.

Madame Atomos addressed her followers: "The extraction went as planned? He is unharmed?"

"Yes, Madame, we broke into his house at night, and drugged him in his sleep. He should be starting to regain his senses soon."

"Good work. Tie him to the chair and remove the blindfold. I will deal with him personally."

Today was the day that she would use the weapons of America's past to destroy one of them and the weapons of its future to destroy them all.

The man was tied to a chair and the bag removed from his head. He was tall and thin, with brown hair and eyes. His head lolled from side to as he regained consciousness.

"Good morning, doctor," said Madame Atomos. "You may be wondering where you are, what has happened to you, and why you are here." She slowly walked up to the man and looked down into his eyes. Then, raising her hand, she slapped him across the face. "To answer the first question, we are at the testing grounds for the first atomic weapon. I chose this place as it holds significance to both of us on several levels. This is the spot where your country, and, more specifically, scientists like you, created the tools that have brought much suffering on my county and my people. On a personal level, in a sense, this is where my life truly began—and yours will end."

The scientist mumbled something, but Madame Atomos slapped him again in response.

"Vermin! You will speak when I give you permission to speak! Anyway, I doubt the sedative you were given has yet worn off to the extent of allowing you to speak." Her voice softened. "To answer the second question, my followers have drugged you and brought here so that you may decide how quickly you will die for your sins. You see, doctor, there is still enough radiation in this area to cause a human to become afflicted with radiation poisoning. My men and I are immune to these effects. You, however, are not so fortunate."

The doctor mumbled something slightly louder than his previous attempt at speech, for which he was struck again.

"Swine! You will learn to speak only when I command you." Another slap quickly came snapping the man's head to the side. As to why you were brought here, the answer is simple. You have created a new weapon far more deadly than the hydrogen bomb. As such, I hold you just as responsible for the destruction of my homeland as I do those who created the H-bomb. By now, your body is starting to take in all of the radiation that is still floating in the air. Your choice is simple: divulge the secrets of your weapon to me and we will kill you quickly, or remain silent and strapped in that chair until the radiation slowly corrodes your body from the inside out."

Madame Atomos laughed as she walked around the man. She grabbed him by the collar, her eyes filled with rage, and slapped him again with each word she spoke: "DO I MAKE MYSELF CLEAR, DOCTOR?"

She straightened her posture and lowered her voice "Now what do you have to say to my proposition?"

The doctor took a deep breath and slowly raised his head, panting as he spoke. Madame Atomos saw his eyes flash green. Inside them was a rage in them that far exceeded even her own.

"Don't make me angry," growled Bruce Banner. "You wouldn't like me when I'm angry."

Madame Atomos realized at last she was not the most dreadful monster born of radiation.

SF & FANTASY

Henri Allorge. *The Great Cataclysm*
Guy d'Armen. *Doc Ardan: The City of Gold and Lepers*
G.-J. Arnaud. *The Ice Company*
Charles Asselineau. *The Double Life*
Cyprien Bérard. *The Vampire Lord Ruthwen*
Aloysius Bertrand. *Gaspard de la Nuit*
Richard Bessière. *The Gardens of the Apocalypse*
Albert Bleunard. *Ever Smaller*
Félix Bodin. *The Novel of the Future*
Alphonse Brown. *City of Glass*
André Caroff. *The Terror of Madame Atomos; Miss Atomos; The
Return of Madame Atomos; The Mistake of Madame Atomos; The
Monsters of Madame Atomos; The Revenge of Madame Atomos*
Félicien Champsaur. *The Human Arrow; Ouha*
Didier de Chousy. *Ignis*
Captain Danrit. *Undersea Odyssey*
C. I. Defontenay. *Star (Psi Cassiopeia)*
Charles Derennes. *The People of the Pole*
Georges Dodds (anthologist). *The Missing Link*
Harry Dickson. *The Heir of Dracula*
Jules Dornay. *Lord Ruthven Begins*
Alfred Driou. *The Adventures of a Parisian Aeronaut*
Sâr Dubnotal *vs. Jack the Ripper*
Alexandre Dumas. *The Return of Lord Ruthven*
Renée Dunan. *Baal*
J.-C. Dunyach. *The Night Orchid; The Thieves of Silence*
Henri Duvernois. *The Man Who Found Himself*
Achille Eyraud. *Voyage to Venus*
Henri Falk. *The Age of Lead*
Paul Féval. *Anne of the Isles; Knightshade; Revenants; Vampire City;
The Vampire Countess; The Wandering Jew's Daughter*
Paul Féval, *fils. Felifax, the Tiger-Man*
Charles de Fieux. *Lamékis*
Arnould Galopin. *Doctor Omega*; *Doctor Omega & The Shadowmen*
G.L. Gick. *Harry Dickson and the Werewolf of Rutherford Grange*
Léon Gozlan. *The Vampire of the Val-de-Grâce*
Edmond Haraucourt. *Illusions of Immortality*
Nathalie Henneberg. *The Green Gods*
V. Hugo, P. Foucher & P. Meurice. *The Hunchback of Notre-Dame*

Michel Jeury. *Chronolysis*
Gustave Kahn. *The Tale of Gold and Silence*
Gérard Klein. *The Mote in Time's Eye*
Jean de La Hire. *Enter the Nyctalope; The Nyctalope on Mars; The Nyctalope vs. Lucifer; The Nyctalope Steps In; Night of the Nyctalope*
Etienne-Léon de Lamothe-Langon. *The Virgin Vampire*
André Laurie. *Spiridon*
Gabriel de Lautrec. *The Vengeance of the Oval Portrait*
Alain le Drimeur. *The Future City*
Georges Le Faure & Henri de Graffigny. *The Extraordinary Adventures of a Russian Scientist Across the Solar System* (2 vols.)
Gustave Le Rouge. *The Vampires of Mars The Dominion of the World* (w/Gustave Guitton) (4 vols.)
Jules Lermina. *Mysteryville; Panic in Paris; To-Ho and the Gold Destroyers; The Secret of Zippelius*
Jean-Marc & Randy Lofficier. *Edgar Allan Poe on Mars; The Katrina Protocol; Pacifica; Robonocchio; Tales of the Shadowmen 1-8*
Xavier Mauméjean. *The League of Heroes*
Joseph Méry. *The Tower of Destiny*
Hippolyte Mettais. *The Year 5865*
Louise Michel. *The Human Microbes; The New World*
José Moselli. *Illa's End*
John-Antoine Nau. *Enemy Force*
Marie Nizet. *Captain Vampire*
C. Nodier, A. Beraud & Toussaint-Merle. *Frankenstein*
Henri de Parville. *An Inhabitant of the Planet Mars*
Gaston de Pawlowski. *Journey to the Land of the 4th Dimension*
Georges Pellerin. *The World in 2000 Years*
Pierre Pelot. *The Child Who Walked on the Sky*
Ernest Pérochon. *The Frenetic People*
J. Polidori, C. Nodier, E. Scribe. *Lord Ruthven the Vampire*
P.-A. Ponson du Terrail. *The Vampire and the Devil's Son*
Henri de Régnier. *A Surfeit of Mirrors*
Maurice Renard. *The Blue Peril; Doctor Lerne; The Doctored Man; A Man Among the Microbes; The Master of Light*
Jean Richepin. *The Wing*
Albert Robida. *The Adventures of Saturnin Farandoul; The Clock of the Centuries; Chalet in the Sky*
J.-H. Rosny Aîné. *Helgvor of the Blue River; The Givreuse Enigma; The Mysterious Force; The Navigators of Space; Vamireh; The World of the Variants; The Young Vampire*

Marcel Rouff. *Journey to the Inverted World*
Han Ryner. *The Superhumans*
Brian Stableford. *The New Faust at the Tragicomique; The Empire of the Necromancers (The Shadow of Frankenstein; Frankenstein and the Vampire Countess; Frankenstein in London); Sherlock Holmes & The Vampires of Eternity; The Stones of Camelot; The Wayward Muse.* (anthologist) *The Germans on Venus; News from the Moon; The Supreme Progress; The World Above the World; Nemoville; Investigations of the Future*
Jacques Spitz. *The Eye of Purgatory*
Kurt Steiner. *Ortog*
Eugène Thébault. *Radio-Terror*
C.-F. Tiphaigne de La Roche. *Amilec*
Théo Varlet. *The Xenobiotic Invasion; Timeslip Troopers* (w/André Blandin); *The Martian Epic* (w/Octave Joncquel)
Paul Vibert. *The Mysterious Fluid*
Villiers de l'Isle-Adam. *The Scaffold; The Vampire Soul*
Philippe Ward. *Artahe*
Philippe Ward & Sylvie Miller. *The Song of Montségur*

MYSTERIES & THRILLERS

M. Allain & P. Souvestre. *The Daughter of Fantômas*
A. Anicet-Bourgeois, Lucien Dabril. *Rocambole*
A. Bernède. *Belphegor*; *Judex* (w/Louis Feuillade)
A. Bisson & G. Livet. *Nick Carter vs. Fantômas*
V. Darlay & H. de Gorsse. *Lupin vs. Holmes: The Stage Play*
Paul Féval. *Gentlemen of the Night; John Devil; The Black Coats ('Salem Street; The Invisible Weapon; The Parisian Jungle; The Companions of the Treasure; Heart of Steel; The Cadet Gang; The Sword-Swallower)*
Emile Gaboriau. *Monsieur Lecoq*
Steve Leadley. *Sherlock Holmes: The Circle of Blood*
Maurice Leblanc. *Arsène Lupin vs. Countess Cagliostro; Lupin vs. Holmes (The Blonde Phantom; The Hollow Needle); The Many Faces of Arsène Lupin*
Gaston Leroux. *Chéri-Bibi; The Phantom of the Opera; Rouletabille & the Mystery of the Yellow Room*
Richard Marsh. *The Complete Adventures of Judith Lee*
William Patrick Maynard. *The Terror of Fu Manchu; The Destiny of Fu Manchu*

Frank J. Morlock. *Sherlock Holmes: The Grand Horizontals; Sherlock Holmes vs Jack the Ripper*
Antonin Reschal. *The Adventures of Miss Boston*
P. de Wattyne & Y. Walter. *Sherlock Holmes vs. Fantômas*
David White. *Fantômas in America*

SCREENPLAYS

Mike Baron. *The Iron Triangle*
Emma Bull & Will Shetterly. *Nightspeeder; War for the Oaks*
Gerry Conway & Roy Thomas. *Doc Dynamo*
Steve Englehart. *Majorca*
James Hudnall. *The Devastator*
Jean-Marc & Randy Lofficier. *Royal Flush*
J.-M. & R. Lofficier & Marc Agapit. *Despair*
J.-M. & R. Lofficier & Joël Houssin. *City*
Andrew Paquette. *Peripheral Vision*
Robert L. Robinson, Jr. *Judex*
R. Thomas, J. Hendler & L. Sprague de Camp. *Rivers of Time*

NON-FICTION

Stephen R. Bissette. *Blur 1-5. Green Mountain Cinema 1; Teen Angels*
Win Scott Eckert. *Crossovers* (2 vols.)
Jean-Marc & Randy Lofficier. *Shadowmen* (2 vols.)
Randy Lofficier. *Over Here*

HEXAGON COMICS

Franco Frescura & Luciano Bernasconi. *Wampus*
Franco Frescura & Giorgio Trevisan. *CLASH*
L. Bernasconi, J.-M. Lofficier & Juan Roncagliolo Berger. *Phenix*
Claude Legrand, J.-M. Lofficier & L. Bernasconi. *Kabur*
Franco Oneta. *Zembla*
L. Buffolente, Lofficier & J.-J. Dzialowski. *Strangers: Homicron*
Danilo Grossi. *Strangers: Jaydee*
Claude Legrand & Luciano Bernasconi. *Strangers: Starlock*